Marooned

Lost and Found Series
Sunny and Kit

Louise Jane Watson

Foundations Book Publishing
4209 Lakeland Drive, #398, Flowood, MS 39232
www.FoundationsBooks.net

Lost and Found Series: Marooned
Louise Jane Watson

ISBN: 978-1-64583-096-2
Cover by Dawné Dominique Copyright © 2022

Edited by: Dr. Nathan Fayard
Formatted by: Laura Ranger

Published in the United States of America
Worldwide Electronic & Digital Rights
Worldwide English Language Print Rights

To Mum and Dad, my biggest cheerleaders, love you!

Table of Contents

Marooned

Pinky

*H*er concentration was split between balancing on the piece of floating orange foam and nervously eyeing the approaching leaden-blue wave.

Up, up, up.

Then a stomach-swooping down again.

At the height of the swell, she noted a bank of dark clouds on the horizon and, once again, no land in sight. Back down in the trough, her thoughts were as depressed as the oncoming weather front.

There had never been a situation she couldn't run, jump, or fight her way out of. But out here, her modus operandi was useless.

Ugh. She coughed out another mouthful of salt water.

And the day had started so well...some sunshine, some romance, some new friends.

Speaking of, she once again studied the unconscious human she was currently riding atop.

Nope, no change. Time for another proof-of-life check.

Digging a sharp claw into some white, pruned flesh, the little cat was heartened to hear a moan come out of the body.

Good.

Nothing much else she could do except hold on, wait, and be grateful she had nine lives.

She'd be happy to allot one to the human, but that was not how it worked.

Chapter 1
Sunny

n a dusty Fijian shuttle bus traveling from the airport to the harbor, Sunny experienced love at first sight.

He whistled at her from one seat over, dark eyes flashing with mischief. Then he turned away, giving her a view of his glorious back.

Oh wow—he's gorgeous!

She reached out a tentative hand, the urge to touch him overwhelming. The owner of the parrot shook his head.

"Oh no, honey, I wouldn't. He's a beautiful boy, but he'll nip you to pieces."

The girl sighed and sat back. Beauty and danger. Fiji was just as magical as she thought it would be.

The parrot-fancying girl was Sunny Evans.

Sunny didn't need to look in her bird book to identify the exotic creature in front of her.

"Red-throated Lorikeet," she whispered to herself.

The parrot turned back and gave her another cool look.

"Hi," she said to it.

The parrot didn't reply. Instead, it studied her, seeming to track a rivulet of perspiration that was dribbling down her weary face.

The reason Sunny was dripping with sweat, and drooping with exhaustion, was that she'd been traveling for almost 40 hours. She had another ten to go before she made it to the remote atoll she would be calling home for the next few weeks.

The airport bus moved through the green island interior, passing low, thatched buildings that were dotted with blue tarps like rain hats on shaggy heads. The parrot watched his reflection in the window, angling his head from one side to the other and giving himself glassy kisses. As the highway turned a corner, the thick vegetation fell away to reveal the ocean. A herd of wild horses

3

ambled along the shore, nudging through heaped seaweed with their long, whiskery faces.

On entering the city, the bus pulled up to the harbor stop. The parrot and its human hurried down the steps, disappearing into the marketplace. Sunny got up more slowly, being careful to collect all her luggage, making sure she hadn't left anything behind on the hot bench seat.

"Your first time in Fiji, dear?" the woman next to her asked as they lined up to disembark.

"Is it that obvious?" Sunny laughed, holding out her white arm, comparing it to the older woman's golden brown one.

"You be careful not to burn; the cloud cover can be deceptive—don't want to ruin your vacation."

"Thanks! I'll definitely take care." Then, puffing out her chest a little, she added, "I'm actually here for work—I'm going to a research station where they study the effects of sea debris on ocean creatures."

The woman, not really listening, patted her hand. "Well isn't that nice; enjoy your trip."

"I will, thank you...ouch!"

Something jabbed Sunny in the back, and she stumbled slightly. Turning, she saw a boy behind her. He was holding a wooden crate that contained two ducks. She smiled at the boy, and then at the mallards. Sunny liked ducks.

She had decided, around the age of nine, to appreciate ducks as much as possible.

Her elementary school peers had pointed out that with her short legs, splayed feet, and wide eyes, Sunny had all the makings of a person who looked particularly duck-like.

Sunny was a remarkable person in many ways, and the way she decided to own the nickname, "Quackers," and throw herself into anything duck-related, spoke of a resourceful mind that saw a problem, then found a solution.

Nobody could hurt her feelings if she herself embraced the duck. And, as her dad pointed out, she could always tell the other kids to "duck off."

Sunny looked like her dad, but no one had ever teased Sunny's dad about his appearance. Welsh folk were known for stout bodies and short legs. Nothing wrong with that; it made working the hilly land much easier.

And if Sunny sometimes found herself wistfully watching long-legged women, she immediately gave herself a stern talking to, reminding herself about her life's priorities.

And one of those was to not waste time on vanity. Another was to experience other cultures.

"Vinika," Sunny said to the bus driver as it was her turn to exit. Pleased to be putting her newly learned Fijian to use, she stepped down onto the cobbled plaza, where her glasses instantly steamed up from the humidity.

Moving to one side to defog, she let the other passengers get out, and when she could see again, took in the view around her. Bright south pacific light was flooding the square. Rows of market stalls lined the edges, where clusters of people gathered around to inspect glistening sea slugs, brilliant bougainvillea, and strange jellied green berries. Tourists milled and took photographs, and beside a long pier, taxi drivers called out, angling for business.

Two little boys threw pebbles at a clamshell. They cheered when one landed in its target. Sunny gave them a congratulatory yay. From their perch on a low wall, the boys gave her four thumbs up then took aim again. She watched a huge ginger cat race across the square hot on the trail of another yowling stray. It was all so steamy and lush and intense that a resulting wave of exhaustion came crashing over her. Spotting a palm-dappled bench, she picked up her bags and made a beeline for the shady spot.

Squeaking as hot wood met sturdy thighs, Sunny sat back and tried to get her bearings. She was in the harbor market square, and the first long pier on her right would be where the supply boat

5

would leave from. Bikes and buses zipped along the frontage, weaving between visitors and fruit-sellers. On the bay, fishing boats and water taxis chugged across a backdrop of cruise ships and container vessels.

Bit of a change from Seattle, she thought.

Sunny had spent the last six months hunched over a drawing board in a chilly but agreeably cheap artist studio, working on the final project of her fine art degree. The air in Seattle was often fishy and salty, but never as warm as this. With her eyes closed, Sunny pictured the huge terrestrial globe that hung high up in the art school atrium. The northern hemisphere was perpetually covered in thick dust, but that dust fell away as it rounded the curves toward the equator.

I'm officially out of the dust realms, she told herself, pulling her hair away from her sweaty neck and feeling glad she'd spontaneously chopped several inches off last week with the shears at the bakery. The heat was making her eyes sore, so she closed them. The light left bright spots dancing behind the lids.

The air, she thought to herself, felt as scorching as when she pulled pastries out of the industrial oven at work.

An image of her floury apron popped into her mind. It was going to hang, unused, on its peg for the next three months. It gave her a pang of very mixed emotions—happy to have a break from the bakery, worried about how the new girl would work out in her old position, and a little lonely to be so far away from her friends.

Must email Clive and Dennie, let them know I got here safe.

Clive and Dennie were her bosses at Bagel Bubbe, the bakery where she worked in Seattle in the early mornings before college. They were more than bosses, though. They, along with their incontinent beagle Brisket, were her best friends. They were the ones who'd convinced her to come on this trip,

"All work and no play..." said Dennie,

"Makes Sunny..." said Clive,

"A dull goy!" they chorused, "it's time to take a leap..."

6

Talk about leaping! Sunny opened her eyes just in time to see a brown projectile headed her way—a flying, furry something was approaching with startling speed. The creature trailed a length of rope, and a barefoot young man was vainly attempting to catch hold of the end. The fur-ball leapt onto Sunny's bench, and before she knew it, she had a monkey in her lap.

"Gee-boy! Gee-boy! Get back here!" yelled the pursuer, but Gee-boy was having none of it.

Bouncing out of her lap, Gee-boy knocked the water bottle out of her hand, dousing her and her paper itinerary. Watching the retreating escapee and frustrated handler, Sunny blinked several times, then burst into laughter. This time three days ago she was in the rain, wrestling with a rat who'd jumped out of the shop dumpster onto her chest, causing her to spill rancid oil everywhere. If you have to tussle with wildlife, doing so in the tropics was much more pleasant.

Rooting around in her huge tote bag, she pulled out her camera. What a shame she hadn't gotten a picture of either the monkey or the bus parrot, but there were plenty of other wonderful things around to snap. If she wanted to record every part of her journey, she'd better get on with it and capture some of Suva before leaving for the atoll.

Wait one minute...

She focused on a nearby tree that, if not hosting Gee-Boy himself, was at least the perch of a family member. Smiling, she lined up her camera and snapped the monkey as he relaxed on a flower-laden branch.

Not Gee-Boy, she thought, *no red collar.*

The monkey sat up then skipped down his perch, going tree to tree around the plaza, probably on the hunt for some snacks. Sunny tracked the monkey's progress, with her eye glued to the camera lens. Finally settling in a Kauri pine tree, the monkey became obscured by an unfortunately placed human head. Peering around the compact camera, Sunny could see a man in a dark Panama and shades sitting in the way of her shot. She waited a moment to see if he would move, but he didn't. Sunny stood up and stepped closer, zooming in and hoping the monkey would move instead.

Come on, sweet boy, she thought, *let me see you!*

Once she had captured the perfect picture, she'd better hustle and head to the supply boat. Soon it would be time to leave for the art residency, her first lucky break in forever.

Kit

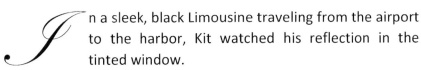

n a sleek, black Limousine traveling from the airport to the harbor, Kit watched his reflection in the tinted window.

He reached for the console to get a drink, but then realized this ride didn't come with cocktails. It was the smallest limo he'd ever been in, but apparently stretch (and decent service) wasn't a thing on the tiny island of Fiji.

Oh well—time to get used to roughing it anyway.

He pressed his head back into the leather and closed his eyes. It had been a long trip and he still had nearly ten hours of travel ahead of him until he made it to the remote atoll he would be staying on for the next few weeks.

The Limousine moved through the lush island interior, but Kit was completely oblivious to the passing scenery. He spent the journey trying, and failing, to sleep.

Surely just one stretch limo on the island wasn't too much to ask?

Finally, the car pulled to a smooth halt. They were now at the Suva plaza, the driver informed him, next to the harbor. Apparently, he had to be dropped here, as the hire car company didn't have permission to drive on the—pier? Jetty? Whatever harbor-type thing non-tourist boats docked at.

Whatever. It meant he'd have to brave the masses. He was pleased that nobody could see through the windows of the car (that was one point for the crappy ride), and he took advantage of the moment to scope out the scene.

The scene was filled with people. Too many people.

Heaving groups of red-faced, photo-taking tourists, and rows and rows of bored-looking trinket-selling locals. Kit saw a particular group of pink visored older women swivel in his direction. Saw them point and nudge.

Limos and chauffeurs often got the gen pub excited.

It's not like I could have taken the bus, though, Kit thought to himself.

The driver got out, and seconds later, opened the rear door, allowing bright, south pacific sunlight to pour in over the warm leather, and Kit's face. Kit winced and put on his black fedora and dark glasses, hoping they would both obscure his face and help his pounding head.

Sighing, he got out of the car.

He could feel the eyes of the granny brigade focus on him and studiously ignored them. Kit was very used to curious eyes. He waited as the driver retrieved his oversized MontBlanc suitcase from the trunk. On its receipt, Kit gave the chauffeur both a nod and a generous wad of local currency, then immediately turned away. After a quick scan, he spotted a table tucked in an empty, shadowed corner of the square. He had some time to kill, a horrendous hangover, and a need for anonymity, so if he could spend the next 30-odd minutes in a discreet, undisturbed spot, unbothered by autograph hunters, that would be perfect.

Sweeping the dry pine needles off the bench seat, he sat and rested his elbows on the warped tabletop. A row of trees rustled in the breeze behind him, adding a piney scent to the fresh, salty air. The smells were so different from the exhaust fume-tinged ozone of Los Angeles.

He swallowed a couple of Xanax, rested his tender head on his hands, and took in the scenery. For a while, he watched two cats engage in some energetic courtship, and then he was amused by a boy on a battered skateboard freaking out a tourist, her overly tanned bosom swelling with indignation as he pulled a sweet ollie right in her path.

I used to ollie that well.

He missed it—cruising along on a board, practicing tricks. Skateboarding had been nixed for a while now. Too easy to break a bone and send productions into an uproar.

The suffering ex-skateboarder was born Otis Kitson, but was known the world over as Nicky 'Kit' Kitson—pretty much the most "A" of all the Hollywood A-listers.

A favorite guest of late-night TV hosts, Kit spent as much time mingling with the younger British royals as he did with fellow Hollywood elite. He'd consistently beat out Robert Pattinson for the title of "Sexiest Man Alive" three years in a row.

But now, he was headed off for a few weeks of zero glitz and glamour. No staff, no security, and none of the luxuries he'd grown used to.

"Nicky playing normal with the normies," his agent had called it.

Alexis, his on-again-off-again girlfriend, had called it ridiculous.

"'Method acting' was extremely last decade," she'd told him. Everyone was doing *practical aesthetics* in Hollywood now.

"Isn't practical aesthetics just a bikini wax?" he'd drawled.

"Don't be ridiculous, Nicky!" Alexis snapped, at the same time flicking through a copy of *Oh-Wow!* magazine and pausing to admire a feature about herself, "...all your stupid trips are such a waste of time."

But that's what Nicky Kitson loved about his research trips: a break from Hollywood, both mentally and physically—it was time where no one discussed flattering camera angles or which new exercise fad would make his pecs even more pronounced.

On this trip, he was going to learn about life on a remote scientific research station, and he was honestly really looking forward to it. Remote atoll, some nerdy scientists to pal around with, and no cell service—just what the doctor ordered.

Well, what the doctor had really ordered was that he up give up booze for a while; his liver needed a little vacation as well. But that was still up in the air; several bottles of single malt whiskey were packed in his luggage, just in case.

Loud, uncontrollable laughter cut through his thoughts as, across the square, a girl was flinging her arms around and obviously having a hilarious time. A monkey had escaped from its owner and was now leaping along a bench, using the girl as a springboard. He watched her water bottle go flying and the paperwork in her hand flutter to the ground. She was still chuckling as the monkey disappeared into some bushes.

Then she sat back and lifted her face up to the sun.

Her limbs were a firmly indoor pallor, but even from this distance Kit could see hot patches forming on her nose and cheeks.

Clueless tourists, thought Kit. Her mottled red and white skin was making Kit both wince and worry about his own complexion. He pulled out a tube of lotion and dabbed it on the parts of his face not covered by his shades, then took his hat off momentarily and wafted himself. It was very hot, but the lily of the valley-scented lotion was cooling on his skin.

Looking up at the girl again, he saw she was doing the same, wafting a sheet of paper in front of her face. She looked like the 'before photo' in an *Oh-Wow!* makeover section, he decided. Her limp brown hair was styled as though she'd hacked it off with some kitchen scissors. She had thick-lensed glasses, stubby nails, and pale limbs. No makeup either, or jewelry—apart from a clunky charm bracelet around her wrist.

Natural, wholesome, and unadorned wasn't exactly a thing in his circle.

She was now rooting around in a large tote bag, finally pulling out a digital camera. Lifting it to her eye, she panned around the plaza.

Kit saw the moment she spotted him.

11

He saw her freeze, lean forward, and zoom her camera straight at his face.

The black hat, glasses, bandanna combo obviously wasn't the cloaking device he'd hoped it would be.

Sighing, he looked away.

Earlier that year, a photo of Kit vacationing in Barbados, wearing frayed white shorts, white shirt, white bandanna, white fedora, and white framed shades, had become an instant 'Nicky Kitson' classic look. The style was copied by fashionable young men the world over as soon as the sun came out. Reversing the color palette had been his stylist's idea. Now that he was in the tropics, Kit realized all black might be super stylish, but it was also super good at absorbing heat.

Should have stuck to my guns with the white outfit, Kit thought crossly.

He turned back toward the girl, and couldn't believe it. She was still at it!

Just take the damn photo already!

Having very little privacy was the price of fame—he knew that; he wasn't an idiot, but he definitely had a preferred way for fans to act. Basically, he wanted them to just take a snap or two from a distance. They'd be slightly embarrassed to be photographing him but unable to resist getting digital proof that they'd been in the vicinity of superstar Nicky Kitson. His least favorite fans were those who trailed him for blocks, then demanded a selfie, as though his fame gave them some kind of ownership over him. Or those fans who were too timid to approach but just stared and photographed, stared and videoed, stared and stared until Kit was forced to move.

He watched the girl stand up, camera still trained on him, and start to take some steps closer.

Yep! Kit thought, his scowl deepening, *here she comes...well darling, not today, I'm not in the mood.*

He got to his feet and clicked up the handle of his shiny black rolling luggage. The wheels caught on an uneven cobblestone as he tugged at it, making Kit trip and stumble, stubbing a toe, which his expensive athletic water shoe did nothing to soften. Wincing, he glanced up and saw the girl still had her camera trained on him—she had probably just recorded his clumsiness!

Ugh, she'll probably sell the video. All the trashy celeb websites devour stuff like that, and I'll be a meme by the end of the day.

Regaining control of his luggage, but not his temper, Kit took off along the seafront, annoyed with the fan-girl and annoyed with life in general.

I cannot wait to get away from it all, he sighed. *I'm ready for some peace and quiet.*

Chapter 2
Sunny

*S*unny was delighted that the man across the way had moved. Now she could focus on the tropical bird that had just hopped onto the branch to join the monkey. She combed mentally through the bird book she'd borrowed from the library pre-trip. Ah! If she wasn't mistaken, this was an azure-crested flycatcher! The beautiful blue feathers on the head were a dead giveaway!

Sunny loved bird watching, a passion she'd shared with her father, Glynn. As a boy, her father had spent his weekends camped out on the side of Pen y Fan in Wales. Eyes glued to an ancient pair of binoculars, a paper of toffees in his pocket. He'd diligently noted observations in a well-thumbed birding guide. He had passed both the bird book and his birding passion down to Sunny. Together they'd spend his occasional free weekends wading through knee-high Trinity County thistles and poison ivy to their makeshift bird-hides in the woods. On Monday mornings, back at her Northern Californian high school, when her friends would tell her about the latest thing on *YouTube*, she'd nod uncomprehendingly, then try to excite them with the news she'd glimpsed a Wilson's warbler. Her peers were seldom impressed.

Watching a petrel circle overhead, Sunny reflected her interests had always been profoundly more webbed-feet than website. But, despite it not winning her many cool points at school, her love of birds and animals had paid off in the end. Her final art project for her degree had been a huge sheet of handmade paper covered in a map of the wildlife she saw across the city. Beautifully painted, the depicted birds and animals shone with character. Her clever brush captured the wariness of a golf course fox, the mischievous spirit shining from the eyes of squirrels, and the solemnity of the muskrat that lived in the bioswale.

During the thesis gallery exhibition, the Dean of Students had introduced her to a woman who had fallen in love with her art piece.

"I'm Elsa Stokes, Dr. Elsa Stokes," the woman said. "I couldn't make head nor tail of most of this stuff," she waved an arm airily around the gallery, "but your work—just lovely."

Sunny hid a smile as the doctor pointed dismissively at a giant concrete tampon sculpture.

"Oh, err, thanks."

Dr. Stokes had gone on to explain that she was a staff board member with the Research Association of Marine Biology Oceanwide, otherwise known as RAMBO. This was a non-profit that had sponsored several environmental art programs at the university. Dr. Stokes had then told her about a brand new program they were developing, a residency with RAMBO at their newest South Pacific research station.

She'd asked Sunny if she was interested in the position.

Then she'd told her how much the position paid—an unheard of $12,000 for three months! Plus accommodation and travel...this was a rare thing in the art world; it really was a dream come true!

Better not miss this boat!

Sunny felt she often missed the metaphorical boat; she was certainly not going to miss the literal one. Standing up and trying to ignore the brutal nineteen-hour time difference, she gave her bracelet a habitual twist for good luck and headed off to find the correct pier.

Approaching the end of the long jetty, panting a little in the hot sun, Sunny was delighted to see Dr. Stokes, resplendent in cargo shorts and a SpongeBob SquarePants Hawaiian shirt, gesturing wildly at a young man holding an awkwardly shaped parcel.

Elsa Stokes stood on the wharf next to the supply boat, nearly a foot taller than the sailors and dockworkers around her, all of whom were busily unloading boxes from a white delivery van. Dr. Stokes had the excellent posture of a woman who often knew she was the cleverest person in the room and wasn't afraid to own it. A six-foot-tall woman has only one real choice—her equally tall mother had told her—accept that eyes will always be on you and stand tall and proud.

As Dr. Stokes' magnificent head looked up and down from paperwork to packages, Sunny could hear her brusque voice instructing the crew to "take care now" of various assorted items.

Sunny gave a wave and called out to get her attention. "Dr. Stokes! I didn't know you'd be here!"

As far as Sunny knew, all the scientists were already at the island and she was to be the only passenger on the supply boat. But those plans had obviously changed. She could have handled figuring out the trip on her own, but having Dr. Stokes there let some of the tension leave her shoulders. It would make everything a little less challenging.

Also, she thought, it would be great to spend some travel time with the marine biologist. So far, she'd only met Dr. Stokes once, at graduation; all their other communication had been through email. Email that had as a sign-off under Dr. Stokes 'name —*Why did the two algae never have sex? Because they had a planktonic relationship*—which amused Sunny greatly.

"Aha! Sunny! Bang on time. Wouldn't have expected anything else!" Dr. Stokes declared cheerfully.

The scientist gave off an air of practical sense and minimum fuss, and that was Sunny's kind of person.

The supply ship also looked practical and no-fuss. Quite old and modest in size, but obviously organized and well cared for. Australian pop music was playing from a radio perched on a cabin roof, the singer crooning about a 'bevvy in the arvo'.

For a moment, Sunny watched the crew move fluidly along the narrow bulwark, bags and boxes held high above their heads. Their bodies rippled and swayed with the motion of the boat, completely adapted by years spent at sea. Dr. Stokes though, still kept a sharp eye on their progress, making sure the precious lab equipment was handled correctly.

The boat had a regular schedule to deliver food and goods to the outlying islands. This trip, though, was chartered to deliver a carefully crated array of apparatus to the research station, along with three passengers.

The final item the crew carried aboard was a heavy, brand-new plankton dredger that Dr. Stokes was particularly excited about. She called over to a cheerful-looking boy.

"Hey Farhan, can you get Sunny settled aboard—look after her? I want to see where they are putting that..."

Without waiting for Farhan to agree, she hurried off, shouting, "Hey there, have a care!" to the disappearing crew.

Sunny looked at her appointed guide and returned his welcoming smile. He took her backpack, lowering it to the deck, then offered his hand to help her aboard. Before this, the only boats she'd been on were a shallow aluminum rowboat for river fishing and the swan-shaped paddleboats at Six Flags. This was to be her first actual ocean voyage. Sunny paused and checked out the boarding bridge. It was made out of metal and seemed sturdy, and there were rubber pads at each end to stop it from slipping. Seemed safe enough.

Crossing the divide from land to sea, she stepped down onto the bobbing deck. This was it, the final leg of her journey.

"Come sit over here." The boy called Farhan gestured to a shaded patch of deck.

Lowering herself down, Sunny looked around at the bustling crew, feeling a bit awkward and trying to keep her body and her backpack out of the way. Everyone but Sunny and Farhan looked incredibly busy.

"Am I keeping you from your work?" she asked the boy. "Don't feel you have to babysit, or can I help in any way?"

"Nope, you've nothing to do other than enjoy the trip," Farhan told her.

This was not normally how Sunny rolled. Usually, she was the one getting things done while others sat about, but taking Farhan's word for it, she leaned back and let the warm deck soak into her tired bones.

Relaxing next to her on the warm floor, Farhan told her he was going to use the excuse of being her "guide" to take a break himself.

"And in that spirit," he said, "let me give you an orientation!"

He asked how much she knew about boats. "Virtually nothing," she'd replied, so he'd gone on to explain that they were presently sitting at the stern, which was at the aft of the boat. Sunny nodded.

"The front is the bow, right?" she said, then added she had never been clear which side was port and which was starboard.

Farhan grinned at her, "Oh, that's easy, just ask yourself—is there any port left?"

"Port is left—clever! OK, next question—poop deck?"

Farhan rolled his eyes and called her a dork. Then he and Sunny had a very enjoyable time as they sat together in the shade and he taught her all about ship parts and sailing terms. She decided her favorite was 'scuttlebutt'.

"The water barrel is the butt, and a hole in the barrel is the scuttle," Farhan informed her, "and sailors would gather around it to drink water and gossip..."

"Hence the term! I love it!"

Farhan had just graduated from the University of Hawaii and was helping out on his uncle's boat before heading off to Sydney for his graduate studies. He would be studying Ocean Sciences. The next thing he decided to enlighten Sunny about was the Polynesian Triangle.

"The three corners of the triangle are New Zealand, the Easter Islands, and Hawaii," he explained, "it's ten million miles of ocean, and we are in the middle of it."

The vastness made Sunny's head spin.

He told her that the area had a thousand atolls scattered around, but sometimes one of the low-lying islands would just disappear.

"That's like rising sea levels disappearing, not Bermuda Triangle disappearing, right?" she asked him with a grin.

"Yep, and anyway, the Bermuda Triangle is in the North Atlantic, so don't worry about mysteriously vanishing on this trip."

They laughed together, and then Farhan pointed out the last member of the crew who had just arrived and was currently trotting along the boarding bridge.

The ship's cat—Pinky—was returning from a very enjoyable shore leave, and just in time, as the captain was preparing to cast off. Sunny was fascinated.

"She just comes and goes on her own?"

"Sure does; Pinky is amazing, always comes back to the boat just before we set sail. She never misses a trip; we don't know how she does it."

He beckoned the cat over and petted her head.

The cat turned its pink nose to Farhan and butted it against his hand. "Uncle thinks of her as a good luck charm," he continued, "she turned up a couple of years ago and has been on every voyage since. Uncle's never had a spot of trouble since she's been a crew member." He bent low and nuzzled the cat with his face. "Ooh, that's tempting fate! Shouldn't we knock on wood or something?" said Sunny.

"Nah, I'm totally confident in old Pinks! I don't think the boat would actually start if Pinky wasn't aboard!" The cat allowed Farhan to pet her for another minute, then stood up, stretched, and meowed.

The next moment, the ship's engine rumbled loudly and a couple of the crew raced over to the stern, reaching out to undo the ropes that were anchoring the small ship to the dock. Sunny looked from the departure bustle, then to the little cat, who blinked slowly back at Sunny with a knowing expression.

"Well!" said Sunny, "that was..."

The rest of her words were drowned out as the ship's horn gave a long, loud hoot. The sound gave her a surge of adrenaline, setting her heart racing.

Sailing on an ocean with no land in sight was going to be just fine, she told herself. Farhan had made this trip a hundred times, and the lucky ship's cat was right there.

It was all going to be plain sailing.

Kit

*A*pproaching the supply vessel, Kit's heart dropped down to the bottom of his very expensive athletic water shoes. The photo-taking fan-girl from earlier was boarding the boat. He couldn't believe it; a tiny island in the middle of nowhere, what were the odds?

Kit then admitted to himself the odds were high. He was very famous, after all.

Oh well, just have to give her the legendary Nicky Kitson freeze.

Rolling up with his suitcase, which by this time had lost its glossy shine under a layer of red Fijian dust, and still limping a little from his stubbed toe, he was greeted by a statuesque woman in an extraordinary shirt. She held out a hand, and Kit shook it, wincing slightly as her powerful grip squeezed his bones together.

This was the scientist who was going to be accompanying him to the research station—a Dr. Elsa Stokes. His team had arranged for her to be there to make sure he had a smooth passage. Dr. Stokes had been scheduled to be at the island two weeks ago, but Kit's manager had thought the exceedingly sizable donation into the Research Association of Marine Biology Oceanwide funds should come with a personal guide. The RAMBO board had agreed—a six-figure donation certainly warranted the personal touch—so Dr. Stokes was volunteered to be tour guide.

Kit watched her glance down at her watch and not comment on his lateness. They say the tide waits for no man, but in Kit's experience, large amounts of fame and money usually got the tide to be obliging.

"Welcome Mr. Kitson," she said briskly.

Then looking at her watch again, she added, "You're late."

Kit blinked. Then smiled slightly. No ass-kissing, that was different!

"Please, call me Nicky."

Dr. Stokes was wearing a SpongeBob watch to match her SpongeBob shirt, but instead of making her look ridiculous, it made her a little intimidating. A woman who could rock that look was not someone to mess with, Kit thought. She also didn't seem at all excited to meet him.

Handing his case off to a waiting crew member, Dr. Stokes led Kit aboard, saying the captain was anxious to set sail, which Kit rightfully took as another scolding.

Seeing the drab fan-girl nose-to-nose with a laughing young man, he looked away and asked the scientist to lead him to a private cabin, somewhere he could lie down and not be disturbed. She snorted a little and pointed a finger bow-ward, saying this wasn't a pleasure cruise and maybe there would be some space for him at the front. Then she abruptly turned on her heel, heading into the dark hold and leaving Kit on the deck, not sure of what to do.

Okay then, thought Kit.

Nonplussed, he wandered cautiously through the ship until he found a quiet place on the fore deck. It looked like a good spot to keep a low profile and hopefully sleep off his excesses from the day before. Easing himself down onto the hot deck, he rested his back against a cabin wall.

Yep, get some zees. Coming here straight from JT's party was probably not the best idea.

As Kit yawned, he exposed a perfect set of white, even teeth and a slightly yellow tongue. Alexis had set him up with a nutritionist, who had in turn set him up with immune-boosting turmeric shots and pre-flight infrared saunas to combat the effects of jetlag.

"So important that international travel doesn't tax your body," said Jurgen, the naturopath, "and more importantly, your epidermis!"

Feeling the sun on his face, he again pulled the vial of moisturizer from his pocket and gently patted it into his skin. As he did, his thoughts turned back to Alexis and her latest *Oh-Wow!* feature, an interview accompanied by lots of shiny photos.

"Talking Sparkle with Meghan Markle!" trilled the headline.

Kit had rolled his eyes as he'd looked at pictures of Alexis trying on diamond rings.

"Meghan naturally suggested the stone be a princess cut, but we'll just have to wait and see!" Alexis' quote was emphasized in the middle of the text by large pink, curvy font.

The article concluded by noting she was currently 'just looking' but hinting she might have a Nicky Kitson ring on her finger very soon.

Yeah right. Fat chance...

Alexis was launching a new line of fine jewelry at the end of the summer, so Kit knew the magazine stunt was just part of her press plan, and he rather admired her cheek. Neither of them had the slightest interest in or intention of getting hitched—they'd actually called it quits (again) just before he'd left for this trip. Alexis was pissed at him for missing a premiere that she had targeted as a good photo op for her new business. The film was about blood diamond mining. Kit had pointed out that maybe that wasn't the best place to promote a new diamond jewelry line.

"You should go to the new *Bugs Bunny* premiere instead."

She'd looked at him blankly, "What?"

"Talk to the press about 24 carrots jewelry. Come on, babe! Carrots! Get it?"

She growled and turned away.

"Oh babe, chill out for once," Kit replied, then offered to get her a drink. "Wanna beer?"

"Carbs!" she snapped. But after a pause and thinking about burning calories, she said, "I'd go for a bump, though…"

Alexis was humorless, and Kit's dad-joke habit really got under her skin. That just made Kit want to crack crappy jokes all the more.

"Oh, go away to your stupid research trip," she'd shrieked at him, "I've got real work to do."

Yes, Alexis did have real work. And she was also a real piece of work.

When they'd first started dating, Alexis had just launched her beauty product line. There had been a series of articles in the press, all about her mother's cancer diagnosis and how the stress of the diagnosis was taking a toll on her (Alexis') skin.

It was miraculous, Alexis had said, that something like a loved one's cancer battle could be the inspiration for an empowering line of lotions for ladies under stress. Her new range would help get you through those stressful times without adding any new wrinkles.

Kit had met Alexis' mother, Barbara Balantine had swirled a martini, and quite casually admitted she'd never had cancer. "I don't mind helping Alexis out with her little projects." She'd sighed. "The poor thing didn't quite inherit the family business skills, you see…"

"What a caring mother you are, Barbara," Kit had said, rolling his eyes at Alexis. But Alexis was too busy flouncing off and then slamming the door to notice Kit trying to give her support.

Kit didn't agree with Cold Mother Balentine, as he called her. Alexis was smart, and her manipulative cunning was kind of impressive, and she was crazily successful because of it. Alexis was all drive, hair extensions, and long legs—but no laughs—and nothing was ever allowed to get in the way of what she wanted.Her manipulative cunning was kind of impressive, and she was crazily successful because of it. Alexis was all drive, hair extensions, and long legs—but no laughs—and nothing was ever allowed to get in the way of what she wanted.

23

Rolling the small tube of lotion between his fingers, he thought one of the problems in his life was the lack of laughs.

Everyone took *everything* so very seriously in Tinseltown—even when it came to humor. After hearing Alexis' complaints, one actor friend had offered to workshop some jokes with Kit, give Kit some better material for his banter.

With what Kit felt was great restraint, he mildly turned down the offer with a brusk, "I'll pass."

He was quite happy to have one piece of his life unpolished and a little bit dumb.

Kit sighed. His life just wasn't much fun. More than that, Kit was dissatisfied—deeply dissatisfied—with what he was doing. It was confusing because he liked acting, really, but he often despised Hollywood. He was adrift, ungrounded.

What did he want?

He didn't think it was Alexis and the A-list set. That thrill-ride had quite definitely peaked a while ago, and it also wasn't being the next James Bond (which his agent Mattie was currently pushing hard for). None of that was going to fill the hole in his soul, so what would?

I need a change. Maybe do more theatre?

Kit did love Shakespeare, but that still didn't feel like the right thing.

I think I need a really big change, but I have no idea what.

Maybe hanging out with a handful of scientists, who didn't give a shit about his fame and fortune, would help him get his head straight.

Chapter 3
Sunny

arhan had told Sunny the journey to the research station would take eight hours and they would be arriving at the atoll some time after sunset. As they talked, she petted Pinky—the lucky charm cat—and that's when Farhan had noticed the lucky charm bracelet she wore on her wrist.

"What's this all about?" he asked, picking up her wrist and examining the jewelry.

"My dad made it for my mom. He was a locksmith, so he was great at metalworking. He made this locket on it, see," she indicated a charm shaped like a padlock. Opening it up, she showed him that inside the locket, behind thin glass, was a tiny picture of her parents on their wedding day.

Snapping it shut again, she continued with her story.

"It became a wedding anniversary tradition—over the years he made more charms."

She took the bracelet off so Farhan could examine it more closely.

"That's cool!" He peered through a tiny magnifying glass.

"He made that so they could always see themselves together—he was a bit of a cheeseball. There were about twenty charms for it by the time they died. Mom couldn't wear all the charms at once—it got way too heavy—so I'd help her pick out a half dozen every few months to change it up."

"What's this one?" Farhan asked, fingering another piece.

"A miniature lock-picking tool—because mom had unlocked his heart."

"Yes, cheesy, but very sweet."

"That basically summed up my folks. I miss them and their cheesiness all the time."

25

Farhan paused, looking at Sunny, a gentle expression on his face.

You said they passed. "Do you mind me asking , when did you lose them?"

"They died at the same time, when I was 18." She took a breath, looking out across the ocean. "The furnace broke down, making carbon monoxide leak into our house; it killed them while they slept, Steve Irwin as well."

"What?"

"Oh, sorry." She smiled at him. "Steve Irwin was my dog. I was away for the weekend on a school trip, so escaped getting killed too."

"How awful. I'm so sorry."

"Thanks. I won't lie; it's been really hard. But now, seven years have passed, and I can talk about it without getting choked up. I do wish they could see me now, though—heading off on this adventure—they'd be so happy for me."

Her parents had always marveled at Sunny's drawing talent and had fully encouraged her to follow her art dreams. They knew Sunny well enough to realize she would find a way to make a career in the arts and still pay the bills.

Farhan gave her arm a squeeze.

Sunny smiled back at him; it felt like she and Farhan had somehow become instant friends. It was rare for Sunny to feel at ease with new people. Sunny was especially intimidated by charismatic charmers. The golden people who breezed easily into every situation, charming and collected, and always the hub of something exciting.

But with Farhan—who had charm by the bucket-load—she immediately felt at ease.

Sunny wasn't sure why her social anxiety was dialed down, but she liked it. Maybe it was getting away from Seattle, which wasn't the friendliest city in the world, or maybe it was just Farhan. She was about to ask him about his family when a voice from inside the dark cabin yelled out Farhan's name.

He looked at her and winked. "Busted! Well, duty calls—better see what's going on." He stood and put a hand on her shoulder. "I'll check on you later—you OK? Need anything?"

"Nope, I'm 100% content."

And she really was.

Left alone to sit at the stern, Sunny pulled out her camera and took a few more photos, sketched Pinky the cat, munched on a tired sandwich (she'd bought it in Honolulu when she'd changed planes; the spam was definitely beginning to shrivel), and then with a sigh of pleasure, decided to get out a book to read.

She'd brought two books in her hand luggage; one was for research and one was for pure pleasure. The first was the autobiography of Marianne North, a Victorian botanical painter, called, very inspirationally in Sunny's mind, *Recollections of a Happy Life*. She picked up the book, held it for a moment, then put it back into the bottom of the bag. She pulled out the second book instead.

Sunny had been all work and no play for several years now, so this moment of having nothing to do but stroke a cat and read an old favorite was sheer bliss. After her parents had died, she'd lived paycheck to paycheck. Not having any savings, she'd been working nearly full time at the bagel shop all the time she had been doing her degree. She was very glad to keep her student loans low, but she was exhausted from four years of 4 A.M. starts followed by full days of college classes—and all the extra work those entailed.

Time for a comfort read.

Sunny stroked the well-worn cover of *The Incredible Journey*. Her mom had adored it as a child and passed her old hardback copy on to Sunny. So as the boat chugged across the ocean, Sunny became wrapped up in the adventures of three animals far away from home.

The sun moved down the sky and the shadows shifted. Sunny unconsciously shifted with them, engrossed in her book and keeping

27

in the shade. The breeze was pleasant, and the monotonous tone of the engine lulled her into a completely relaxed state.

She was so engaged with the story that she didn't notice Dr. Stokes standing in front of her with two sweating bottles of cold beer.

"Beer, dear?" Dr. Stokes said, making Sunny jump, dropping her book, and making the skinny cat leap off her lap.

"Oh, lovely." She smiled and thanked her, then pressed the cold glass to her hot cheeks.

Joining her on the shady patch of deck, Dr. Stokes invited Sunny to call her Elsa. "You're part of the family now, dear! We've talked for years about getting an artist to join us at a research station, and I'm so glad it's you."

They chinked their matching bottles of Fiji Gold, which confusingly proclaimed itself to be 'refreshingly gold' on the wrinkled printed label.

"Cheers," said Sunny.

"Cheers—I think you'll fit in marvelously."

"I hope so! I'm grateful to be here," Sunny replied. "I've always wanted to travel, but thought I'd have to save for years before I could! And now I get to see all the amazing nature, and have weeks and weeks to draw—I just can't believe it! I truly can't wait!"

Sunny knew she was gushing, but everything she said was true. Getting this art residency was going to be absolutely life-changing.

"Well, not much more waiting to go; we're over halfway to the island now."

"Whoa, already?"

Elsa checked her watch. "Yep, and there should be a meal served soon. After that, just another few hours..."

Sunny eyed the second hand of the SpongeBob watch ticking past the Krusty Krab and suppressed a smile. Elsa noticed her noticing.

"This is all my Rachel's doing!" she indicated her cartoon-decorated outfit. "Rachel—that's my daughter—thinks it's hilarious to give me SpongeBob merchandise."

Sunny smiled, but a little blankly, not really understanding the joke.

"You know, what with SpongeBob's nemesis being plankton and all," Elsa continued.

Again, Sunny tried not to look as confused as she felt, but Elsa saw right through her.

"You know who SpongeBob is, right?"

Sunny said she did but still didn't quite understand the connection. Elsa went on to explain more of what she did in the research team.

"My field of focus is plankton—phytoplankton, not zooplankton."

"Err, of course," nodded Sunny.

"Of course, indeed! The world of the dinoflagellate is infinitely richer than holoplankton."

Elsa took another glug of the Fiji Gold. "I have to admit, though, I nearly got turned off dinoflagellate completely after a bout of food poisoning—puked my guts up for days!"

"Err...I didn't know you could eat plankton," Sunny said.

"Some types you can, but that wasn't the problem in this case," Elsa corrected her. "No, the problem was I ate a fish that had been caught straight after a storm."

Elsa looked a bit green at the memory of the story, but Sunny encouraged her to continue.

"OK, you asked for it. Storms kick dinoflagellate off the reef, making it a quick and easy snack for the fish, but also making a toxic fish supper for humans."

"Oh no! But don't fish always eat plankton?"

"Yes, dear, but there are many, many types."

29

Sunny realized she had never actively thought about plankton before. Elsa, being an expert on the subject, was happy to share several more plankton facts with Sunny.

"Did you know plankton can be autotrophic?" (Sunny didn't, and she didn't even know what autotrophic meant). "And that dinoflagellate can swim ten times their body length in just a second?" asked Elsa. "I don't suppose you do, but it's true."

Elsa looked out at the horizon, a content smile on her face.

"Even the simplest things are teeming with mystery," she said. "People get caught up with all the big stuff, but it's the small things which really teach us about life."

Elsa patted her on the knee, and Sunny surreptitiously got out a pencil and wrote "remember the Tao of Stokes" on her sketchpad and circled it several times.

Remember to look hard at the small stuff.

Elsa cut through her thoughts, "Talking of small, teeming things, the islands are riddled with ruddy mosquitoes, lots of dengue fever. You did get all your shots?"

"Absolutely."

"Jolly good. I'm the first-aider for the trip, and I don't want to waste any time mopping fevered brows!" Elsa barked out a laugh.

Sunny grinned back at her. "There will be seven of us total on the island, right?" she asked, "Does everyone have dual positions?"

Elsa laughed again, "On a trip like this, when we are a small group, everyone pitches in. Our water chemist is also going to be the main cook."

Sunny told Elsa she would be happy to help in any way she could. The older scientist nodded. "That's one of the reasons we chose you, could tell that you weren't going to spend all day tick-tocking or whatever it is the kids spend their time doing these days—you're much too sensible."

Sunny gave a mental sigh. *Sensible Sunny, that's me.* Sometimes Sunny felt as though she'd skipped being a 'young person ' altogether. Burying your parents at 18 had a way of making one grow up fast.

Elsa was still talking about the research station personnel ahead of them. "Oh, and we had a last-minute addition to the party, so we will be eight, not seven."

Then she added, "The eighth person is also doing..." she paused, and Sunny was surprised to see a mischievous look on her face, "artistic research. But they work in a very different medium to you!"

Sunny was pleasantly surprised to learn another artist would be at the station, "Cool, this other artist, are they already on the island, or are they coming later?"

It would be sweet to have another artist to share ideas with, but she didn't understand why Dr. Stokes (no—Elsa, she must remember that) had such an amused look on her face.

"Oh, he's aboard with us right now; come on—I'll introduce you!"

Sunny couldn't believe she'd missed another artist being aboard the boat with her. He must have boarded when she was hanging out with Farhan.

Oof, hope he doesn't think I was being aloof and cliquey!

Scrambling to their feet, Elsa and Sunny, with Pinky at their heels, walked along the narrow deck to the front of the boat. With a new sense of social confidence, Sunny decided she was going to do her best to put this artist at ease, the same way Farhan had done for her.

Turning the corner to the stern, she saw a glamorous man. He was sprawled on the deck, his back resting against a cabin wall and small snores coming from his perfectly sculpted nose.

Elsa and Sunny stood and looked at him. Sunny thought that with his black shirt, shades, bandanna, and a Panama hat, he looked like a dashing, but fast asleep, bandit.

All that black doesn't seem like a terribly good idea, she thought. *As an artist, he should definitely know that black will absorb heat not reflect it!*

31

Sunny decided she definitely hadn't seen him board, but there was something a little familiar about him. How curious. Also, his clothes looked extremely expensive. She didn't know any artists who made enough money to splurge on designer labels. And if she wasn't mistaken, his fingernails were manicured; she could see the sunlight glinting off a coat of clear varnish.

High maintenance much? Probably a trust-fund baby.

Sunny then gave herself a two-second talking to about being judgmental.

Elsa and Sunny lifted their gaze from the figure, and their eyes met. "Well," said Elsa with a shrug, "I guess I'll introduce you when he wakes up."

Then she turned on her heel and disappeared into a cabin, leaving Sunny standing in front of the slumbering figure.

Am I supposed to follow her? Should I go back to the stern?

Sunny gave herself a little pat on the back for calling the back of the boat the "stern" and then told herself to stop overthinking things. Just find somewhere to sit, maybe do some more sketching and not stress out.

In fact, the fast asleep guy would be great for a life drawing study. The light-play of his muscles was interesting. She should take a snap of him, so she could reference it for her sketches later...

Kit

The booming voice of Dr. Stokes had roused Kit, but he kept his eyes closed, not wanting any kind of company. After a couple of minutes it went quiet again, and he decided it was safe to move. He opened his eyes to find his on-board super fan staring at him in a decidedly beady manner. She couldn't see he was conscious, his green eyes being hidden behind his shades, so he kept perfectly still and observed her observing him.

She had perched on the life jacket chest opposite him and was staring intently, eyes bulging slightly behind her thick glasses. Kit, who was used to intense scrutiny, could see her checking out every inch of his body.

He then watched her shuffle around in her bag and pull out a damned camera again.

Geez, give it up lady—what is she thinking!

Enough was enough. As she focused her camera and lined up her shot, he murmured,

"Please don't."

The girl's eyes opened wide, and she looked embarrassed.

Well, good, thought Kit, *she should be embarrassed.*

He sat up while the blushing girl in front of him apologized. As she hastily put away her camera, he slowly lowered his sunglasses.

"I usually charge for a close-up."

The girl laughed nervously. Kit watched her chew on a slightly chapped bottom lip, take a breath, and then stutteringly introduced herself.

"Hi, um, my name is Sunny. Um, Dr. Stokes, I mean Elsa, was going to introduce us, but she went back inside..."

She trailed off as Kit narrowed his best penetrating gaze at her. A gaze that he had perfected to say, "Go Away."

The girl didn't go away though; she was fiddling with her charm bracelet and looking down at her dusty toes. Her face had flushed a dull red to compliment the burned tip of her nose. He watched her swallow then look up again.

"Um, you're going to be at the research station too, I hear?"

Stubby fingers kept twisting the bracelet around and around as though it was a string of worry beads. Her nervous energy was tiresome. Kit pushed his sunglasses back up his perfect nose.

"I'm a painter," she said, much to Kit's disinterest, "I'm going to be doing nature studies there. Err, Elsa, said you were also an artist..." she struggled on.

Kit did think of himself as an artist. Embodying a character was an art, an art he was really good at. From the moment he'd shrugged off his past life in the backwoods of Washington state as Otis Kitson, and emerged hungry and eager in Hollywood as Nicky Kitson, acting had been the one thing he had been really good at.

His first speaking role had been that of a young poet trying to escape a tyrannical family to follow his dreams. Kit's audition had been the talk of the town. His beautiful face and the pain and anger he had summoned up when reading for the part had delighted the row of casting directors.

He'd had plenty of experience to draw on.

Kit thought it was a good thing acting had taken off, as he was pretty useless at everything else.

The boat motored on, rising and falling on the swells, and the girl shifted to keep her balance. Kit watched her screw herself up to speak again.

"So, err, what kind of art do you do?" she asked.

Her face was completely guileless.

Kit had had every intention of tipping his hat back over his eyes and ignoring this girl, Sunny, for the rest of the journey. But then he realized she was either an excellent actress, or she was one of the very rare few that didn't recognize him. He didn't think she was faking; he actually believed that she didn't know who he was.

Deciding this could be entertaining, Kit made up a reply to her question.

"I guess you could say I do… performance art."

The girl smiled back at him, saying," how interesting," but with a slightly fixed grin.

Kit laughed internally. He thought about the last piece of "performance art" he had seen at some gala or other. A performer was dancing on crushed up eggshells for 45 minutes while reading off a list of ingredients from a boxed pancake mix. In another part of the museum, a girl had spent the night facing a blank wall while whispering about her daddy issues.

"Yeah, performance art—that's the real shit, right? The one true art," Kit said, completely straight-faced.

She gave him another strained smile.

They dropped again into an uncomfortable silence, and Kit watched her shifting on the metal locker, beads of sweat pooling on her upper lip.

"Your nose is burning; did you know that?" Kit told her.

The girl put her hand up to her face.

"I know; it's so hot. My sunscreen is packed in my luggage, though."

Kit reached into his shirt pocket, pulled out the tube of cream, and tossed it at her.

"Here."

She fumbled the container, and it rolled underneath the life-jacket locker. Instantly dropping to her knees to scrabble around and find it, she gave Kit a view of a large bottom in straining shorts with some kind of candy wrapper stuck on the center of her left cheek. He could also see a red line of flesh, where the strap of a sensible money belt dug into her waist. Huffing, and with an air of modest triumph, she finally straightened up, showing him the tube clutched in her hand.

"Got it!"

Looking at the label, she raised her eyebrows above the rim of her specs. "Wow, fancy. I'll just use a tiny bit. Thank you."

He watched her squeeze out a small pea of ointment and rub it into her nose, giving a little sigh of pleasure as she did so.

"Oh, that feels good."

The little cat, who had been observing all this, wandered over to the girl and gave a raspy lick to her newly creamed nose.

She gave a small nervous chuckle, "She must like the caviar content!"

Then, handing the lotion back to Kit, the girl said, "I didn't know that caviar in a sunscreen was a thing! It seems…" she quieted, and Kit watched her struggle to find the right word, "…luxurious."

35

"A friend gave it to me."

"Oh, that makes sense. It's not really the kind of thing you buy for yourself, is it?"

Kit supposed expensive lotions were not the kind of thing she would buy for herself. She was definitely more Marshalls than La Mer.

The girl struggled back onto her former perch, and the cat jumped up beside her. Kit looked away. He tended to avoid cats.

It wasn't that he was a cat-hater, far from that—he liked cats a lot—but, it was complicated.

When he was in the company of a cat he started to feel things he'd rather not feel. He started to feel something, rather than the mindless vacuum he normally aimed for.

The cat looked at him, looked him in the eye. Kit looked away, paused, then looked back again. The cat lifted a blonde paw (one paw was pale and the other a mottled brown) and licked it, almost looking amused, as though she could sense his inner turmoil.

Yeah, yeah, he told the cat silently, *I'm a mess. We both know it.*

The cat blinked in agreement, and Kit felt his guard slipping down.

Damn it, cat!

He sighed. *I'm such a sucker.*

The memory he'd tried to keep buried deep in the back of his brain started to surface. Kit consciously pushed it back down, gave another sigh, then asked, "Who's the kitty?"

The girl picked up the skinny, and apparently very amenable, creature, goofily making it wave a paw.

"This is Pinky—the ship's cat."

She pressed the little furry body against her sticky face.

For the first time that day, Kit gave a genuine grin. It was directed at the cat.

"Hello, Pinky."

Looking up from the furry face back to the girl, Kit could see her responding as he acted a little friendlier, which instantly put Kit back on the defensive. Mustn't give fans an inch, or they'd bite off your whole arm, he thought, totally forgetting that he'd just decided that Sunny wasn't a fan-girl at all.

"I don't think she's a ship's cat in the traditional sense," she was saying, "apparently, she just adopted this boat as her home. I mean, all ships used to have them, cats I mean, to keep control of onboard rodents, but I don't know if that's why Pinky is here," she babbled on. "I mean obviously there are still rats and mice, but I bet they don't get into the stores like they used to..."

Kit raised an eyebrow at her rattling monologue.

"...I guess maybe they do, the rats especially, but you'd think the packaging would be more robust these days. But maybe not; I mean cardboard isn't rat-proof, is it?"

She gave Pinky the cat several more firm pets.

"...I did see some wooden crates being loaded too, and a metal flight case..."

Her voice trailed off, and Kit looked at her with a coolly raised eyebrow.

"Do you always talk so fast without stopping for a breath?"

Sunny grimaced and flushed again, "Only when I'm feeling awkward," she muttered.

At that moment, a voice called out across the boat, and Kit saw a young crewmember waving in their direction.

"You OK, Sunny?" said the slight, wiry boy, jumping down from a ladder and heading in their direction.

"Yes, thanks, Farhan," Sunny smiled back.

Farhan gave her a grin, then nodded in Kit's direction. "Sir," he said formally as he disappeared through a dark doorway.

Kit saw how the girl's face lightened when the boy called to her and then clouded again when it turned back to him. He could tell by her flicking eyes that she was trying to figure out a polite way to exit this scene when suddenly a dark shadow passed over them, and her gaze changed focus.

"A booby!" she gasped, "how lovely!"

37

Kit followed her gaze. "Doesn't look like any booby I've ever seen."

He wiggled his eyebrows at the double entendre, making her blush some more.

As seemed to be her habit, she started to gabble about random facts again to cover up her embarrassment.

"Well, the booby got its name because *bobo* means stupid in Spanish. They're perceived as stupid because they are so easy to catch. In stories, shipwrecked sailors are always eating them..."

Just as she was trailing off, a huge bang blasted around the boat, and the accompanying jolt knocked the girl off her feet and straight on top of Kit.

"What the hell!"

He shoved the girl out of his lap, not noticing her head bounce off a metal stanchion, and scrambled to his feet.

Again he yelled.

"What is going on?"

Chapter 4

Sunny

Time seemed to slow, then stop altogether.

She was sprawled on the deck, Pinky on her stomach, and she was completely confused. What had just happened? Why did her head hurt?

Slowly she pushed herself onto her knees, then stood upright on shaky legs.

Above her, the booby was flying away with heavy, measured wing flaps, and she could feel the cat frantically winding itself in and out of her legs.

Her head was swimming.

Turning toward the bridge, she swayed and held tight to a rail. In the bridge, she could see the shadowed outline of the captain clutching a radio handset. Beside her, the obnoxious performance-artist-man was yelling and clambering to his feet. Sunny tuned him out.

The sky was so beautiful—the setting sun was sending streaks of pink and gold into the blue. *I'd use ultramarine to paint it, with cadmium orange and maybe permanent rose.*

A second later, a siren started to blare. Sunny blinked, and just like that she began to come back to her senses. A crewman flashed by, racing out of the galley, and heading somewhere down toward the engine room. A series of pops tattooed loudly as hot rushing air hit her face.

It smells weird, kinda sour, she thought. Still dazed, as alarms wailed all around her.

The next moment, another explosion rocked the ship, blowing out a window, allowing thick oily smoke to come pouring out onto the deck, muddying the beautiful ultramarine blue into a gloomy Davy's gray.

A loud tannoyed voice broke through the chaos.

"All passengers and crew put on life jackets and assemble at the life raft station immediately!"

Sunny heard a voice beside saying, "here, here," and a hand proffered her a fat orange vest from the metal locker she had been sitting on just minutes before. The smoke was making her eyes water, and as she blinked, Pinky clawed at Sunny's leg. The stinging pain made her jerk, and she put on the jacket the man handed to her with clumsy fingers.

Come on! Get it done up, get it together, Sunny!

She fumbled and failed do up the jacket. Never had her fingers felt more useless.

Damn it! Mom? Mom, help me!

A few years ago, she'd often talked to her parents in her head, but over time that habit had slowed.

Looking around, she saw that the boat was a chaos of smoke, yelling, alarms, and rushing bodies. Sunny's eyes watered as the toxic fumes bombarded her senses. She coughed several times, then shook her head.

Get it together. It's an emergency. You've got to focus!

Finally managing to slot the black plastic buckles together, she bent down, looking to pick up her tote, but then ignored it in favor of the small cat, who bucked and struggled, but didn't manage to escape Sunny's grip.

To her left, she could see a small group were assembling by what was probably the lifeboat. Putting out her hand, she tugged on the black shirt of the man who had handed her the life vest.

"Over there," she yelled, nodding her head towards the group.

He was buckling his own jacket and quickly clipped it together and nodded back at her.

The cat was trying to battle its way out of her arms once again, but Sunny just gripped harder, ignoring the hissing and scratching.

Quit it cat!

An Evans' would put up with any amount of pain to save a pet. Finally wrangling Pinky, she turned her body toward the escape route.

But the next moment, she froze.

Through the smoky porthole a few feet in front of her, she had caught a glimpse of a non-moving figure lying on the cabin floor —it was Farhan,

Unconscious.

"Farhan's in there! He's not moving!"

The man was making to join the assembled group by the life rafts, but Sunny's scream pulled him up short.

Flames from the back of the small ship were now traveling forward at an incredible speed. The room where the boy lay was about to be engulfed. Looking down at the cat in her arms, she thrust the animal toward the man. She just had to save Farhan.

"Take the cat, and get help," she screamed, "I'll try and get him!"

Her arms were outstretched as she tried to push Pinky onto the chest of the man mentally readying herself to run toward the flames. The cat, though, was immediately thrust back onto her own chest. She heard the man yell out.

"You go to the lifeboat!"

The next minute he plunged into the smoke-filled doorway that led toward Farhan.

Kit

iving inside the bulkhead, Kit choked on the thick smoke, and his eyes streamed, the combination making it almost impossible to see anything. Fire crackled, and popping sounds rattled around the corridor. It was so hot the air was burning his throat. Taking another painful breath, then pulling his bandanna over his nose, he moved forward, hoping the corridor would take him toward the cabin

41

where Farhan lay. There was a metal door to his left, and by his reckoning, that would be where the boy was. But the door to the cabin was firmly shut, and as Kit put his hand on it to depress the handle, he screamed. The latch was red-hot and immediately seared the skin on his palm. He felt some of his hand stick to the metal as he managed to release the mechanism.

"Aaaahhh!" he yelled again, drawing hot toxic smoke deep into his lungs on the inhale.

The boy. Gotta get the boy.

Gasping, he shouldered open the door. The inside of the steel-hulled boat was turning into an oven, and even Kit's life vest was beginning to melt, the orange terylene bubbling and shriveling when it came close to the walls and gluing itself to Kit's shirt.

As he moved into the cabin, the heat was even more intense, and there was an overpowering smell of diesel. But there, just a few feet away, lay an unconscious body. Kit knelt beside the boy, ignoring the pain of the metal floor on his knees, and decided not to check if the boy was alive or dead. It was of no consequence in that moment—he had no time to think. He just had to get going. Tugging off the smoldering life preserver before the melting plastic started sticking to his skin, he eased his arms under Farhan's skinny frame. The boy was so mercifully light Kit could easily pull him across the floor, over the lip of the door, and with one last heave, out onto the open deck.

Stumbling around in the hazy outside light, Kit bent over and coughed uncontrollably.

The girl was still there, yelling and clutching the cat, and two other crew members were picking up the boy to move him away from the fire. Kit tried to straighten up.

If he could just stop coughing, he thought, everything would be OK.

Another spasm wracked him, and he bent over again, desperate to take one clean breath and beginning to panic. There simply was not enough oxygen in his lungs, and his vision had started to narrow.

The boat, no longer under the dictates of the engine, rolled with the swells, making him lurch and nearly fall as he gasped.

A hand grabbed the back of his shirt and tried to pull him upright.

"Come on!" a voice screamed.

The insistent tugging at his shirt encouraged him to try again to straighten up. Making it almost upright, he could see the girl, now right in front of him. She was shaking him furiously, which wasn't helping things at all. She screamed again, but he couldn't understand what she was saying. The frenzied, clawing cat clamped under her arm swiped at Kit's arm.

"Come on!" She screamed again. This time her voice registered.

Yes, gotta move.

He took a step forward, his arm going around the girl to bring her with him in the movement, but the next second another explosion boomed.

This blast sent them flying, off their feet, off the deck, and over the railing into the swirling ocean below.

Chapter 5

Sunny

*S*unny's life vest shot her up to the surface like a champagne cork. Spluttering and terrified, she spun around, trying to get her bearings. The boat was towering above her, high on the crest of a wave, while she was low down in the trough. Kit, who didn't have a life jacket on, was still coughing uncontrollably and thrashing in the water close by. A yard further out, Pinky was valiantly paddling to stay afloat.

Sunny began to swim toward Kit and Pinky, the saltwater stinging her eyes and burning her nose. She reached Kit first and tried to grab hold of a flailing arm. It was useless; the man was completely out of control and fighting invisible sea demons. Sunny trod water for a minute to assess the situation; the cat was still paddling away, holding her own, but the man was slipping under the water repeatedly.

She swam up behind him, thinking to slap him, bring him to his senses, but as she reached out toward him, a meaty fist shot out in her direction and locked onto a hank of her hair. The strong arm went down into the water, and with it went Sunny's head.

Beneath the waves, she desperately tried to pry open the gripping fingers.

I'm going to die. I'm going to die.

Then the hand rose upwards again, breaking the water and allowing her to gasp what air she could. She spun and scratched and screamed, but within a few seconds, she was once again dragged down by her hair.

Please. Breathe. Help!

The hand holding her down suddenly released its grip, and she surfaced, taking huge gulping breaths. The man had passed out and was floating on his back, his nose barely above the water. Sunny stretched out a hand and clutched the collar of his shirt. The moment of calm gave Sunny a chance to look around. Pinky was a small, dark spot in the waves, the sodden fur making her look like a tiny seal. Half remembering her water safety certification from summer lifeguarding at the municipal pool, she held Kit around the neck, then paddled on her back toward the tiring cat.

"Pinky, Pinky, here..." Sunny was a strong swimmer, but her whole body was trembling. Nevertheless, there was no way she was going to pause until she had the cat, as well as the man, safe in her clutches. She kicked herself closer to the cat. Kit's head still lay in the crook of her armpit as she tried to coax the cat to board her floating body as well.

"Come on, kitty, please..."

Another wave pushed the cat closer, and it clawed itself onto Sunny's chest, hissing and spitting ungratefully as it did so. Having momentarily saved the man and the cat, Sunny's head sank back on the raised collar of her life vest.

She closed her eyes. Her mind blank, like a fuse had blown from the surge of extreme energy. She let herself float—the cat making mewling sounds and the man making no sounds at all.

Minutes passed. Her brain flickered back to life—but barely.

So tired.

A wave broke, sending water across her face, up her nose.

She coughed and tried to keep her eyes closed, but the waves jostled her shoulders—sprays of water set her spluttering. In the slap of water she imagined her dad's soft Welsh voice saying, "Come on now, Sunny-bach, rhoi'r ffidil yn y to!"

Don't put the violin on the roof, she thought to herself. It was one of her dad's favorite sayings. It meant, basically, don't throw in the towel.

Evans never threw in the towel.

Sunny opened her eyes.

"Rhoi'r," she croaked and opened her eyes.

"Fidel..." She swiveled herself, the man, and the cat around until she saw the ruined, burning ship, now further away and completely enveloped in flames.

"Yn y to," she gasped. Then taking another breath in, she screamed as loudly as she possibly could.

"Hhheeeeeeyyy!"

She screamed, forcing air through her aching throat.

"Heeelllllppppp!"

She screamed, though the tissue in her esophagus felt like it was being torn to shreds.

"Heeeerrreeee!"

But the flaming hull, silhouetted against the setting sun, just kept shrinking. On and on she screamed until no sound was able to come out of her wrecked throat. The flame-engulfed ship was just a speck on the horizon. It was no good. The ship was gone, the crew was gone, everything was gone. The man was unconscious, and she was alone, supporting his body and also acting as a life raft for a half-drowned cat.

Night was falling, and she was floating in the middle of the Pacific Ocean with no land in sight.

*****

Hours passed, and Sunny fought to stay awake. She was constantly checking that Pinky was balanced on her chest and that the man's nose and mouth were clear of the water. She had tried and failed to check his pulse, but the odd moaning noises he made convinced her he was alive. He had to be alive. He had to be.

And she had to keep him that way.

A billion stars were in the sky. The sickle moon shone a soft milky light onto the surface of the water, and a watery luminescence surrounded them, like they were floating in a halo. But even with that illumination, keeping watch on her charges was not easy. Her eyes were in a terrible state, the salt water constantly irritating them and her glasses long lost to Davy Jones. She wanted so desperately to close her sore eyes, shut them and keep them closed, but she knew she mustn't. If she closed her eyes, she didn't think she'd ever open them again.

As they drifted, so did Sunny's thoughts.

Do fish sleep?

Do they close their eyes?

Mustn't close my eyes.

She was so very tired, and the waves seemed so much bigger than they had when she'd been on the boat. The water was warmer than the outside air, but still Sunny felt chilled to the bone—and thirsty, so thirsty. The little cat sat a few inches from her face. Pinky had been letting out intermittent pitiful meows. Now she nudged her head toward Sunny, butting her gently on the nose. The small contact propelled Sunny to dig deeper, further into her dogged determination. It wasn't a matter of stamina—that had long since been used up. Now it was all raw willpower.

Slurring her way through *10,000 Bottles of Beer on the Wall*, she made it through the night, Pinky balanced on her chest, and one arm threaded through the man's shirt—so as not to let him go.

*****

Sunny jerked awake, almost casting poor Pinky back into the water. She'd fallen asleep for a moment, dreaming of her sweet dead dog, Steve Irwin. In her dream, he had been dog-paddling next to her, his warm eyes encouraging her to keep going. As the light was now breaking on the horizon, she turned in a slow circle, squinting and searching for any sign of help. But the three-sixty degree sweep revealed nothing—no land, no ships, no planes—though even if there had been, she probably would not have seen them with her blurry vision.

47

All around, above, and below was just vast, empty blue space, and Sunny had absolutely no idea what to do. Sunny Evans, queen of comprehensive planning, was at a complete loss.

She looked at the man in her arms. He had groaned and muttered several times through the night but never returned to full consciousness. Now though, he started coughing again.

Kit

*K*it woke suddenly and in complete panic. He tried to wrestle away from whatever was attached to him but couldn't fight it off, unaware that his struggles sent Pinky flying and Sunny under the waves.

"Stop!" cried a voice, "stop!"

But in his desperate state, he couldn't process anything. Kit had descended into hell; he couldn't breathe, he couldn't see, and everything hurt. Hands were beating him, always beating him. He couldn't take it any more. The monster. He could never escape the monster, and now it was trying to drag him down into the ocean, and he fought it off with all his might. He could never win, but this time he'd go down fighting. As the creature surfaced again, Kit swung, his head rolling with fear and delirium. His skull met something equally hard, and abruptly the frenzied pulling stopped.

All was quiet.

Salt water splashed in his face.

He was in the ocean, he thought. And, oww, his head—what the hell?

Then he saw a body floating in the water, brown hair waving out like seaweed, and swam a couple of painful strokes to meet it. Trying to grab the body, he let out a cry.

His hand was agony. What was going on?

"Help!" Kit screamed to the empty horizon. "Help!" he screamed again uselessly, then he turned back to the floating body. It was in a life vest, which kept the head above water.

Where was he? Who was that?

The whole situation became even more bizarre when he realized a very soggy cat was paddling in the water next to him.

Kit yelled and yelled, hoarse screams tearing his throat up.

The floating body returned to consciousness.

"Hey..." it croaked, "hey—s-stop."

He turned to the rasping, whispery voice, seeing it belonged to the girl from the boat.

"What—you—what happened—what?"

Her mouth was trembling so much it was hard to make out her words.

"I thought you were dying, and we were going to be alone," she gibbered, grabbing an exhausted Pinky, who was paddling furiously to keep afloat.

Kit thought the girl was bordering on hysteria, so calming his own breathing and trying to repress his own total panic, he slowly repeated.

"What happened? It's OK—I'm OK; I'm not dying—but what happened?"

As they floated on, she described to a dazed Kit the explosions aboard the boat, his rescue of Farhan, and the blast that knocked them overboard.

Kit swallowed, the salt water burned, and his throat was parched. When he tried to generate some saliva, his mouth barely moistened. In a very raw voice, he tried to comfort her.

"They'll know we're missing. They'll look for us."

They will, he thought.

If the others on the life raft made it, then half the Navy will probably be looking for us.

If the others made it.

The girl nodded, but her face didn't show much hope.

"I guess, but I haven't seen or heard anything—no planes, no boats, nothing. We've been drifting all night. I thought the night would never end..."

She paddled her feet to close the gap between them.

"I've had my arm through your shirt so you wouldn't drift away. We should do that again, shouldn't we? We can't split up..."

Her voice was gravelly, and Kit could see a small ring of saltwater boils forming on her neck where the life jacket had scrubbed her tender skin raw.

"You held me all night?" he asked incredulously.

In answer, she just maneuvered herself behind him and threaded her limb through his shirt again. Then leaning back, Pinky settled back down on top of her, and the three of them floated as a unit.

The sea swells grew and waned, with the threesome completely at the mercy of the current. Mostly floating in silence, Kit got lost in his own thoughts. The girl was also quiet, but after what was possibly hours, she whispered to Kit,

"Are you thinking about sharks?" she asked.

Kit had been thinking about sharks.

He'd been thinking about them too much and was consciously trying not to kick his legs because perhaps still limbs would not present such a target. The girl was doing the same, barely making a splash in the water any time she very carefully shifted.

Kit just looked at her but said nothing. What was there to say? After a while, she looked away and they quietly floated on.

A little later, a sudden, heavy, tropical rain shower stirred him from his daze, and Kit raised his mouth to the sky, grateful for every swallowed raindrop that fell into his parched mouth.

"I don't even know your name," the girl murmured. "If we are going to die out here, I should know your name..."

Kit was quiet for a minute, then said, "My name...my name is Otis Kitson, but call me Kit."

He paused for a moment; they drifted some more, then he continued, "I'm sorry, I don't think I can remember your name. You told me before, but with everything since then..."

"Sunny, my name is Sunny Evans," she whispered.

Sunny. His mind sang the lyrics to the old Bobby Hebb song.

Kit tried to shake himself out of his delirium by concentrating on his floating partner.

"Sunny? Weird name. You have hippy parents?"

Sunny

They were probably minutes from being eaten by sharks, but the man, Otis Kitson, Kit, was ragging on her about about her name. Sunny would have laughed if she'd had the energy. Here they were, the sea was poised to swallow them whole, and they were conversing about nicknames.

She didn't often tell people how her name came about—it was kind of a strange way to acquire a name. But right here, right now, in the middle of the ocean, feeling embarrassed was the last of her worries.

"I'd never describe my parents as hippies," she said, "just plain, hardworking folk."

She could picture her mom's comforting face vividly. It felt like only yesterday that she'd kissed her parents goodbye to go on a high school trip for the weekend, only to come home to dead parents.

"My mom had a difficult birth with me. It took ages, I was born face up, not face down, and that is a really painful way to give birth. After I was born, the midwife said I was delivered 'sunny side up'..." she paused, "...Mom and Dad called me Sunny while trying to agree on a proper name, but eventually they just settled on Sunny for good."

Kit, who was literally settled on Sunny, murmured, "Sunny. Hmm, good thing they didn't call you 'over-easy.'"

Sunny sighed.

They drifted more, and all sense of time and place vanished. At some point, Kit said he could see the hazy outline of a ship on the horizon. But they agreed not to use up their strength yelling and waving; the ship was too far away. Better to keep still, keep quiet, and keep from attracting the attention of whatever may be lurking beneath.

Kit asked Sunny what had happened to his hand. He said it didn't feel too bad when it was submerged, but as soon as the air hit it, he felt sick with pain.

Sunny shook her head slightly.

"Don't know," she said. She didn't particularly care about his sore hand. Her whole body was a mass of aching and burning. Her face was on fire, her eyes and throat were gritty with salt, and her head throbbed incessantly.

They had been floating in an arrangement that was like toppled dominoes. Sunny, in the life vest, lay floating on her back with the cat on top of her. Kit, also on his back, rested his head in the crook of her armpit. To pass the time, and to stop herself from getting hysterical, Sunny had started to tell rambling stories. She told Kit of her life growing up in Weaver Creek, her adventures with Steve, the dog, the good times with her best friend, Betsy. She told him how Betsy's family had decided to move abroad, leaving Sunny starting tenth grade without her BFF.

She told him about her loving mom and dad, and she told him how they died and how it still seemed unreal that they were gone. She told him how she'd gone to live with her mom's best friend Andrea and had saved money by working at the town diner until she had enough to move to Seattle. She told him that when her phone rang, she still fully expected it to be her mom, calling to regale her with all the latest Weaver Creek gossip.

She talked until her parched throat insisted she stop.

So, she asked Kit about his life.

Kit just gave her the briefest of snippets about his Ellensburg childhood. A quick mention of how he didn't get on with his dad, "...so I left. Left to L.A. to try and make my fortune. My Mom died when I was little, so I never really knew her."

"Oh, that's so sad!" Sunny murmured.

She couldn't imagine growing up without a mom. Mom's were who taught you how to exist in the world. How to take care of yourself. How do you learn that without a mom? And what about having a dad who wasn't your biggest cheerleader? Your confidant, your foundation?

The conversation petered out, so they floated some more in silence.

As the sky started to darken, Sunny noted the changing light.

"The sun is nearly down again. What do you think about praying?" she asked Kit, through lips that were chapped and bleeding. The skin on her face was shiny and tight, burned a red that was almost eggplant purple. She felt deathly ill. She thought praying might not be a bad idea.

Sunny's family were the Christmas-and-Easter-only type of churchgoers, but those visits had ensured she knew the Lord's prayer.

"Sure, it certainly isn't going to hurt," Kit replied.

Into the gathering gloom, she whispered out words to a God that she was not really sure existed.

Kit

*L*ooking at the endless sky, Kit thought odds were good that he would soon know whether there really was a heaven—or a hell. His throat was on fire, and his tongue was beginning to swell.

That's not good.

The swelling made it difficult to swallow, and the gagging feeling triggered a memory, sending his fevered brain back to his childhood, back to when he was Otis Kitson, "useless" Otis Kitson.

He remembered being delirious with thirst while locked in a small storage shed on the edge of the rundown property that his family lived on, five miles outside of Ellensburg.

Kit's father, Zach, was a bully of the first order. Zach along with his brothers, Kit's uncles, Jason and Jude, spent their days dealing stolen car parts, poaching, and drinking vast quantities of beer. The three men had little time for young Otis Kitson; he cried during hunting trips, whined about things like food and clothing, and had actually had the gall to spend time hanging out with the son of the local sheriff. One day Uncle Jason discovered Kit had befriended a stray cat and had caught him feeding it scraps. This was the perfect opportunity, the three men decided, to make Otis a real man.

Make the boy kill the cat.

Kit and the flea-bitten cat were locked in one of the many rundown outbuildings in the family compound—with no food or water—and Kit was not to be released until the cat was dead. For the first few hours, Kit had paced furiously around the barn, listening to his father and his uncles cracking beers and jokes. Determined not to let them win, Kit spent the remainder of the 48-hours digging with his fingers to get below the shed foundation. The cat waited, big-eyed and trusting. Even though the cat was just a collection of bones, fleas, and mange, Kit knew this cat wanted to live. It was relying on him, so he dug. He dug through the night and all the next day. The foundations were deep, way deeper than he expected, but he dug on and on.

His aim was to dig a hole big enough to release the cat, and hopefully himself.

But that wasn't to be.

When Zach, Jason, and Jude finally unlocked the doors on the third day, Kit was unconscious, fingers bruised and bloody, but the cat was gone, through the narrow shaft Kit had carved out. As Kit lay in the dirt, his body shutting down for lack of water, he heard his father spit and cuss.

"Waste of space; what did I do to get such a candy-ass punk for a son. Worthless, completely worthless..."

The words of his father sank deeply into Kit's nine-year-old psyche, and the idea that he was of no worth to anybody—that he should just give up and die—swam to the surface from time to time. Making a success of his acting career had made the voices a little quieter, and when they got loud again, self-medicating with gin or cocaine, parties and girls, dumb jokes, and fast cars helped. But in the quiet swell of the ocean, the voices were very loud.

So very loud.

And I'm so tired.

Kit thought about all he had achieved in his life, and it all seemed pointless, vapid.

My life has been useless. Of no use to anyone. I am worthless. Dad was right; he was always right.

Water splashed over his face again, brine shooting up his nose. He coughed, but thought it would be equally easy to just inhale the water into his lungs.

Maybe it is time to let go.

Another wave washed over his face.

What's the point of anything?

"He that is born to be hanged need fear no drowning..." Kit mumbled to himself.

Maybe he was born to be drowned. At least he needn't fear being hung.

Can't fight fate.

He was so tired. The sky had turned to a deep navy blue after the sun had disappeared in a flash of orange-gold; the sunset had been beautiful—not a bad way to leave the planet at all.

A star shot through the sky overhead; Kit watched its trajectory and nodded to himself—time to let go.

"Goodnight, Sunny. Goodnight, Pinky," he said quietly.

He carefully eased himself from Sunny's floating body, kicking his legs to move himself apart from the girl and the cat. The next big wave and he would just inhale, breathe in the water and let himself sink. Let go of trying.

All of a sudden, Sunny, who had been mumbling nonsense to herself, must have noticed he was floating away. She spun around.

Kit closed his eyes and laid his head back on the water.

A hoarse cry floated across the ocean.

"No! No, don't give up, don't! You can't—you can't leave us alone!"

Kit opened his eyes and raised his head a little. Sunny was attempting a feeble backstroke, trying to catch up with him as he was floating away. He couldn't make her chase him, so he reluctantly kicked his way back toward her. As soon as she was within range, she grabbed hold of his foot and croaked out, "Please don't leave us alone. Promise me! Please!"

Kit straightened up, trod water, and looked at her. She was a mess, her right eye bruised and swollen, crusty matted hair surrounding her burned face—skin that was so taut it stretched to the point of almost splitting. She looked pitiful, not unlike that stray cat Kit had dug an escape route for. Boils ringed her throat, but her eyes were still filled with a desire to survive.

How is she still fighting, he thought? How? How does she have that much will to live?

They looked at each other through the gloom of the night, rising up with the swells and sinking again into the troughs. Then Kit closed his eyes.

I should stay with her until we die, he thought. *There's no way out of this, but she shouldn't have to be alone out here.*

He opened his eyes again on hearing a meow. Pinky and Sunny were looking at him, eyes huge. Waiting.

Waiting to see if he was done. Waiting to see if he was going to abandon them.

He knew he couldn't do it. Couldn't leave them out here alone.

Paddling closer, putting his face inches from hers, Kit looked into Sunny's eyes.

"O.K. I won't give up until we both agree there is no hope."

He nodded, to himself, to the cat and to Sunny.

"I can do that; I can promise you that. No checking out until we are all ready to let go."

56

Kit nudged himself back into position, head leaning against her shoulder, and Sunny cradled her arm around him.

"Thank you," she whispered "Thank you, thank you, thank you."

"No need to go overboard with the thanks Sunny," he replied. "No need to go overboard...heh, heh," he coughed out weakly.

She didn't reply.

But once the threesome was settled again, the little cat stretched out a small sandpaper paw-pad and rested it on Kit's shoulder.

The light weight of Pinky's paw almost felt like a benediction.

*****

The sky eventually lightened once more, the morning sun warming their battered bodies. Thirty-six hours after they'd become shipwrecked salt-water waves were still the constant seascape.

The first thing that notified Kit that something was different was the smell. The animal part of his brain was tapping on his cerebrum, trying to get its attention. A few moments later, Kit 's front brain woke up; it noticed a musty, sharp scent that mingled with the saline. In the next second, he became aware that the sound of the sea was changing, gradually getting louder until it almost reached a roaring pitch—roaring then fading, roaring then fading. The ocean was gathering its forces to combat something, a resistance of some kind.

The reason for the rhythmic noise became clear as, focusing his salt-crusted eyes, he could just make out a landmass. The rhythmic noise was the waves hitting a reef several hundred yards out from the land.

Sunny floated on her back, perhaps sleeping, perhaps unconscious, and when Kit tried to rouse her, she just moaned and her eyes remained closed. Frantic, Kit thought they were going to drift straight by the land if he didn't do something. Uncoupling himself from Sunny, he pushed her floating body, plus cat cargo, in front of him. Wincing, he brought his burnt hand up to her life preserver, threaded it through the strap, and then began to swim with every last ounce of his energy.

His muscles screamed, the island seemed 100 miles away, but he kept going.

One.

His arm would arc over his head and then break through the surface, a one-armed butterfly stroke.

Two.

His arm plowed down, then circled. The water felt as thick as molasses.

One.

Two.

One.

Two.

His one goal was to reach the nearest break in the coral rim— the one goal in his life, the only thing that mattered.

One.

I can do this.

Two.

I promised...

If he could just reach the break in the reef, they would live.

The current, though, had different plans. For what felt like hours, Kit battled the motion of the sea. Never in his life had he pushed himself so hard. It was too much. Kit was at his breaking point. His father's mocking laugh sounding loud in his head.

Knew you were worthless, boy...

"No!"

Shouting out loud was a mistake. The next minute he was choking on water. He was crying. He was failing. He was worthless.

But somehow his arm once more circled through the water.

Just one more stroke, Kit thought. *I can do one more stroke.*

Time after time, he was on the point of conceding but then would rally again, thinking about the unconscious girl who had kept him afloat for an entire night while he was out of it.

I owe her. Just a bit more; just a bit more.

The water tugged them backward, a huge wave sucking them further from the reef.

No!

Kit thought he must be hallucinating, because now he could hear a voice saying something about putting violins on a roof.

Violins or not, it was no use. It was all over. There was no way he could make up the lost ground, but then, just as Kit was resigning himself to failure, the giant wave rolled back again, casting them closer to the gap. Closer and then, as Kit laughed hysterically, miraculously through, into a bay of calm blue water.

Don't stop.

Though the urge to just stop, just float in the calm water, was nearly all-consuming, Kit worried they could get dragged back out again as easily as they'd been pushed in. With the tiny amount of energy he had remaining, Kit kicked his legs, moving shoreward until, finally, his feet touched the sandy bottom of the bay. From there, he just crawled, crawled until they were in the shallows. On his knees, he gave Sunny and Pinky one last push onto the wet beach, and then he collapsed beside them.

He'd done his part. He'd dug the tunnel and given them an escape route.

Now he had absolutely nothing left.

59

Chapter 6

Sunny

*S*unny's throat was dry and swollen. She was hurting all over, and it felt as though she was still moving up and down in the ocean, though apparently she wasn't as she could feel solid ground under her body.

We're on land, she thought in amazement.

Sprawled on the hot white sand, Sunny felt like she never wanted to move again, but forcing herself, she rolled over. Kit was lying next to her, but Pinky was nowhere to be seen.

She shook him feebly, croaking. "Kit, Kit, we're on land! Kit, wake up!"

As she twisted her head, the skin on Sunny's neck was scraped by the edge of the life vest. Her muscles felt like jelly. With pruney fingers, she fumbled at the thick black clips and released herself. Casting the jacket aside, she peered myopically around the shore.

She couldn't see the little cat but did see an expanse of white sandy beach fringed with swaying deep greens. Amid the natural palette, Sunny could also see jarring, unnatural colors dotting the shoreline. These unnaturally hued objects were heaped in tangles where the highwater mark was on the sand.

There must be people here! Those are man-made objects!

Sunny shook Kit's shoulder, this time with a bit more vigor. "Please, Kit, wake up!"

Then, "Pinky! Puss-puss-puss."

Beside her, Kit groaned and heaved himself up onto an elbow.

"I'm awake."

He reached out a hand to steady himself, but then shrieked in pain. Sunny looked at him and winced when she saw the burned mess of his hand.

"Gotta get out of the sun," she rasped. Every part of her body was being roasted. Nodding to the blurry green line ahead of her, adding, "shade up there."

With a lot of encouragement, Sunny eventually got Kit to drag up the wherewithal to move, and they slowly crawled up from the shoreline to the shade of the trees. It was only a matter of thirty feet, but it felt thirty times that. The passage took up all the energy they had, and as soon as they were out of the sun, they both passed out again.

When Sunny came to a second time, she was totally confused. What was going on? Where was she?

In a flash, it all came back to her, and with it the rocking motion of the sea that still lingered in her body. Leaning over, she retched, dry heaves tearing at her throat as her hands clawed at the sand. After a while, her stomach calmed and the nausea passed. She sat back up, panting, sweat streaking her face and sending salty rivulets into her mouth.

The taste of her sweat made her even more aware of her thirst. She looked at Kit, who had slept on through all her heaving.

This was bad. Really bad.

Sunny rubbed a knuckle against her head. She needed to make her brain work, but her brain felt like it was wrapped in thick fog.

What to do?

I'll just rest a moment longer. Then I'll figure something out.

What that "something" would be was not something Sunny could currently compute.

A light breeze picked up, and it felt good on her skin. The sky was not as bright as earlier, and the whole beach cooled as a passing cloud covered the sun.

Gotta do something, she told herself again, but then continued to lay like a beached jellyfish, as though every bone in her body had dissolved.

Dammit, Sunny! Move your butt!

A few moments later, the newly darkened sky began to spit water. Within minutes a soaking shower began. When the first drops had hit Sunny's flaccid body, she hadn't reacted, but then the clouds burst fully and the cool water hitting her skin was impossible to ignore. Sitting upright, muscles protesting, she poked Kit's shoulder.

"Kit! Kit!" she croaked.

Kit slowly opened his eyes, and at her urging, swiveled his head to the sky—mouth agape—but still basically inert.

The light splashing of the raindrops just seemed to increase Sunny's thirst. Not being able to get an actual mouthful of rainwater was so frustrating. Sunny squinted at the beach flotsam.

Maybe she'd find something on the water line they could use? Plastic bottles? Something was better than nothing.

She staggered over on rubbery legs and immediately found a green *Squirt* bottle, the bright color easy to spot in the sand. In the next few seconds, she'd also got two plastic cola bottles. She set them upright, looking dismally at the narrow openings. Then turning, she tripped over more trash, a soccer ball torn almost in half. Grabbing it, she bashed at the rubber to make the gaping hole even bigger.

OK. As soon as it's a little full, rinse it around to get the salt off.

She watched as the ball's freshly sluiced interior gradually filled, aware that the cloud bank above them was quickly moving away. While the rain still fell and she waited for her containers to fill, she swept her hands over her face, trying to rid herself of the salty scum which was on every inch of her body.

Too soon, the shower stopped, but the ball was almost half full. As she gulped down the water, Sunny's stomach lurched. She paused, hoping it would stay down. It did, so she made her way back up the beach to Kit.

"Here, drink."

Helping him up onto his elbows, Sunny balanced the ripped ball beneath his chin and tipped it. Pouring slowly, so as not to waste a drop, Sunny soon emptied the ball and lay back on the ground, exhausted.

The third time she awoke to Kit shaking her.

"Hey, hey."

She groaned and opened an eye.

"Is there more water?"

His voice was hoarse, and the empty ball sat in between them.

"There's more in some bottles," she whispered, "on the shore..." She pointed a trembly finger.

"I'll get them."

Sunny lay back and closed her eyes again until Kit poked her again.

"Here."

She drank from the *Squirt* bottle. There wasn't very much, and she couldn't ration, not yet. She just needed to drink and was gratified how quickly even a little hydration worked on her body. Her fluttering heart steadied, the pounding in her head lessened, and she began to think clearly again.

And the first clear thought was about the wellbeing of the third member of their party.

"Kit, Kit—Pinky—did she make it too?"

Kit didn't speak for a second, and she felt panic blooming in her stomach.

"Kit?"

"Oh yeah, she made it."

Sunny flopped back on the sand, "Oh, oh, thank God. I wish she was here, though. I have this horrible vision of her crawling off, gasping for water."

"I'm sure she's fine," Kit said, closing his eyes again.

Not bothering to answer him—they had no way of knowing whether she was fine or not—Sunny started calling out to the cat in a croaky voice.

The action of shouting was not only painful to her throat, but also to her lips and face. Putting a tentative hand up to her cheek, she hurriedly pulled it away again.

"Aww, ow."

Kit had opened an eye when she'd made the pain-filled noise. Looking at her, he said, "Your face is really burned."

Sunny's face was on fire, but the only way she could deal with the pain was to try to ignore it.

"It's OK," she lied, "but what about your hand? It looks a bit nasty."

Sunny actually thought it looked horrendous. A mass of bulbous blisters circled with angry red scorch marks.

She moved over to his side and gently examined the burns.

"The salt water was probably good for it, but try to keep it out of the sand."

Kit just lay back and closed his eyes again. "Where do you think we are?"

"Farhan told me there were hundreds of unpopulated atolls out here, far more than populated ones."

She sighed pessimistically, but then she remembered all the trash on the shoreline. "But all the garbage on the shore, maybe that means this island is populated. Trash on the beach will equal people—yes?"

"Nah, more likely that this stuff was headed to the South Pacific garbage patch and got stuck here instead."

"Like us."

"Yeah, like us."

Kit had kept his eyes closed throughout this conversation, and it didn't look like he was going to move anytime soon. Sunny, though, willed herself to stand up, being feeble and giving up were not in her vocabulary.

I'll make an SOS sign.

She plowed her way up to the tree line to look for fallen branches to spell out the letters.

64

At the tree line, she got her first blurry look at the foliage.

"Coconut trees!"

She lobbed a few in the direction of the man and then made another exciting discovery.

"An aloe vera plant!"

Sunny grabbed at a long prickly leaf and examined it. A trickle of gunk was seeping out of the bottom. Squeezing the meaty body of the leaf, Sunny managed to extract a decent-sized glob of gel and smoothed it on her face. It felt so good. Snapping off another leaf, she took it over to Kit and smoothed aloe onto his badly burned hand while he just stared up at the sky.

"Did you see I found coconuts?"

Sunny could see Kit just wanted to lie there and do nothing, but she was determined to keep him engaged.

"How can we open them? Do you have any ideas?"

Nothing.

Over the last few years, Sunny had noticed that her tolerance for hard work was normally higher than the people around her. Her parents had valued a strong work ethic and self-reliance. Inactivity wasn't part of the Evans 'way, and this had translated into Sunny's compulsive need to fill her hours with industry instead of idleness. And in this situation, everyone should be pulling their weight. It was definitely not the right time to lay back and do nothing.

"I'm going to make an S.O.S. sign. Can you help?"

Again she got no response.

With a groan, Sunny staggered back to collect branches from the tree line and started dragging them down the beach to spell out a giant distress signal while the man lay in the long shadows of the setting sun.

Doing absolutely nothing to help.

Kit

".O.S. read the large, crooked letters.

The rising sun cast a golden glow over the newly constructed signage. Kit hadn't looked at it the day before, but as he'd awoken this morning, the network of logs—spelling out the distress signal—was the first thing he'd seen. The girl next to him was still asleep and snoring gently. He studied her. She'd got them water and aloe and made the S.O.S sign, all while he'd lain in the sand, unable to do anything.

He should probably feel guilty about letting her do all the work, but he just felt numb.

Well, mentally numb but not physically numb—unfortunately. He was in pain, and he was hungry and very thirsty.

Shit.

Shit, shit, shit.

It was kind of a miracle they had survived, but at that precise moment, Kit was of the mind that he'd rather have succumbed to the waves. Probably.

Swimming with the fishies—that sounded kinda nice right now. Deep in the cool water, nothing to do but dart around and munch on whatever it was fish ate.

His mind was slipping between their unnerving reality and a place of otherworldly illusions. One minute he'd be aware he was lying on a beach after a shipwreck, the next, it would be like the most intense acid trip he'd ever had, where literally nothing made sense. His life was pretty weird, but in a predictable way. Acid took him to completely unpredictable places.

A bit like being shipwrecked on an island.

Shit man, this trip is wild.

The girl shifted, then rolled over and slowly sat up.

Once upright, her face hovered over him like a red balloon.

"Hey," she said, then leaned to one side and picked up one of the coconuts. "Got to get into these."

Kit didn't reply and didn't move. He knew that wasn't cool, but every effort felt just too much. Sunny coughed, then mumbled something about electrolytes and milk. Her voice was gravelly. Kit turned his head toward her; she looked like shit.

"Nice job on the..." Kit flapped a feeble hand toward the log sign laid out further along the beach.

She nodded while feverishly examining the nut in her hands.

Kit looked at the last dribble of water in the plastic cola bottle between them and regretfully suggested she drink it. It was only fair. Maybe it would rain again soon. The aloe gel had helped the raging pain in his hand a little, but he was just so tired. He noticed the girl's hands were trembling.

"You should rest—you don't look too good."

That was an understatement. Her eyes were crossed, and she was panting for breath.

"No, no, got to open coconuts, drink the milk," she gasped, but the next second she flopped back on the shaded sand, looking half dead.

Nearly every part of Kit wanted to join her, lay back in the sand and do nothing, but a small, annoying part of his brain wouldn't let him. If she was tagging out of this two-person game of survival, the brain-part told him, that meant that he'd been tagged in.

Kit groaned and rose cautiously, avoiding the use of his right hand. He then picked up a lump of coral rock and placed the coconut between his feet. With a pessimistic feeling that this wasn't going to work, he bashed the nut and rock together and was not at all surprised when the rock crumbled to dust under his pretty feeble force.

He gave a deep sigh.

"I guess I'll look under the trees, see if I can find a better rock."

Not getting any reply, Kit reluctantly headed up the beach. His legs felt like jelly as he wobbled toward the trees, trying to keep vertical.

Just pretend I'm in The Bahamas and I've been on a bit of a bender.

He had spent time on more tropical beaches than he could count, staying in high-end resorts or private villas, but this tropical beach was very different. There had been no teams of local workers out in the early morning to rake up the seaweed and garbage from the shore. There were no cute servers bringing iced drinks and fresh towels. No cold showers and sunshades, just unrelenting hot sand, and flies, and trash. Finally stepping into the tree line, he was immediately thankful that he still had on his high-end, lightweight water shoes. The ground was covered in various spined plants and sharp rocks. He hadn't noticed if the girl had footwear on; she'd struggle if she didn't have any. The treed canopy made everything darker though not much cooler. Kit stood for a while, minutes, just listening to the rustling sounds in the undergrowth and flapping in the trees. Long lengths of vines were draped from the treetops, like climbing ropes in a gym.

Sweat poured down his face, and he felt faint. He put his left hand out to a rough trunk for support and closed his eyes. The jungle noises intensified; buzzing insects, cawing birds, and wait, wasn't that a cat's meow? He opened his eyes in time to see a tortoiseshell tail disappearing into the thicket.

"Hey cat, come here, little kitty."

What was the cat called? Pinky, that was it.

"Pinky, Pinky cat…"

The cat didn't return. Kit turned over his options, go further into the forest to look for the cat? Get back to the coconuts? The girl, Sunny, would probably want him to follow the cat, and at least he was in the shade, so he moved forward with a grunt and pushed through the bushes, hearing another encouraging meow in the distance. He followed the cat noises for several minutes, glancing back now and then to make sure he was leaving a discernible path to return by. Sliding past an annoyingly sharp boulder, Kit was on the point of giving up and heading back when he heard a new sound; rounding the corner, he was met by the most marvelous sight:

Pinky the cat, calmly washing her paws as she sat next to a large, clear pool of water.

"Pinky, you little beauty!"

A small spring was feeding into the pool, making the surface move gently. Kit staggered forward and dropped onto his knees. Putting his good hand into the cool water, he scooped some up and was beyond ecstatic to find it perfectly fresh. Plunging his head forward, like the most enthusiastic of apple-bobbers, he pushed his face into the pool and slurped mouthful after mouthful until his thirst was finally sated. Next, he dipped his burned hand into the water; the terrible heat faded immediately. Wishing he could have a bucket of cold water permanently around his hand, Kit studied the rest of the clearing. On the far side of the glade was a tree weighed down with red fruit, and if he wasn't mistaken, they were lychees!

Forcing himself to get up from the water, he limped over the rocks toward the tree and picked a dozen of the low-hanging fruit, loading them one-handedly into the scooped-out front of his shirt. Deciding to leave Pinky—she was obviously quite content—Kit retraced his steps back to the beach.

He found Sunny half-heartedly trying to beat two coconuts together.

"Hey, weren't you supposed to be resting?"

Pulling out his marsupial-pouched shirt, he showed her his harvest.

"Ooh, what are those? How do we know if we can eat them?"

"They're lychee—100% edible," Kit replied, making a proffering motion with his tee-shirt.

She grabbed a fruit and bit down.

"Ugh! Are you sure?"

"You've got to peel them first. I can't because of my hand."

The girl nodded and then stuck in a stubby fingernail. The skin was pretty tough, so she tore at it with her teeth instead. Instantly sweet juice ran down her chin.

"Oh heaven," she sighed, "let me get some for you."

Sunny peeled, or rather bit, several more of the small fruits and fed them to a grateful Kit. He chewed and swallowed, then broke his other news.

"I also found a spring with fresh water." Nodding his head to indicate that he'd like another lychee, he added, "and I found the cat—she's fine."

"What! You asshole! Why didn't you say that first!" Sunny rammed a lychee into his mouth in a decidedly forceful manner, making Kit a bit irritated.

She should get her priorities straight. Food and water were more important than the whereabouts of the cat. He opened his mouth to tell her just that.

"Sorry, sorry," said Sunny. "I know you probably think I'm an idiot, worrying about a cat instead of being grateful you found food and water…"

She looked up at him with red-rimmed, pus-crusted eyes.

"But Pinky is part of our team, it's like…" she paused again, "it's like, the only way we can do this is if we work together, look out for each other."

"And that includes looking out for Pinky," Kit replied, his voice neutral.

"Right," said Sunny. "She survived the sea with us. She, she," Sunny's voice trembled, "she kept me going. Without her, I wouldn't have made it. I really don't think I could have made it."

Kit thought back to the little cat, holding onto Sunny's life jacket by her claws, hour after hour, day after day. Sunny was right. Pinky had kept him going too.

Kit apologized and said he would take her to the waterhole. There they could drink and wash, and see that the cat was OK.

"Thank you," she answered, wobbling onto her feet.

Leading them up to the tree line and then along the newly beaten path headed toward the spring, Kit became aware of tiny whimpering noises behind him. Turning around, he saw Sunny hopping on one bare foot and biting her lip, eyes full of tears. Her other foot had an array of spiky things sticking out of it.

She waved him on. "I'm fine; keep going."

"Don't be ridiculous."

With his left hand, Kit pulled out as many of the burrs impaled in her foot as he could and then looked at all the other hazards of the forest floor.

Crouching down, he made a gesture with his good hand, "Climb on my back."

"I really don't think you're in a strong enough state."

"Get on," he barked, just wanting to get back to the pool and lie down again.

Her weight wasn't comfortable on his sore muscles, but it wasn't too bad. He put his left hand behind him, under her ample bottom, to keep her in place, but kept his right hand well out of the way, not wanting it further mangled. The trek lasted only a few minutes more, and pushing past the sharp boulder that marked the entrance to the glade, the scene was just as Kit had left it. Except now Pinky cat was stretched out on a rock, warming her furry belly in a shaft of sunlight. Sunny dismounted and sat on the edge of the pool, calling to Pinky. Her punctured feet dangled in the water as she bent at the waist, scooping cupped hand after cupped hand of fresh water into her mouth.

"This is amazing. We should bring the ball and the soda bottles here."

"Agreed," agreed Kit, collecting more lychees and depositing them with Sunny for her to peel.

Pinky roamed over but refused to eat any of the lychee Sunny tried to feed her. Kit washed his silk bandanna in the clean water then handed it to Sunny, asking her to bandage up his palm. First, she squeezed more aloe on the burns, then gently wrapped it in the silk. In return, Kit picked the rest of the splinters out of her feet.

"We're like a pair of monkeys grooming each other," she said with a weary smile, and then went on to tell Kit all about her plaza experience with Gee-boy the monkey.

"I know," said Kit, thinking back to his annoyance when he'd thought she was stalking him. "I was there."

"Oh!" she exclaimed, "I didn't notice you at all, how funny!"

Chapter 7

Sunny

he rest of the afternoon was spent recuperating. Sunny reveled in the simple pleasures of washing the slimy film of saltwater from her skin, getting fully hydrated, gorging on fruit, and napping, all of which contributed to her feeling way more capable.

Too soon, the spa day was coming to an end, and she knew they had to get back to reality.

"The sun's going to go down soon. We should go back to the beach. The sand is soft-ish and free of thorns."

Kit nodded, seemingly quite happy to let Sunny do all the decision-making, and bent down to allow Sunny to clamber onto his back once more. Bidding a temporary adieu to Pinky, they trekked back through the forest to the beach. This time Sunny was more relaxed riding on Kit, so she took the time to gaze around. Horribly nearsighted without her glasses, she could still only make out rich blurry greens and bright pops of color around her. At one point, she tapped Kit on the shoulder.

"Stop, Shhh!"

Within the jungle tapestry, Sunny could make out a blur of squawking reds and yellows. Was it a parrot?

Kit said he wasn't sure but hoped Polly was easily catchable and tasted like chicken.

She agreed. The lychees had been sweet and refreshing but had also ignited her hunger rather than quenched it.

The light across the beach was fading quickly, so Sunny picked out a sheltered spot of sand and decided that was as good a place as any to call home for the night. Laying her weary body onto the sand, Sunny looked up at Kit a little uncertainly.

"Sleep?" she asked.

"Sleep," he agreed, flopping down beside her.

The air in the space between them felt cool. Kit shifted so that his back rested against Sunny's side. Sunny lay still for a moment, then with a sigh snuggled into Kit's side, the need for comfort and warmth outweighing the awkwardness and embarrassment. The air had a slight chill now, and the sand was not particularly soft, but she had spread out the life jacket so they could both use it as a pillow, which helped a little bit.

In the darkness, her stomach growled loudly.

"I wish we had been able to have our dinner on the boat before it exploded—Farhan said they were going to serve fish cutters."

The thought of the soft white bread sandwiches, with slabs of fish steaming inside, made her mouth water non-stop.

"Tomorrow, we can look around, see if there are signs of life, maybe a burger stand," Kit mumbled, obviously on the verge of sleep.

"Good idea," replied Sunny, "and I'll start planning out how to build a shelter, oh, and see if I can figure out fire. I should also go through the beach flotsam, see what else there is that we can use."

Kit wasn't listening, loud snores coming from his still body. Sunny also lay still, and without someone to listen to her practical planning, fearful thoughts flared up in her brain.

Are we going to make it? Did anyone from the boat make it?

She desperately wished she could hear her parents' voices, that they would answer her from wherever it was their spirits now existed.

But she heard nothing, so finally, she banished all the worries to the back of her mind, instead, making a mental to-do list of tomorrow's plans, and then sank into a deep, exhausted sleep.

*****

The next morning Sunny awoke to a trilling meow. Opening one gritty eye, she saw Pinky sitting on the sand beside her. Between

Pinky's paws lay a very dead, slightly mauled seabird with clownish, custard-yellow feet and a fat pointed beak.

Heaving herself up onto an elbow, she petted the cat's head.

"Why, thank you for the present; what a good girl you are, what a good girl!"

Pinky purred delightedly and nuzzled her head against Sunny's hand. Her fur was still slightly sticky from the ocean. As Sunny was considering how best to tackle the dead bird, the body next to her jerked violently.

"Ahh!"

Kit sat bolt upright and sent Pinky running.

"It's O.K.," Sunny reassured him, "you are on the beach—remember?"

He twisted his head around in several directions, then slowly seemed to regain focus.

"Oh right."

His eyes focused on the pile of gory feathers next to Sunny.

"Shit. Did you catch that?"

"Nope." Sunny knuckled the last vestiges of sleep from her eyes. "Pinky delivered it as a morning gift."

She passed him one of the soda bottles that they'd filled with spring water, then got on her knees and shuffled nearer to the dead bird. Kit leaned in, taking a closer look. "What do you think it is? How shall we eat it?"

Sunny poked the carcass with her finger.

"I think it's a Brown Booby. It's a bit mangled, but the yellow feet are pretty distinctive."

She could hear Kit's stomach rumble.

"And what's your opinion on eating raw seabird?" he asked.

"We'd get parasites and food poisoning, probably."

Kit lay back down again.

"Well, fire was on our agenda," Sunny said as she dusted the sand off her hands and stood up. "So, I guess it's time to see what I can do about it."

She looked down at the man, who had closed his eyes again. Sighing, she had a conversation with herself about whether it was worth trying to get him motivated. He'd done great the day before, finding water and fruit, but now it seemed he'd just stopped trying again.

Sunny wondered if he was in shock; he seemed almost catatonic at times.

She prodded him firmly with her toe.

"Get up."

He groaned and ignored her.

She poked him again. Nope, she wasn't going to put up with this.

"Stop being pathetic! Get up and help me—now!"

Kit

*S*couting around for fire-starting sticks, Kit was feeling very weird; nauseous and confused. His hand hurt like hell, and he just wanted to lay on the sand and rest. And anyway, neither of them knew anything about starting fires with sticks. That kind of thing required wilderness know-how, and Sunny had already admitted she didn't know how to make a bow-drill or whatever it's called.

Grabbing a few dry branches, Kit's head spun, and he felt like his legs might give out. He slowly made his way back to Sunny, who immediately squatted next to the stick pile and started talking at him about fire again.

"Friction. It's all about friction. I'm pretty sure you do a backward and forward motion, super-fast, one stick rubbing on top of another flat piece of wood," she said.

"Have at it then," Kit replied, lying back down on the sand.

He closed his eyes, but even with them firmly shut, he could feel her scowling at him.

"My head hurts," he said.

"You think mine doesn't?"

He felt a stick poke into his stomach. "Rub. These. Sticks. Together," she said, emphasizing each word with another prod.

"I don't think I can; my hand is too damaged. I need to lie down."

Even as he said the words, he knew they sounded pretty pathetic. His body just didn't want to do anything. Summoning all his willpower, he sat back up again.

"Geez—alright, alright."

Sunny pushed the sticks toward him, saying, "Here," and then mumbling, "Darn, we'll need tinder too."

Kit sat blankly for a moment, then realized he might actually be able to be helpful. He dug around in his shorts pocket with his left hand, then pulled out a small pulp of notes.

"Tinder?"

Sunny took the pile from him, and he watched her smooth out the mashed banknotes over her thigh.

"Whoa, Kit, great!" She looked up at him. "There are hundreds of dollars here...sorry we have to burn it."

Kit looked at the wad that was such a tiny drop in his ocean of wealth.

"No problem," he said, "I've got money to burn—literally."

The girl gave him an appreciative smile and handed him some of the pieces of wood and more gently suggested once more that he take a stab at rubbing them together.

Then she paused, a strange look on her face. "Oh! I forgot; I'm still wearing my money belt. I've some cash in there too."

Kit watched her dig beneath her shorts, releasing the sturdy plastic clip of the belt and pulling it out. From inside the zipped pocket, she produced her passport, some crumpled banknotes, a water-bleached photo of her mom and dad and Steve Irwin, and a soggy white explosion that had once been a tampon.

"If we dry this out, it'll be excellent tinder!"

77

She waved the tampon in front of his face, and Kit batted it to one side, unable to deal with her enthusiasm. But as he did so, his eyes focused on something else, the bracelet on her wrist.

He grabbed her arm.

"Your bracelet! Is that? I don't believe it!"

They looked down at the tiny magnifying glass on the charm bracelet and yelled in unison, "Fire!"

Focusing the sun through the small lens took a lot of patience. Sunny took charge of propping the glass in the perfect position and instructed Kit to add more tinder if smoke started to appear. Kit lay on his stomach, concentrating on the torn paper. Smoke had appeared, but the banknotes had refused to catch fire.

"It appears I don't have money to burn after all," Kit said, propping himself onto his elbows.

Looking over to Sunny, he gave a weak smile. "Hey Sunny! What do you call a girl who sets fire to bank loans?"

Sunny ignored him and started fiddling with the binding on the passport. "I guess paper money has some kind of coating so it won't be flammable," she muttered to herself.

"Bernadette."

"Makes sense, but it's not very helpful to our situation..." Sunny continued on.

"Bernadette," repeated Kit.

"Bernadette," he said a third time.

Sunny finally looked at him. "I get it," she said, then told him to concentrate.

The passport was more successful; the stiff outer cover and laminated ID page just shriveled, but the rest of the inside pages burned easily. Slowly, so slowly, a tiny wisp of smoke rose from the pile. Kit blew on it gently under Sunny's urging, and suddenly the ember took hold, the tinder going up with a whoosh. Sunny added one dry stick after another until the fire grew and they could sit back, confident in their success.

"We gotta cook that bird," Kit said. "I can't do anything else unless I eat."

Sunny nodded and deftly plucked the feathers off the booby, then handed it to Kit, telling him to drive a sharp straight stick through the body.

"Me?" He looked at the limp dead bird with a shudder. Sunny was obviously way more capable and outdoorsy than he was.

"Yep, I'm going to get more firewood—you skewer it, then prop it over the flames."

She stood, wincing slightly, to head up the beach.

"Here." Kit kicked off his shoes, suggesting she wear them so her feet didn't get further punctured, then waved the bird and the stick at her again, hopefully.

"Bird! Skewer!"

She flapped off in the too-large shoes, and Kit speared the booby while mumbling "winner, winner, chicken dinner" to himself.

While he rotated the carcass over the fire, Kit watched Sunny make several trips to the tree line. She brought armful after armful of wood back to the fire pit, then arranged it into a neat pile. Watching her work, Kit felt like a lazy ass and decided he was being a bit of a jerk, but he didn't have the energy to do anything about it.

Mmm, Jerk chicken.

Damn he was hungry. The smell of cooking meat was making his mouth water, and it took a lot of restraint not to just grab it off the skewer and wolf it straight down. When Sunny eventually sat down again, he could hear her stomach growl.

"Do you think it's cooked yet?" He asked her.

"Let me see."

She poked at the meat and declared it was close enough. Tearing apart the bird, they found the meat was a mixture of charred and nearly raw, and they agreed it tasted absolutely sublime. Kit licked his fingers and chewed on a piece of breast bone and for the first time since they had washed up, he felt his brain begin to work again. Sunny was poking the bits of offal that were left over from their dinner.

"Next time, we gut it first, can't believe I forgot," said Sunny.

"Sure," Kit agreed. He'd be quite happy for her to pluck and gut if all he had to do was tend it over the fire.

They washed down the meal with water from the soccer ball, and when only the most unappetizing pieces were left, Sunny set the remains aside, saying they would be a perfect thank you for Pinky.

Then she caught Kit totally unawares. "So I can't stop thinking about you doing performance art. Not to be rude, but it seems an," she paused, "unlikely fit for you."

Kit had no idea what she was talking about.

"Did I remember that right?" she asked. "On the boat, you said you were a performance artist."

Ooh right.

"Uhm, I actually don't do 'performance art' as such," he replied, "I do more traditional, straight acting."

Sunny nodded. "Oh, I see. Or at least I kinda see. Why were you doing an art residency if you are an actor?"

Kit gave her an almost-truth. "I got sent to the island to do research for a new production."

"Oh cool, kinda like an acting research residency?"

"Yeah, right. Like that."

He watched her face as she nodded.

Lying back on the sand, Kit decided to change the subject in a way he knew would distract Sunny completely.

Getting shit done.

"OK—what's next on the agenda?" he asked.

Sunny blinked a couple of times and then gave him an encouraging smile. A smile accompanied by a look of relief in her eyes. Was he being so pathetic that just showing just a modicum of enthusiasm was enough to lift her spirits?

Sunny began to talk, listing off the things she'd obviously been thinking about.

"The SOS sign is OK—if rescue planes fly over, they'll see it. And now we have fire. We can collect green leaves to add and make a smoke signal."

He watched Sunny turn and squint at the center of the island.

"We also have to see if the island is inhabited—it would be ridiculous to just sit here with a resort just around the corner!"

A rocky ridge was visible toward the center of the island, its peak pushing out through the jungle canopy. Sunny said they could get a view of the entire island if they climbed it.

Assessing their wrecked state, Kit couldn't see them handling a trek through the jungle at the moment. It sounded like a lot of work.

"I think we need to rest more before doing any hiking."

Sunny said she didn't agree; getting the lay of the land was important.

"It's been, what three, four days? We haven't seen any sign of rescue operations, so we have to be proactive."

Kit thought about the outside world. His agent and staff were probably coordinating a huge rescue effort. His disappearance would be the biggest story in the news, without a doubt.

We'll probably be rescued really soon.

In fact, now he came to think about it, he was surprised they hadn't been rescued already. Kit felt strangely mixed about being rescued. When he'd floated out at sea, he'd been completely ready to slip off the old mortal coil. Now, though, he was glad to be alive—mostly.

But the idea of being rescued and jetted back into his reality was not exactly appealing. He could too easily picture the circus his arrival back on terra firma would cause. He hadn't told Sunny he was famous—what was the point? But maybe he should mention it so she would know that people were going to be scouring every corner of the earth for him.

Eh, it can wait.

This can be a retreat from reality for a while, he thought.

"If I can borrow your shoes, I can go right now," said Sunny, "be back before dark."

He watched her squint at the trees. She bit her lip.

"But I can't see very well," she said. "I might not be able to see anything useful when I get to the top of the peak."

"So," said Kit slowly, "I'm the one with good eyesight, and I'm the only one with shoes, so really, I'm the one who has to go scouting."

Sunny nodded, "I hate to say it, but I think you're right."

Did she hate to say it because she thought he was incapable? Kit knew he was perfectly able to go into the jungle and look for help; he just didn't want to.

"Why don't we wait till tomorrow?" he suggested. He would probably be more willing to do it after another day of rest.

Sunny shook her head.

"No, you should go today. And go now, so you have as much daylight as possible." Then she added, "Please?"

I should probably be a better survival partner while we are here. He imagined Sunny being interviewed by Oprah and telling the world that he'd been useless on the island.

Sighing and thinking about news headlines, Kit stood and shook the sand from his shorts. Sunny looked at him from her seat on the sand. He'd expected to see triumph in her face, she'd got her way, but instead Sunny's burned face just looked plain miserable.

Now what?

"I'm getting mixed messages," he said, "do you want me to go or not?"

"Yeah, you should definitely go, but I'm worried. What if you get lost or hurt? You could fall off the rocks or something like that. What if something happened? If you didn't return, I don't know if I'd be able to find you." She looked out toward the ocean. "Stupid, unpredictable accidents happen. You can't plan for them. I don't know how best to take precautions, you know, to make sure you come back safe."

Kit scratched his head. *What was Tom Cruise always saying in that movie? Oh yeah...*

"Hope for the best, prepare for the worst.." he said to her, a little flippantly.

"Sometimes you don't even know there is something to prepare for..." she replied. "Sometimes you have no idea that the worst thing ever is just around the corner."

Kit thought she was referring to their being shipwrecked, but as she looked back up at him, her face was carved with a deep, deep grief.

Gas leak, parents. Shit.

He could see why she might be extra worried about unpredictable accidents.

Poor kid. Time to grow a pair, I guess.

"Look," he said. "I'll be really careful, and I won't take any unnecessary risks. And I'll make every effort to be back before dark—I promise."

He smiled at her, but Sunny didn't look any happier.

"Anyway, you won't be alone—you'll have Wilson."

"Wilson? What are you talking about?" said Sunny.

He picked up the battered soccer ball. "Wilson—like in the movie *Castaway*!"

She smiled weakly. "Yep, I'll have Wilson. I'd rather have Tom Hanks, though."

As she turned away, Kit could see the miserable look return to Sunny's face. He thought back to the promise he'd made as they'd floated so close to death, out at sea.

Putting out his good hand, he patted her on the shoulder.

"Look, we are in this together, from start to finish. I solemnly promise I won't take unnecessary risks." He gave her another awkward pat, then added, "I'll be home before you know it. "

"Home," said Sunny, giving a deep sigh.

Kit grimaced. "Yeah, wrong word choice. I'll be back at basecamp before you know it. Better?"

"Much," she replied.

"And I promise not to say "I'm going out, I may be some time..."

Sunny looked at him blankly.

"Captain Oates? Antarctic explorer? Famous for disappearing on an expedition?" Kit said. "Nothing? Ah well, probably for the best."

Then, having made sure Sunny had enough water and fruit for the day, and after depositing the leftover seabird offal with Pinky, Kit set off on his own expedition into the wilds.

Chapter 8

Sunny

*K*it disappeared into the blur of greens that made up the island's jungle. Sunny tried to put the idea of ill-fated polar explorations out of her mind and get down to some work.

Sunny's long vision was pretty terrible. So was her middle vision, actually. Basically, anything beyond an arm's length was horribly out of focus. This didn't mean she was incapable, she reminded herself; it just meant she needed to get up close to things.

She had settled on beachcombing as the first task of her day. This seemed like a safe option with some instant gratification. There were drifts of potentially useful items waiting to be collected, and organizing and 'Macgyvering 'were just the kinds of things Sunny loved doing.

Limping to the water's edge, she plopped down and started sifting her fingers through the sand, pulling out plastic bottles, fishing twine, and any other objects worth examining more closely.

The first noteworthy find was a battered toothbrush. Just one toothbrush.

Sharing a balding, garbage toothbrush with a virtual stranger, versus no toothbrush at all, she mulled. Both were pretty gross options. Shoving the toothbrush in her back pocket, Sunny gleaned on, collecting several plastic pots, a fishing buoy, more plastic rope, a long-dead cigarette lighter, and a baby's pacifier.

The highlight of her search was when she spotted a hint of bright Kelly green under some seaweed. Tossing the weed aside, she revealed a flip-flop in almost her size.

"Welcome to the 'QVSeashore' Deal of the Day!" she announced to the empty beach, holding the shoe aloft.

As she sat back, admiring her one shod foot, Sunny felt the skin on her face and arms prickling as her sunburned flesh reacted to the hot rays. Not wanting to be blistered further, she hobbled back to base camp to organize her loot and lunch on lychees and water. After lunch, red-faced and sweating, she made shelves from rocks and branches. The first shelf became a health section, which was basically the toothbrush, some aloe vera leaves, and also a rusty disposable razor.

Hmm, that should probably be in the potential tools section.

She switched it to a different shelf that also held the long-dead lighter and plastic barrels from several ballpoint pens. Next to these, she put yards of fishing twine, which would need to be unknotted, and a piece of ratty fishing net. In the kitchen section was a slatted plastic spoon, formally a scoop for cat litter, several plastic containers, the pacifier, and the lid of a squeezy yellow mustard container. The final section was shelter-building equipment.

Here lay coils of blue plastic rope that had made her fingertips bleed as she attempted to detangle them, and a section of curved plastic, also blue, that looked like it had once been part of a storage barrel.

What do you think, Dad? This a good start?

Her dad could have made an excellent shelter. She was sure of it.

Why is the majority of plastic made in this blue color, Mom? Do you think it's so it's a bit camouflaged when it ends up tossed in the ocean?

The clothing section of Sunny's shelves was empty, seeing as it currently only consisted of the green flip-flop, which was on Sunny's left foot.

I could weave a sun hat, she thought, but what I really need to find is another shoe. As she thought about her footwear problem, Pinky came to visit. She pulled the little cat close and ate some more fruit as she wondered how Kit's expedition was getting on. She felt like she couldn't get an accurate read on Kit. Some people you met, and within a few minutes, you had the gist of them. But Kit was one of those opaque people who didn't reveal much.

When he'd confessed to her earlier that he was an actor and not a performance artist, she hadn't been surprised. Performance art was about revealing things about yourself, but with acting, your real self was always in disguise.

I have no idea what Kit is capable of.

He hadn't shown any areas of survival strength yet. Sunny wondered if that was the shock or if he was really as useless as he made out. She sent up a little prayer to her parents.

Can you guys keep an eye on Kit? —I'm kinda worried...

Kit

One hour into the jungle expedition and Kit was going crazy.

Gnats and flies worried at him. Even though he kept his mouth closed, they still found their way up his nose, into his eyes, and even his ears. The further away from the beach he got, the denser the clouds of midges became. The air was humid and thick and had him sweating constantly. He'd already drained his water bottle and hoped he'd come across another source of clean water during the hike; otherwise, he was going to have an awful thirsty return journey.

He was using a stout stick to beat the trail and had initially made good headway, but now the going was much tougher. Occasionally he rubbed his face in the condensation that dripped off fat, dark green leaves, wetting his lips, the tepid water giving a moment of relief from the heat and annoying flies. The floor of the forest was a blanket of tree debris, small spiky growths, and coral rock. This is definitely not something to do barefoot, Kit thought, deeply thankful for his expensive, fancy footwear once again.

He hadn't grown up with money. He'd grown up with hand-me-downs and Walmart-pilfered-goods. If Kit had wanted money, he knew never to ask his father and instead had done odd jobs for neighbors and, as he got older, sold weed, nervously secreted from his dad's grow-house, to the other kids at high school in Ellensburg. Kit very rarely thought about his childhood. The few times he did, were usually from the comfortable leather chair of his very expensive therapist's office.

"Trust issues," said Francis, the therapist. "Of course you have trust issues. You grew up not being able to trust your family, and if you can't trust your family, then whom can you trust? No one!"

Kit often thought Francis should have gone by 'Frank, 'so blunt were some of his observations.

Kit staggered on.

"Just a short trek," she said. "Just climb to the top of the peak and look around," she said. "It'll be no big deal," she said.

"Yeah, right."

While he was muttering to himself, Kit finally came face to face with a steep rocky cliff that meant he had reached the peak. The rockface was dotted with shelves and ledges, and remembering his promise to be careful, Kit methodically scouted around to find the best access rather than just attempting to scramble straight up.

Finding a reasonable spot to start, Kit began to climb in an ungainly, mostly one-handed manner. He could use the fingertips of his throbbing right hand, but because the cliff was not too shear, he didn't have to use that hand too much.

He'd done some climbing in Yosemite, spending weekends there with a professional climbing coach to get in shape for the mountain scenes in *Fury of Flames*—the TV series which had catapulted him into stardom. The technique came back to him, and he climbed slowly and carefully, taking his time to test handholds and footholds before moving on to the next section.

Left hand, left foot, right foot, pause. Left hand, left foot, right foot, pause.

"Slow and steady wins the race," his climbing instructor would tell him. Then would go on to remind him never to get too comfortable; things could change in a split second.

The ledge under Kit's right foot started to crumble. Instinctively Kit reached out his right hand to cling onto a tuft of spiky roots. The sharp foliage burst the blanket of blisters that covered his palm. The red-hot pain almost made him vomit, and a cold sweat broke over his body, on top of the hot sweat that was already there.

He couldn't let go of the tuft, so he clasped it until his foot found purchase again. Then he let out a long groan and, using his tired core muscles, pressed himself into the cliff face.

His whole body was trembling. Kit stayed frozen in place, terrified of trying to continue and terrified of trying to get down. He just wanted to keep his balance. After a while, his racing heart began to calm down, and he could think a little more clearly.

So—that was nearly curtains.

If he had fallen, would he have died? The fingers on Kit's left hand dug deeper into the shelf above his head as he pictured himself, back-broken, on the jungle floor.

Sunny would be on the beach. Night would fall, and he wouldn't have returned. She'd be frantic. In the morning, she'd probably set out to find him, in her bare feet. Kit imagined her bloody and hobbling, calling out and desperate. He imagined himself, broken and unconscious at the end of her search. There would be nothing she could do for him, just sit with him until he died.

I hope she'd take my shoes...

A bird settled on a tree just a few yards away and cocked its head.

"What are you looking at?" Kit asked it, making the bird take off in fright, shooting straight past Kit's head. The bird almost caught him in the eye, the shock nearly making him lose his grip again.

Drenched in sweat, dehydrated and full of panic, Kit thought he could see his father—blood shot eyes, sneering expression and all—hovering over him.

"What you looking at, boy?"

The voice echoed in Kit's head.

"Trying to see what real work looks like?"

And then there was his Uncle Jason, laughing and throwing a beer can straight at him.

Kit flinched.

It's not real, just a memory.

He remembered the beer can hitting him. It was full, smacked him hard on the eyebrow. Eyebrows, he'd suddenly learned, bleed a lot. He had bled and bled, blood running down his face and all over his one good sweatshirt, and then down onto the shredded linoleum floor. Kit's father turning to his brothers, asked, "What did I do to deserve such a worthless piece of shit?"

What you looking at...worthless piece of shit.

Present-day Kit felt his body tremble, brace for blows.

That's not my life anymore—get it together Kitson.

He remembered that day so clearly. The brow above his right eye tingled, as though his body was remembering as well. Young Kit had bitterly regretted stepping into the kitchen where his father and uncles were sitting around the table. Very much regretted seeing the heaps of prescription bottles and strange white packages strewn like Aladdin's heaps of gold and pearls. He had not wanted to hear the men laughing about how easily they had broken into the medical clinic one town over.

This was a bigger job than the brothers usually pulled. They decided they had to be sure young Otis Kitson could keep the secret he'd stumbled into. Wouldn't rat them out.

The beating was just a taste of what he would get if he ever spoke of this, they told him.

Kit had tasted blood from his split lip and loose teeth for over a week, until the injuries slowly healed. His mind had a harder time recovering. The voices in his head kept telling him he should have fought back, but he hadn't. He was worthless, just like dad had always told him.

Kit's young brain built a wall to block off these feelings. In the last decade, the wall had threatened to crumble, but Kit found he could shore it up by avoiding any kind of strong feelings.

Any kind of excessiveness helped with that; partying banished his father's voice.

Halfway up a rock face in the middle of the jungle was no party.

"Ahhhh!" A massive cry rose up from somewhere deep inside Kit. He screamed at the jungle, at the rockface, at his father.

I can do this. I'm going to finish this climb, see if there is any help to be had, and if there isn't, I'll do it. I'll be enough. I'll make sure me and Sunny survive—or die trying.

There was going to be no easy win for his dad, no easy out for Kit. He tightened his finger-hold and heaved himself up another couple of feet.

Easy now, just a bit further.

The trees crowded him, but he could see they would soon thin out, just another yard or so to break through the canopy. A final grunt and his head pushed through the overstory. The sudden disorientating brightness almost made him lose his grip again. Kit swayed slightly with the treetops and allowed the breeze to cool his face.

Yes!

From here, he could see almost the whole circumference of the island. He could see trees, rocks, sand, and sea. But not a single sign of human presence.

No.

Might as well keep going.

He climbed higher, all the way to the peak. Then, flopping down on a flat, gently angled slab, he caught his breath and looked around again. He could see the beach cove where he and Sunny had washed up and the crooked S.O.S. sign on the sand. The bay of the cove was encircled by coral reef. At the end of their cove was a rocky outcrop, with white foamy waves breaking over the boulders. The other end of the cove had a tree line that went all the way down to the water. Three-quarters of the island perimeter seemed to have just sheer rocky cliffs separating jungle from ocean, and their cove was the only way to easily reach the ocean.

Thank God we washed up on this side, not against the cliffs.

There were no ships on the sea, no other islands in sight, and nothing to show human activity for as far as the eye could see. He sat back on the rock slab, thinking about the agencies that were buzzing around the South Pacific trying to find him. If he wasn't famous, they'd probably already be declared dead. But as it was, his fame and fortune would guarantee a truly epic search.

If he wasn't famous, he wouldn't have been on the boat in the first place.

He thought about Sunny, floating with Pinky, alone in the sea.

Thank God I was there.

Suddenly it struck him. His life had been a series of events that led to him being washed ashore on this island, with a half-blind girl and a skinny cat.

Thank God!

Or actually, thank Brian!

It's all thanks to Brian.

Kit's best friend Brian had spontaneously decided to leave Ellensburg and move to LA. Kit had hitched a ride. They lived in the smelly VW van for months. During the day, Kit had gone to open cattle calls for acting jobs—mostly getting work as an extra—and in the evening, he'd chopped vegetables for a pizza place. His first big break came pretty quickly, and his dazzling good looks had as much to do with it as his acting skills. That first role, playing a poet in the indie film, had led agent Mattie Matthews to Kit's door with an offer to represent him.

Mattie was extremely ambitious and soon had Kit reading for bigger and bigger parts. The thing that shot him into the Hollywood stratosphere, though, was the lead role in *Fury of Flames*. Playing the heroic main character in the TV show of the decade had decidedly changed Kit's life. The TV show had run for four years, and his career now felt like a juggernaut that had no brakes and was racing down a mountain.

Out of control, and inevitably ending in a crash. Clambering slowly back down the rock face, Kit concentrated on controlling this descent. Feet back on the ground, to Kit, the jungle seemed even darker and even more strange. It was time to get going.

"Once more unto the breach, dear friends!" He shouted aloud, causing a fluttering of wings in a nearby tree. The climb had been exhausting, but Kit also felt energized. He was going to try his best to be of help to Sunny. He was going back to their camp a new man.

Well, maybe not a new man, he acknowledged to himself, *but at least a better version. Kit 2.0.*

At the last minute, he pocketed a couple of rocks. They were made of the same sharp stone that he'd just climbed, and he wondered if they could help with the coconut situation.

Sunny would know.

Sunny.

The unfamiliar feeling of having faith in someone else was peaceful. He just knew he could rely on her, trust her.

He pictured Sunny on the beach, probably beavering away to make a deluxe cooking system or construct a full-blown escape raft.

He set off, and as he walked on, he thought about his island companion some more. With her shaggy brown hair and squinting eyes, she'd pulled all those logs into the SOS signal, tongue sticking out between chapped lips. Her short legs and determination gave her the air of a hobbit, Kit decided. He could just imagine her tending fields of turnips in the Shire but also being very brave when thrust into the middle of a bizarre adventure.

I'm really going to step up my game. Sunny has to survive this.

She needs the chance to live a full life. Rescue more cats, paint a massive collection of paintings, go on bird watching trips.

Maybe she'll get married, he thought. *Married to a plumber called Roger. Or she could work in an animal rescue shelter and paint pictures of the rescued cats to sell in the shelter gift shop.* Kit grinned at the life he was conjuring up for Sunny and then decided to improve her lot by giving her a contract with an art gallery, which sold her nature paintings for vast amounts of money. He also decided Roger would also have a job to do with animals. He figured Sunny would like a partner who she could talk nature with.

Park ranger? What do they do?

Images of Yogi Bear danced through his mind. "Hey, hey, hey," he said to the jungle.

Hmmm, do Sunny and Ranger Roger have children? Yep, she'll have rowdy twin girls, who are always covered in scratches and mud, and a studious son who goes bird watching with his mom on Saturdays.

Inventing Sunny's future gave Kit added determination as he trekked on. The journey and climb had taken him several hours, and his throat was parched. More than parched, he was dizzy from dehydration, and his whole body was beyond exhausted.

Water soon. Rest soon. Just get back to the beach. I can do this.

The sky was darkening rapidly. The trip must have taken hours. Definitely longer than they had expected.

Once again, he thought about Sunny, waiting for him on the beach.

"I have promises to keep, And miles to go before I sleep, And miles to go before I sleep," he said out loud.

Robert Frost. Hmmm, frosty beer.

He walked on, one foot in front of the other.

Don't worry, Sunny. I'll be back soon. Promises to keep...

Chapter 9
Sunny

*S*unny was worried.

The sun was going down, and Kit still had not returned. Promises to be careful were just empty words. Anything could have happened. Kit just didn't seem like someone she could rely on.

She sat alone on the sand and thought about the *Castaway* cracks he'd made. Sunny was the Tom Hanks of their particular situation, and Kit was the Wilson, she thought. Like the rubber volleyball in the movie, Kit was some company (for which she was grateful) but not much help.

Picking up the disposable razor, she set to work again. If Kit didn't return, she'd have to look for him in the morning.

When Kit arrived back at the cove, she didn't notice him at first. She was concentrating on her project and moving her arm back and forth in a frenzy, huffing and puffing with effort.

"Come on, come on," she muttered to herself.

A second later, she nearly jumped out of her skin as Kit made his presence known.

"Sorry I'm late m'dear, the traffic was 'ellish," he drawled in a terrible British accent.

Sunny looked up, and on seeing Kit's grinning face, a wave of relief washed over her.

"You found help!"

His grin faltered. "Err, no."

Sunny slumped. She couldn't think of another reason Kit should look so happy. His face, thus far, had shown just a perma-sulky-glum expression.

"So what did you find?" she asked, "surely something helpful?"

He came over, threw his staff and empty bottle on the sand, and then raised his hand, making a V sign with his first and middle finger. "I found some inner peace Sunny...inner peace."

Sunny wondered if peyote grew on the island. "Did you get high somehow?" she asked him.

Kit laughed. "I got so high! I climbed to the highest peak...looked all around, then deep into my soul."

Sunny couldn't make head nor tails of what Kit was saying. Sometimes it felt as though he was just playing the role of a "shipwrecked person #2."

"Stop being an idiot—tell me what you saw! Does that mean you managed to climb to the top?"

Much to her relief, Kit seemed to calm down. Swigging from Wilson, Kit filled her in with as much detail as possible. He told her about his journey and how no signs of civilization could be seen from the rocky peak—no ships or other islands on the horizon—and the island itself was enclosed by a coral reef.

Sunny tried not to let his report dishearten her. "Finding people was a long shot. I think we would have heard boats or engines or something, but..." Sunny took a deep breath, then slowly let it out. "But I really did think you might see a nearby island. I'd thought we could put up smoke signals and someone would see them. I had it all planned."

But now you adjust to circumstances and make a new plan, she told herself.

Picking up a strand of blue plastic twine, she twiddled it between her fingers. "The reef is good news, it'll keep the sharks out of the bay, so we can fish without worrying, and even swim."

They had not discussed going swimming, but now that she had thought of it, the idea of ocean water on her skin sounded nothing short of heavenly.

Kit was looking thoughtful. "Tourist information said beaches in Fiji were perfectly safe for swimming." Keeping his eyes on the ocean, he continued, "so I imagine it's the same for here."

Sunny looked at Kit, pleased Kit had remembered that bit of information. "That's good to know. And with the water so shallow and clear, on the very remote chance a shark was about, we'd see it anyway," she added.

Kit nodded. "I'm in 100% agreement!" He stood up and put out his hand to help Sunny up. "Swim time?"

Sunny gave him a weary smile. Some R&R in the ocean sounded amazing, but first things first. "I wish. But we really have to figure out the coconuts. Nourishment is more of a priority than swimming." She gestured to a neatly stacked pile of coconuts that she'd arranged next to the newly stocked plastic stores.

To try to hack open the coconuts, she'd taken apart the battered disposable razor. She thought that if she could make a groove in the tough outer shell, then maybe that would allow a big whack with a stone to split the thing.

Working with the tiny rusty blade was frustrating, and she hadn't made much of a dent. But it had been worth a shot.

Kit looked at her labors, then said he'd brought some more rocks for them to try. He pulled them out of his pocket, and she immediately took one out of his hand.

"Hmm, these might work..."

They were definitely better than the coral and limestone they'd been working with.

"You bash at one nut; I'll bash the other."

She rolled him a coconut and immediately set to hammering, while Kit studied his nut and said in his best gangster accent, "Tough nut to crack, aintcha."

To the rhythm of their beats, she asked Kit to tell her more about the jungle, the birds he'd seen, the vines, and the plants.

"Please tell me you found bananas or something?"

"Nope, sorry."

"We are actually, one hundred percent, marooned, aren't we?"

"Yep," Kit agreed. "I'm afraid we really are."

He gave her a pat on the leg, and she told him to get back to hammering while striking her own coconut with even more force.

"These. Stupid. NUTS!"

Kit looked a bit startled by her yelling.

"O.K. O.K.—back to business," he said.

Sunny was trying not to get too irritated with him, but it was difficult.

"Hey, Sunny?"

"Yes?" she replied, not looking up.

"Get this, we are marooned, and your face is doubly so..."

Bash, bash, bash. Sunny pounded on the hard husky shell. *Mustn't pretend this is Kit's head, she told herself sternly.*

"So why is my face doubly marooned?" she eventually asked him, as Kit had stopped work again and was obviously waiting for her to reply.

"Because it's so red! It's 'maroon-ed.' Maroon-ed."

Sunny decided that even though Kit wasn't a big help with their survival, his stupid jokes did actually help keep things light—in the same way a court jester would as the King was trying to formulate battle plans.

She watched him left-handedly bashing at the coconut in his lap and suggested he experiment with striking different points on the hull.

"My hands need a break," she told him. "You keep working."

Sunny flexed her cramped up fingers and took the opportunity to show Kit all the things she'd found on the beach while she had her break. Kit seemed a mixture of impressed and entertained by her finds.

"We can take turns sucking on the pacifier if things get too upsetting," he told her.

Maybe I need to think laterally? Could we put the nuts on the fire and burn through the shell? That would probably evaporate the liquid, though.

While Sunny was deep in thought, and deliberately not paying Kit any attention, the coconut in his hands suddenly broke in two, pouring clear, sour liquid down his hand.

"Whoa!" he yelled.

"Kit! Watch out! Sunny dashed forward with a plastic bottle to try and catch some of the milk.

"I did it!" said Kit gleefully.

Ignoring Kit's yelps and whoops, Sunny looked at the two halves of the open nut. It seemed like striking hard on the bottom with one of the flinty stones was the key. The diet of lychee was already making them dash off into the bushes with rather too much frequency, so adding another source of food was a massive relief.

Passing Kit another couple of coconuts to work on, she suddenly shivered. The skies were darkening, not with nightfall but with rainclouds. Soon another hard shower began to tumble down. Sheltered under a large-fronded tree, Sunny munched on a hard lump of coconut and thought about how to construct their shelter.

"My Dad built our bird-hide out of old pallets," she said, wiping her coconutty hands on her shorts. "I realize that's not helpful, but thinking about building a shelter makes me think of my Dad."

She felt Kit give her shoulder a squeeze.

"If your dad were here now, what do you think he would do?"

Sunny looked off into the distance, thinking about her quiet, incredibly handy dad.

"Oh, that's a good way to think about it. He would know exactly what to do, build a shelter and probably a bunch of Swiss Family Robinson-style contraptions too."

She tried to imagine her little stooped father on the darkening beach. "I've already started on his first steps by organizing tools and supplies."

Sunny put on a gruff Welsh accent. "Sunny-bach, the key to a successful project is PPPPP," she quoted.

"PPPP? —what is PPPP?"

"You left off a P," Sunny corrected him. "It stands for—'proper preparation prevents poor performance'—and, if you don't do PPPPP, then you are most certainly a twmfatt." She wagged her finger at him and gave a mock scowl.

"Twmfatt?"

"That's Welsh for idiot, Kit-bach."

"And bach?"

"It means 'dear.'"

"Well, Sunny-bach, we'd better tend to the fire before the rain puts it out completely!"

"Oh no!"

Sunny couldn't believe she had forgotten the fire. She must be exhausted, and Kit was forever distracting her. She leapt up and rushed to save the dying embers from the drizzle. Kit sat sheltering, calling after her that she was a real twmfatt. As she fanned the flames, added dry wood, then brought some flaming branches to where he was sitting, she was counting furiously to ten, trying not to explode at him.

The thought of shoving the burning wood into his lazy face was very temping.

"What do you want me to do?" he asked her while she moved things around to keep the fire sheltered from the rain.

"Show some initiative," she mumbled to herself.

Eventually sitting back down, Sunny knew she had to figure out the shelter-building plan. A roof over their heads would go a long way to making things more bearable, and if there was rain, they could have a fire in the shelter entrance.

The rain stopped as abruptly as it had started, and their clammy, damp clothing was unpleasant. The rescued fire was puny and didn't really help to dry them.

Shelter, hmmm.

She closed her eyes to imagine the forces of wind and rain that might beat against their shelter. *We also need to consider where it* should be sited. What do you think, Dad? We should use an A-frame, right?

Yes, they'd use an A-frame. That would spread the weight of collected branches better...

As Sunny shared her thoughts with Kit, he threw in the odd suggestion, making it obvious he didn't have any construction experience. She was going to be foreman on this project, and Kit's role would be that of laborer. His assistance would be handy, as long as he was willing to pay attention to the details, follow her lead, and not mess things up.

The fire slowly grew again until it had enough heat to be comforting.

"Let's call it a night."

"I'm still hungry," Kit complained.

"Then open more coconuts tomorrow, or figure out fishing, or find a banana grove!"

He was beginning to drive her nuts, but at least when he spooned his body around hers, she was very grateful for the warmth. As she lay with his body wrapped around hers, she thought back to when she had first seen him on the boat. Her initial impression had not been favorable—he'd snapped at her for photographing him and then mocked her. He'd looked outwardly beautiful, even though he was dressed ridiculously, but his manner had been so cold and off-putting.

Sunny was glad that he'd warmed up a bit...and that he was warming her up a bit.

Maybe the ocean water had scoured away some of his cold, hard edges, allowing a warmer nature to come out.

"I feel better than I did this time yesterday, Kit," she whispered into the dark night.

She felt Kit's arms tighten around her as he replied.

"Me too, Sunny, me too."

Chapter 10
Sunny

heady mix of seashore ozone, wild ginger, and burning feathers filled Sunny's nose as she woke. Rolling over, she saw Kit constructing their breakfast. Chunks of coconut, a plastic bowl full of lychees, Wilson brimming with water, and on the wooden skewer stick, a tiny bird.

Wow! He's really trying!

Kit greeted her with a smile. The proud look on his face was not unlike the look Pinky gave when she sat with a bird catch at her feet. Speaking of which, Sunny looked at the bird...

"Pinky?"

"Yep, but we should really get her to rustle up several dozen more of these if we want a satisfying breakfast. I think it's some sort of hummingbird."

"Hmm, I don't think so—not here." Sunny stretched her arms and then twisted from side to side. "Maybe a Zosteropidae, a Fiji white-eye perhaps? They're nectar-drinkers, kinda like hummingbirds."

"How do you know all this stuff?"

"Book I read on the plane," she replied, then thinking about the journey from Seattle added, "or should I say planes. I had four different flights to get to Fiji—over 24 hours of travel! Was it the same for you?"

Sunny watched Kit turn to attend to the breakfast again. Still looking away, he answered. "Nah, my journey was a bit easier. Anyway—have you got any more bird facts you'd like to share before breakfast?"

Because sharing bird facts was one of her favorite things, Sunny immediately dismissed Kit's travel from LA to Fiji. Instead, she told him that a human would need to eat around 250 pounds of meat a day if they had the same metabolism as a hummingbird. Kit, roasting the chunks of coconut on rocks next to the fire, laughed and said he was glad to just have an average human metabolism.

While she moved the virtually bristleless toothbrush around her mouth, Sunny observed Kit's cooking technique. She'd have to give him some pointers on bird plucking. She didn't interfere, though. He needed to learn, and there was no better way than by actually doing things yourself. Finally, he announced the meal was ready. The tiny bird was mostly charred, but the texture was good alongside the lychee and coconut. As they ate, Sunny shared some food thoughts with Kit.

"We need to expand our diet. There's bound to be more fruit here somewhere, maybe bananas or something like that, and maybe some of the seaweed is edible. But the big thing we should do is fish. We have fishing line, and we can find something to make a hook."

Kit nodded. "Good idea."

After clearing up from the appreciated but not very satisfying breakfast, Sunny told him they had to prioritize their workflow. One thing Sunny was a firm believer in was a well-ordered to-do list; organization was the key to success in her book. Talking over what the options were, they both agreed—fishing first, shelter building after. Food was the priority.

Sunny went to her stores to pull out some lengths of fishing line and gave Kit her bracelet to fiddle around with—he was trying to form a hook with the tiny bracelet lock pick but not having much success.

"Argh and dammit! This won't bend, and it's not at all sharp."

Sunny wasn't surprised; her dad wouldn't have made any charms that could have hurt her mom. Mildly, she suggested he look along the shoreline for something else to use.

"Put the bracelet back in the money belt; then we'll look through the refuse on the shore."

Kit nodded, picking up the money belt from Sunny's shelving. As he unzipped it, Sunny's eyes narrowed, following the motion of his hand.

103

"Wait! The zipper! If we can take the zipper loop off and break it open, I bet that would make a super hook!"

Kit shook his head and handed the pouch over to her.

"Sunny-bach, I have come to the conclusion that you are the brains of the island."

Sunny flushed. She never considered herself the foremost brain of anything, anywhere. It wasn't embarrassment that made her blush, though. It was the daunting realization that she probably was the brains of this survival operation.

She looked at Kit, who was smoothing back his hair with a wodge of coconut oil. Sunny suddenly realized that he reminded her of that hilarious film about the vacuous male model.

Zoolander! That was it.

As Kit smoothed coconut onto his eyebrows, (presumably to groom them?), she stifled a sigh.

It would have been really great to have someone equally resourceful to work with, but at least Kit had muscle. She gave the zipper a hard twist, broke the loop into a sharp-pointed U shape, then showed Kit.

He gave her a thumbs up. "Fish supper, here we come! Hooray for protein!"

Kit

Kit had told Sunny that there was a rocky outcrop at the end of their cove, and she'd decided that this would be the best place to fish from. Before heading off to the far end of the beach, she'd bossed him about to get ready for the day.

"Find a bendy sapling to use as a fishing pole, then go to the water hole and fill the bottles and get fruit to take with us."

Follow directions, don't mess it up, Kit told himself.

When he returned from doing his appointed tasks, she then asked him to spread more aloe gel on her back and shoulders.

104

Looking at Kit as he heaped aloe goo into his hands, Sunny realized he actually looked paler than when they had arrived on the island. She commented on it, and he looked a little embarrassed.

"Spray tan fading, that's all."

That made Sunny laugh out loud.

"Aah, the hardship of shipwreck life! Your manicure looks like it needs a little work too!"

"Yeah, yeah..." Kit said. "Turn around."

As he rubbed in the sticky gel, she told him her face was a little less painful today. He winced every time he looked at the series of blisters that stretched across her cheekbones and around her throat, but the purple undertones of her skin were changing to a slightly healthier reddish-brown.

Her nose, though, was still bright red with shafts of white skin peeling off it, and he couldn't resist reaching over and tugging off a loose piece.

"We should use this for fish bait!"

"Ugh, gross, though not a bad idea if we can't find anything else."

"I was joking."

"Many a wise thing spoken in jest, and all that," she replied.

"Many a true word, not wise thing. Shakespeare said it best, 'Jesters do oft prove profits,'

He could see Sunny rolling her eyes at him.

"You are very well read," she said, but the tone of her voice suggested she was not particularly admiring of literary leanings.

Whatever.

At the rocks, Sunny scouted around until she found what she determined to be the perfect fishing spot. The hot afternoon had not a breath of wind, and the boulders were almost too hot to walk on. Sunny dipped one foot, then the other, in a rock pool, sighing with relief. Kit took out the fishing line and the zipper hook, and holding them in his hand, peered down into the water, which was teeming with tiny fish.

105

"Careful!" Sunny chided. "That hook is worth a billion times its weight in gold!"

Kit looked at the fishing equipment in his hands, then looked back at Sunny. "How do we attach it? Do you know any knots?"

Of course Sunny did. Kit handed the hook and line over to her. "This is your department then."

As Sunny wound the line along the length of the wooden pole, then applied a perfect clove hitch to it, she told Kit to look for bait. Sunny said he might find some kind of critter down in the wet sand.

Kit knelt and dug half-heartedly. "I don't see anything, Sunny."

"Deeper, you've gotta get down to the waterline. Put your back into it," she yelled back. "If you want to eat, find some bait!"

Geez, she was bossy.

Soon he was soaked in sweat, but with the motivation of eating some protein, he burrowed on until he reached the water table. Sunny called out encouragement from time to time.

"You're doing great, Kit. Keep it up! At this rate, you'll soon get to Timbuktu."

"Yeah, very supportive."

"No, seriously, it said in the in-flight magazine that if you dug a hole right through the earth from Fiji, you'd end up in Timbuktu," she explained.

"Oh great, that's immensely helpful then," he muttered to himself.

When success arrived, it was a bit of a shock. A disgusting, maggoty creature wriggled under his hand, making him shout. Picking it up, he examined it between his finger and thumb. The maggot gave another wriggle, and Kit shuddered.

"Our bait is even more gross than your nose skin."

Holding the maggot up to the sky, he added dramatically, "What have we here? A man or a fish? Dead or alive?"

Turning back to Sunny. "Shakespeare!"

"Indeed," said Sunny, as she came over and plucked it out of his hand. She carefully demonstrated putting the bait onto the hook, then attaching a small pebble with a hole in it as a weight. Looking at the rod, she added, "we really need a lure, something shiny to get their attention."

"The charm bracelet?"

"I really don't want to use anything off there; everything is too precious to lose."

"Shiny seashell?"

"I don't think fish are attracted to shells. They see them all the time—it would be mayhem."

Kit watched her forehead wrinkle in deep thought; the frown lines puckered her crispy, sunburnt skin.

"Something shiny, something shiny..."

The next minute, she turned her back and wrestled under her t-shirt. Turning around again, she had in her hand a surprisingly jazzy bra. Nestled between the cups was a tiny plastic rhinestone heart.

I'd have totally thought she'd be a practical sports bra kinda ' girl.

Kit raised his eyebrow. "Nice bling!"

"Oh, shut it. The sparkly jewel will be perfect!"

As Sunny tugged at the little adornment, she muttered under her breath, "anyway, they were two for one at Target..."

Looping the fishing line through the bead, she handed the tackle back to Kit and told him to put it into the water.

"And keep the line still!" she yelled as she retreated into the shade.

Under the blazing sun, he cautiously lowered the line into the water and then stood motionless, nervous even to twitch under Sunny's beady eyes. As he fished, Kit's thoughts stayed on Shakespeare. His first stage role in LA had been *The Tempest,* and that was all about a shipwreck. He'd played Trinculo, a minor part but a great experience.

It's ironic—I got the part of the jester when I really wanted to play Prospero. Prospero—trapped on an island for years and years,

Kit thought. *But now, jokes on me, 'cause here I am, living Prospero in real life.*

To make the time pass, Kit tried to remember all his lines from the play and found, rather to his surprise, that he could. He'd been fishing for a while without a single nibble, so he called out to Sunny.

"This is the tune of our catch, played by the picture of nobody."

Sunny called back to Kit, asking if he was feeling OK. Was he getting delirious?

"Give it up for a while. Get some shade and some water," she suggested.

"I shall laugh myself to death at this puppy-headed monster!"

Seeing her shocked face, he yelled again, "SHAKESPEARE!"

He could see Sunny shaking her head and laughed. Having decided to give island survival his best effort, his mood had changed dramatically. Kit felt a lightness of being, something he hadn't felt for a long time, if ever.

The day continued, and in the stillness of the afternoon, he could hear his own heart beating in his ear—pumping blood in rhythm with the ocean. He waited some more, eyes fixed on the water. If sheer will could catch fish, Kit would have already caught a creel-full.

Suddenly feeling a tug, he froze. Some ancient instinct told him to wait one moment—one breath in and one long breath out—then, with the snap of his wrist, he yanked the line high out of the water. A wriggling fish hung on the end. *Careful, careful, don't let it get away.*

In a smooth motion, he swung the line round until the fish dangled safely over the rocks.

"A fish, a fish! My kingdom for a fish!"

Sunny whooped and raced over to examine the catch. Hopping from one foot to the other, she passed him the water bottle and told him one fish would do for today. But Kit had the bit between his teeth and was determined to stay until he caught more. The act of waiting, thinking about his quarry, and making minute adjustments to his line placement was kind of satisfying. He liked it.

He *really* liked it when he proceeded to catch four more fish. Sunny had taught him how to gouge out the eyeballs of the first fish to use as extra bait. It was gross, but he did it.

I did it. I'm a fisherman. I can catch fish!

The feeling of pride, more than any film role had given him in recent years, blew him away.

Rolling up the line but leaving the netting on the rocks, he and Sunny tramped back to the camp, mouths watering at the idea of a fish fry. Sunny gave Kit a quick lesson on how to pull fish guts out with a sharp stick and, stoking up the fire, they soon had the fish roasting. The smell was amazing, and the taste even better. Stretching out on the sand, Kit felt almost satisfied for the first time in days.

The only thing that could improve his lot was an after-dinner whiskey, maybe some air-conditioning, and for his hand to feel better.

Unwrapping his palm, he waved his injured hand toward Sunny. "Now we have the fishhook, let's sterilize it in the fire and pop these blisters."

"That's not what you are supposed to do. The blister is keeping it clean—new skin is growing underneath. You can probably keep it unwrapped now."

Kit gave a sigh. He'd been hoping popping the blisters would have sped up the healing; he'd like to get his hand back. But Sunny's slightly annoying "know-it-all know-how" was probably correct.

He tied his black silk bandanna around his neck in a jaunty side-knot, then held his hand up and examined the angry, fluid-filled sacs that covered his palm and the base of each finger. Gently poking at them, he thought about the fresh skin growing beneath—nature was pretty cool. Watching the blisters wobble was like being mesmerized by a lava lamp.

I could lay here and do this for days.

Poke, wobble, poke.

"Watch this, Sunny."

As he looked over to her, he saw she was looking intensely worried and realized this probably wasn't the best time to try and entertain her with his wound.

"What's up?'

"Oh, it's just...we still haven't seen any search planes."

Sunny looked at the piles of trash and fish bones next to her.

"Do you really think anyone's looking for us? I can't help but think that maybe we were presumed dead from the beginning. I'm sure the others only saw the explosion but didn't see us being blasted into the water."

Kit propped himself up on an elbow. "How long since it happened?

She counted back on her fingers.

"It's all a bit of a blur, but I think five days, or maybe four? I guess we should start keeping track, move a stone to a certain place every night so we can mark the passing of time."

Kit thought about a large pile of stones and almost smiled; *each stone would represent a day more of peace*. Then he sighed; Kit thought it highly likely they would be rescued and vowed to enjoy island life until that happened. He was in no rush to return to civilization. For a moment, he wondered again if he should tell Sunny that he was super rich and famous, which guaranteed people would be looking for him. It might ease her mind, he thought, but it might also get her hopes up too much—and then what if it doesn't happen?

Maybe he'd better keep it all to himself.

Thinking about whether or not they had a future off the island made Kit curious.

"What were you going to do after the research station trip?"

Sunny shrugged. "Go back to Seattle, room with Dennie and Clive—I've just moved out of the student dorms. They said I could rent their spare room until I find a new place—and go back to working at the Bagel Bubbe. I had it all planned. I've got a spreadsheet of galleries and shows I was going to apply to. I was going to use my work from the residency."

Sunny looked incredibly glum. "I had the whole of my next year mapped, but now it's not going to happen. Now I'd probably head to Weaver Creek." She looked toward the lowering sun. "Spend some time with Andrea. Make a new plan."

"Who's Andrea again?"

"Andrea and Jerry, my parent's best friends. I moved in with them after Mom and Dad died. So, if we get off this island, I'll go spend a little time with them, then go on to Seattle and take up where I left off."

"At the bagel shop? Why go bake bagels again? Why not just get a studio and work full time as an artist?" Kit thought Sunny's plans sounded a little uninspired—and a lot of grind

"Oh, hello! There is something called "bills" to think of! Making money painting won't be a reality for a long time, if ever. An early baking shift and painting in the afternoons is the perfect setup for me."

Kit sometimes forgot how it felt to have to take money into consideration.

Sunny turned to Kit and asked him the same question. "What about you? What was your plan for after the trip? Tell me about your acting. You're such a man of mystery...spill some beans!"

Ideas of inventing himself a whole new back-story crossed Kit's mind, but he settled for, once again, just giving her the bare minimum. He didn't want to complicate things between them. From long experience, he knew that fame and riches always complicated things. And probably would still do so—even when shipwrecked.

"I told you I was going to do an acting gig in a film. It was an action movie about a pandemic. I was going to play a science researcher. That's why I was out here, to find out what their lives were like on the research station."

111

"Oh wow, that's huge—a film!" Sunny looked up in surprise. "You must be so upset to miss out on that. Would it have made you a star? Was it a big movie?"

Kit rolled over and, with his back to her, said mildly, "It was no big deal. It really doesn't matter."

"I'd hate to play 20-questions with you," said Sunny. "You are the worst! I feel like I have to drag every minuscule bit of information out of you. You never share voluntarily; did you know that?"

She then flicked a pebble in his direction. "Have you always been so squirrelly?"

He rolled back over to face her again. "Squirrely? Is that a thing?"

"You know, you hide your nuts away and don't tell anyone where they are hidden—squirrelly."

"Well, yes then, I've always been squirrelly."

To distract her from any further probing, he made a squirrel face and nut-burying motion.

Settling back into a comfortable silence, they both got lost in their own thoughts for a while. He didn't know what was on Sunny's mind, but Kit was thinking about all the secrets he had kept over the years, all the secrets he was keeping from Sunny—and that he was a squirrel, apparently.

Kit had been in show business long enough to know that exaggerations, secrets, half-truths, and flat-out lies were normal in his world.

First, you'd change your name from something like Otis to something like Nicky, especially if you wanted to shake off your past. Next were the small bendings of the truth; you applied for a call and claimed you were 6 '3", but in truth, you were 6 '1". Or you told a casting director you could absolutely ride a horse and then hoped you could fake it on set. As your fame grew, the lies got bigger, helped along by agents and PR teams. Like the story his agent had leaked to the press, that he was having a steamy affair with his costar on *Fury of Flames* (he wasn't; she was actually in love with the actress who played her handmaiden). One of the more outrageous planted stories involved him having a long-lost brother. Another had him marrying a pop star in a Vegas drive-through chapel.

Being on the island was putting into perspective how artificial and shallow his life had become. He had seen so many famous actors become caricatures of themselves, lives filled with girls and drugs, and aging faces filled with, well, fillers. He was determined that if they ever got rescued, he was going to make some big changes.

Chapter 11
Sunny

*I*n the late afternoon, Sunny sent Kit off to collect yet more fresh water and deposit the fish guts with Pinky. Even though they had fish, lychees, and coconut, she still wanted to expand their pantry.

Mom could figure all this out. She'd know where to look for more food.

Her mom had been an amazing gardener and enthusiastic canner. *I could try to dry the lychee into fruit strips.* The dried fruit from her mom's dehydrator had been the favorite part of her school sack lunches. *Maybe it's too damp here, though. What do you think, Mom?* Sunny considered the seaweed again. She'd never been a sushi fan, but she knew some people loved it. And a girl in one of her classes always had packs of dried nori as her lunch snack. Whether this South Pacific seaweed was edible, Sunny had no idea.

I'll just have to try a little bit—see if it's OK.

She popped a piece in her mouth, crossing her fingers that it wouldn't make her sick.

Chewing cautiously, Sunny thought about her next problem. Being held hostage on the beach for lack of footwear was no good. She was going to have to figure something out.

Looking at all the piles of debris around her, she decided to fashion a second shoe by winding plastic rope into a sole, in the manner of an espadrille. Without a needle and thread, she pondered on how to bond it all together, then realized the answer was right in front of her. Holding the rope over the fire with two careful fingers, she had some reasonable success melting the twine and bonding it into one flat shoe bottom.

As Kit re-entered the campsite, carrying a full Wilson, his face wrinkled. "Ugh, what's burning?"

"The bottom half of my new shoe!" Sunny held up the smoking plastic triumphantly.

"Oh clever, let me help," he said, setting Wilson down in the shade.

Sunny made space for him next to the fire, then held the "shoe" while Kit burned a couple of holes in the sole with a heated stick. Some more blue rope was threaded through the holes, and in the end, they had made a reasonably passable sandal.

"Hold it with two hands," Sunny instructed Kit, "it's not set firm yet."

Kit picked it up by the newly threaded-in strap. The whole thing fell apart.

"Oops!"

Sunny closed her eyes and counted to ten. She then opened her eyes again and looked at Kit. "Have you always had a listening problem?"

"Huh?"

She started to repeat herself, then stopped. "Very funny."

Kit put on a somewhat contrite expression. "Sorry. Let's put it back together, you know—S.O.S!"

"Huh?"

"Save our soles."

Again Sunny said, "Huh?"

"Save our soles..." Kit pointed to the bottom of his foot.

Sunny started winding the melted twine again and muttered, "Save assholes..."

"Language, young lady!"

When the flip flop was once again assembled and melted into place, Sunny held up the finished object.

"It's not going to be very comfy," said Kit.

Sunny nodded. "Better than nothing, though."

She took the homemade shoe and skipped over to display it on the wardrobe shelf. As she did, Kit called out to her.

"You look about ten years old when you skip like that," he said.

115

Sunny stuck her tongue out at him and then positioned the shoe among the stores, making sure it was sitting neatly.

"How old are you anyway, Sunny?"

"Twenty-five," she said, without turning around.

"Hmm, I thought you were younger."

Now she did turn around. "I seem young to you? Immature?"

"A bit."

"That's rude. Just because I'm not interested in pointless things like fashion and pop culture, people think I'm immature, then..." she trailed off, feeling herself get steamed up.

"Sorry, I didn't mean to get irritated. It's just people have said stuff like that to me before. They treat me like a simpleton because I don't wear make-up or have a tinder account. But I buried my parents when I was 18, I have no other living relatives, and I have no financial support, so I don't have the time or the patience to care about vapid stuff."

"O.K! I get it."

"You probably don't, but that's O.K. I'm used to people making assumptions about me."

"I'm sorry. And I was wrong to say you seemed immature, actually..." he paused, and Sunny could tell he was trying to come up with the right words. "Actually, it's more like that you are just—not jaded."

"Jaded?" she asked. "That means cynical, right?"

"No, not cynical exactly. It's more like world-weary."

"Yeah, O.K., I'll agree with that. I'm not jaded, and I don't ever want to be jaded. How can you be jaded, world-weary at twenty-five? Or at any age, really. There's so much out there. I think if you are weary of the world, something is very wrong with your life choices. What's the saying? When a man is tired of life, he's tired of..."

"When a man is tired of London, he is tired of life..." corrected Kit.

116

"Oh, well, I guess if London is an analogy for the world, that fits."

"Samuel Johnson also said, "Human life is a state in which much is to be endured, and little to be enjoyed," added Kit.

"Well, he sounds like a bundle of laughs." Sunny turned back to the shelf and fiddled with a project she had been working on earlier. Pleased with her results, she sat back. On a flat stone in front of her, the baby pacifier now had two pebbles as eyes and a curve of braided grass below as a smile. Dried lychee skins made the face apple-cheeked and a halo of wilting blue flowers completed the scene. She could feel Kit's breath on her neck as he peered over her shoulder.

"What is that...creation?"

"Hmm, it probably falls into the category of assemblage art," said Sunny, moving back slightly. "I haven't got a pen and paper to doodle with, so I'm using found objects instead. I think better when I'm doodling," she told him. She fussed with one of the flowers to make it align better. "I think it's turned into an homage to Giuseppe Arcimboldo."

"Err, who?"

Sunny passed Kit some green seaweed berries and encouraged him to add them to the artwork.

"Did you ever see those old paintings, portraits where the face is made up of fruits and veggies?"

Kit looked blank, so she continued. "Sixteenth-century painter from Italy. Huge influence on Dali, big on turnip noses."

"All I'm thinking about is that Peter Gabriel video from the eighties," said Kit.

"Yes!" said Sunny. "That was totally influenced by Arcimboldo!"

Kit reached over and moved the braided grass mouth so it looked like it was talking. "Sledge. Hammer." Kit continued to play around, making the art piece sing tunes.

"Wah, wah, wah..." he sang.

Sunny laughed. For a moment, she felt completely normal. Talking about art, doodling, almost relaxed. She was also enjoying Kit's change of attitude.

"Why are you less morose now?" she blurted out before she could think better of it.

For a beat, Kit didn't reply.

Sunny took a deep breath and hoped her comment hadn't sent him back into a mood.

But it hadn't. Kit turned and looked at her, "Just decided to embrace island life, is all," he said. Then reaching over, Kit poked her in the belly.

"I realized I couldn't communicate properly in morose-code."

Sunny wondered if Kit's incessant punning was an unconscious tic. Or maybe it was like that whole "sad clown" thing, a defense mechanism of some kind. Or maybe he just liked terrible jokes.

She poked him in the ribs in return. "I'm going to start grading your jokes; that one gets a two."

"Out of five?" asked Kit.

"Out of ten, and that's being generous."

"So, what happens if I manage to get a ten? Do I get a prize?"

"Honestly, if you manage a ten joke, I think it would be me getting the prize." She paused and thought. "But as an encouragement to up the quality, if you manage to get a grade ten joke, you can have an afternoon hanging out at the waterhole and not doing any chores."

Kit grinned. "This should be easy—hope you are prepared to do all the work from now on."

Sunny raised an eyebrow at him. Kit had the good grace to look a little bashful.

They rested by the fire, and as Sunny ate yet another piece of coconut, she leaned back against Kit, feeling like they were maybe becoming friends. Above her, the sky darkened rapidly. Too rapidly. Rain clouds were gathering again. Sunny looked at their pile of building equipment. *Should have done the shelter today,* she thought in frustration. *But I guess the fishing was a success. Can't do everything at once.*

The wind began to whip, making it seem as though this was going to be more than just a quick tropical shower.

Dad? Is this going to be trouble?

After a moment, Sunny decided she needed to take action.

"Move everything up to the tree line," she commanded as she started collecting their supplies and tamping down a nugget of disappointment as she dismantled her neat shelving. Moving everything to the shelter of the trees was better than having it blown all over, but it still seemed a shame when she'd just gotten it all organized.

Kit was randomly throwing things into a heap under a nearby tree, which was quite irritating. Things got lost in the sand so easily. She unburied the cigarette lighter and sighed.

"Can you just go and get more firewood? I'll sort out this stuff."

Sunny transferred their fire under the trees, and it wasn't many minutes later when the rainstorm rolled in. Waves buffeted the shore, and the wind blew, driving rain and wet sand toward them and putting the fire out almost immediately. Kit stretched his arm around Sunny, who was grateful for the warmth and comfort.

"This storm isn't how I'd pictured being washed up on a deserted island," she sighed, snuggling into Kit's warm armpit.

"You've thought about being washed up on a deserted island?"

"Of course!" She looked at him with confusion, "hasn't everyone? You get shipwrecked, and then you have only plucky wits to survive on until rescued."

"Can wits be plucky?"

Sunny rolled her eyes at him.

Giving a snort of laughter, he added, "Well, if they can, I'm sure you have the pluckiest wits of them all!"

Sunny thought he was being patronizing again, but looking at him, she saw Kit had a completely sincere expression on his face.

"Seriously, you are really good at this whole shipwreck thing. To be quite honest, I don't know what I would have done if you hadn't been here."

Very true, she thought, but held that back and instead replied encouragingly, "Oh, I think you could have been fine; after all, you did catch the fish.

Picking at the peeling skin on her shoulder, she shivered. They really must get the shelter built tomorrow. Kit must have been thinking about the same thing.

"What's the plan for the shelter? It would be great to have somewhere dry!"

Pleased that Kit was showing an interest, Sunny discussed her ideas; they could topple a palm tree by setting fire to the trunk, and the roofing could be woven. Perhaps also they could make their own kind of adobe?

Later, after a predictable conversation about Pinky's well-being, they decided to call it a night. As they burrowed down together to sleep, the seas roared, the forest creaked, and the wind whipped sand against their exposed skin.

The last image Sunny had in her head before she fell asleep was a huge pile of stones, marking the days they had spent on the island. And beside it, her and Kit looking old and gray.

Chapter 12

Kit

Neither of them slept well during the night, so as dawn broke, they headed straight to the waterhole to drink, wash, and eat. Returning to the beach, Kit took stock of the disarray. Some large branches had fallen from various trees, and a new delivery of flotsam was lining the high tide mark. A significant amount of newly fallen coconuts lay around, and they also needed to be collected.

Kit shuddered, thinking of the damage a falling coconut could have done to their bodies, and made a mental note that they should not shelter beneath palm trees during a storm again. As he got up to collect the fruit, he tried to lighten the slightly heavy mood of the morning.

"Hey Sunny, check out my nuts!"

He enjoyed making her laugh but then stood patiently as she scolded him for not lining the nuts up neatly.

They kept straightening the camp, and he kept putting things in the wrong place, so eventually, Sunny shooed him away. Walking along the shore, maybe only a hundred yards away, he found something catching his eye. A new piece of garbage, much larger than the norm, had washed up. Trying to make it out, he walked closer. Perhaps they'd get lucky, and it would be a fridge full of steaks and beer, Kit thought wistfully.

The object was red and half-buried in the sand. Pulling it out, Kit thought for a heart-stopping minute that it might really contain steak and beer. He waved at Sunny, then called out to her. This discovery was reasonably momentous for their now very stripped-down life.

"Hey, look at our latest gift from Neptune!"

"What is it?" she yelled back.

Pausing a moment to build up the suspense, he then yelled back, "A cooler!"

With the swagger of a big game hunter, he dragged the box up the sand. The cooler was completely intact. *I can take it with me fishing—keep my catch in it*, thought Kit. *I just need a weird hat covered in hooks and flies, and I'll be a legit angler*. But before Kit could go off and fulfill his fishing fantasy, Sunny insisted they make a start on the shelter. She said she was determined to build today and that shivering through the rain had convinced her shelter was imperative.

Kit sat with Sunny on the sand as she explained her two shelter design options.

"It really depends how long we think we are going to be here. If it's only for a short time, we can do the easy shelter, but if it's for..." she stumbled for a moment, "...for months, or years—then we need to build something more durable."

He looked at her. Discussing their timeline on the island was something they had both avoided. Kit swung his head to look out to sea, where, once again, no ships were in sight. He didn't care one way or another what kind of shelter they built, but saying that to Sunny would probably be irritating. Better to be positive and say they only needed a short-term one—that would have the added bonus of being quicker to build.

He gave the cooler next to him a firm pat—he basically just wanted to go fishing.

"So, how about we make a temporary shelter, then count the days. If we are still here in, say, two months, we set about upgrading it..." he suggested.

"Two months on the island—you think we'll stay alive that long?"

Kit didn't see why not. So far they had been lucky. They'd found food water and avoided any disasters. But anything could happen, he acknowledged. Anything could definitely happen.

In an effort to be positive, he replied, "I really doubt we will be here in two months, but it makes sense to plan ahead."

Sunny nodded. "OK. I was willing to make the permanent shelter, but it would have used up an awful lot of our energy..." Looking at Kit, she added teasingly, "...and you'd really need to step up your fishing game to make sure we were adequately well fed!"

"Well, if you just want me to go fishing now...?"

"Nope—you're the muscle!"

Sunny had decided they would utilize a large, newly fallen branch for the temporary shelter. With much heaving and sweating, they managed to lift it until one end was trapped in the v of some branches on another tree, creating a roughly 45-degree angle. Next, she instructed Kit to drape some ragged fishing nets over the trunk, and then together they wove long branches through the netting until the lattice of twigs became a somewhat rigid wall.

This wall was attached to the ground by several rocks, and Kit was tasked with finding heavier boulders and logs to make it secure. Grunting, he heaved the heaviest things he could find to the building site.

"More dry grass."

However many bunches of the dry, hay-like grass he collected, Sunny would say they needed more. More, more, more.

"This has to be enough..."

She eyed his pile. "We need at least double that."

Kit groaned and pulled himself back to his feet. The shelter was going up remarkably fast, and yet again he was impressed with Sunny's skills and her stamina. He watched as she took some enormous waxy green leaves harvested from nearby foliage and deftly threaded them through the branches. He watched her take the fronds and start weaving them in until they lay like shingles.

"The last time I did roofing was with dad," she'd told him as her fingers moved like a shuttle on a loom. "We were so hot and sweaty by the time we'd finished that mom hosed us down in the yard."

Kit had not learned anything particularly practical from his father, apart from how to dodge a blow and steal copper wire. His dad and uncles were all hunters, but Kit had only once been invited along on their beer-filled, mostly illegal hunts. It hadn't been a success.

Would have been the one helpful skill Dad could have taught me, he thought.

The shelter continued to form, sited at the point where the trees met the sand. Here the earth was a satisfying loamy mixture of sand and soil. Better to build on, but far enough from the jungle to not be living in a permanent cloud of insects. At the base of a tree, Kit set up the storage shelving again, letting Sunny have the task of arranging the stores to her satisfaction. He was quite sure that he would not do it right.

As she lined up the mostly plastic pieces, she told him about her dad's workshop, where every tool had a sharpied outline on a piece of old peg board, and how much she'd enjoyed slotting the tools back into their assigned places. Suprisingly, Kit thought that did sound pretty satisfying.

Maybe one day I could have a workshop. Maybe one day I could be the kind of person who had a workshop and pegboard and tools.

Watching Sunny's meticulous organizing, Kit pointed out that as well as shipwrecked, they had also been shopwrecked.

"Ha ha—not. That's a three-pointer."

As Sunny reconstructed her weird portrait art, he felt an overwhelming sense of peace. It was simple here; just find food, build shelter, be friends. *I never had peace being Otis Kitson, and I didn't being Nicky Kitson either.*

Otis was a shell, a boy never fully-formed. Nicky was also a shell, a façade. Uncomfortable comprehension flashed through his brain; *I act because I can pretend to be someone else—because I don't actually know who I am*

He didn't know what to do with that thought. Normally if he started thinking too deeply, he'd get stoned or drunk to curb it.

124

Fishing—that'll have to be the new whiskey.

"Fishing time now, right?"

"Sure."

Sunny accompanied Kit in his quest for 'catch of the day. 'But as he stood on the rocks, the line remained stubbornly limp. The water was all churned up from the rough night before.

Maybe all the fish were hiding, he thought to himself as he tried to get lost in the peaceful fishing trance. Eventually, he did get a bite, just one solo fish. Sunny said she'd let Kit eat most of it, seeing as he'd done all the heavy lifting that day, and he gratefully took her up on the offer. After the meager dinner, Kit snuggled into the new shelter. Having walls, a roof, and a fire burning just outside was reassuring, but even so, he felt a bit off. Sunny fell asleep immediately, but Kit tossed and turned. Something just didn't feel right.

Sunny

t was still nighttime when Sunny was woken by Kit's arm flying right into her face. Startled, she sat up as Kit moaned beside her.

"Ahhh—it hurts."

He was clutching his midriff and rocking. All of a sudden, he exploded out of the shelter, and Sunny could hear a series of groans and retching outside. The noise set off her own stomach, surges of nausea creeping up her body. *This was going to be bad.*

She made it as far as the nearest tree and, leaning against it, vomited copiously. An awful sour cocktail of coconut, fish, and seaweed coming up. Would it ever stop? Why wasn't her mom there to hold back her hair?

Kneeling in the sand, Sunny was vaguely aware of awful sounds coming from Kit's direction. She waited a few long minutes, until it seemed safe to move. She had to get it together. *Come on, Evans— you can do this.*

"Kit?"

He didn't reply, just continued to moan and retch.

On shaking legs, she stumbled toward him. He was lying on his side, clutching his stomach, and his face was pressed into the sand. Sunny shook his shoulder.

"Stabbing," he sobbed, rolling from side to side.

Sitting on the sand next to him, Sunny waited for her heart to stop racing. Now that her stomach was empty, she was beginning to feel much better. Kit, though, was nowhere near OK.

"Ahhh..." He rocked and sobbed.

Poor Kit.

"No..." he hissed. Shuddering, he started to heave again.

She stroked his back and held the hair out of his face, so grateful she wasn't in such a state. How could she help him?

Water? Yes, water.

Sunny always filled the water bottles up before bedtime, so now she staggered over and collected them from outside the shelter. Rinsing her mouth and spitting, she then took an actual swallow. Her stomach gurgled, but the water stayed down.

Moving back to Kit, she asked, "Can you drink?"

He didn't reply, just continued to heave. How he could still be retching was beyond her. Tears caught in his eyelashes, shining in the moonlight. A huge shudder rippled through his body; then, he started to shake uncontrollably.

Sunny rubbed him on his back again. All she could do was wait it out with him.

Time passed.

Eventually, Kit stopped writhing about. In fact, he was very still. When he didn't respond to any of her questions, Sunny gently pried open one of his eyes. The eyelid contracted against her finger, and Kit looked at her.

"Do you think you can keep down some water?"

Kit paused a beat.

"Yes."

Sunny put an arm under his neck to ease him up into a sitting position. He waved a hand, signaling her to stop.

"No."

He collapsed back, moaning.

The sun slowly rose, bringing with it a cloud of flies that hovered around the mess.

Ignoring the tired aching in her body, Sunny put on her flip-flops and made it down the path to the water hole. She washed and filled all their water containers. Eyeing the fruit, she didn't think it seemed like a good option, for either her or Kit. The idea of the sweet, acidic juice hitting her stomach made her quiver. Wearily she returned to the camp, where Kit hadn't moved.

"Kit?"

No reply.

"Kit?" She knelt beside him and shook his shoulder. He just groaned in response. Stroking his brow, she brought her hand away. Did he have a fever?

Taking off her t-shirt, she dipped it in fresh water and brought it up to his lips, just moistening them a little. He probably wouldn't be able to keep down water, but this might help a little.

As Kit slept on and off, waking to moan or retch, Sunny felt useless. *I guess I'll tidy up.* She tried to straighten up the site, pushing soiled sand away and then burying it, but always keeping an eye on Kit. Pinky arrived on the scene.

"Oh, I see you come by when all the hard work is done!" Sunny said to the little car.

Pinky yawned and snuggled close to Sunny, obviously wanting to lie on her chest.

"Just for a minute, Pinks," Sunny told her.

Just take a minute to rest.

But it was many, many more minutes before she woke again. As she did, she opened one cautious eye and then the other, the palm fronds waved hello above her head.

Beautiful.

Then it all came rushing back.

Kit!

Kit was half in, half out of the bushes. He lifted his head slightly and moaned as she approached.

"Am I dead? Please tell me I'm dead, urgh."

Sunny was so relieved to hear him speak—and make sense—she could have wept.

She passed him some water. '"Fraid you're still living, well, maybe living-dead."

He sat up warily, and with a shaky hand, brought the bottle to his lips.

"Zombie sounds about right."

They sat still in the sand, passing the bottle back and forth, then lay down again.

More time passed, the shadows lengthened, and the heat of the day began to ease.

"Kit?"

"Yeah?"

"You've got to try and move."

"Yeah," he groaned.

"OK, you are going to move on the count of three." She took his arms in hers. "One," she muttered, "two," *come on, Kit,* "three."

They stood, Kit leaning heavily on Sunny.

"Good job–you're vertical!"

Now that he was upright, Sunny led him to the fire, sat him down again, and gave him Wilson and a bunch of dry grass.

"Can you wash yourself?"

He nodded and slowly splashed water over his face and torso, drying it off with the grasses.

"Good."

She helped him into their shelter, where he collapsed down on a bed of more dry grass. Sunny then felt his forehead with the back of her hand.

"You're not hot anymore; that's good."

He certainly wasn't hot; he looked like he was freezing. Kit started to shake.

Dammit, thought Sunny, he looked awful.

She lay next to him, pressing her body into his, but still his teeth chattered. Stroking his back, she started to recite *The Incredible Journey* from memory.

"It all starts when we meet a man called John who lives alone in the wilds of Canada. This place has lakes, woods, and rivers, and hardly anyone lives there..."

Sunny continued on with the story until she felt Kit's body stop trembling and relax heavily against her. His breathing was slow and even.

Good, he's asleep.

Laying in the shelter and looking up at the woven ceiling, she thought about the three animals in the story; two dogs and one cat.

It's just like me, Kit, and Pinky, three animals lost in the wilds. And Pinky is just like Tao, catching food to share with her friends.

That story had a happy ending, she reminded herself firmly, so we can too. Just got to keep going and not give up.

Chapter 13

Kit

When Kit woke, the first thing he was aware of was the scratchy, grassy bedding against his skin. His heart thudded—was he back in the shed? The next sense to return was his hearing, and the first thing he heard was a cat's meow. The cat! He had to save the cat...dig a way out, get under the foundations. He tried to swallow, but his throat was dry and sore. How many days had it been?

Come on Otis, move!

The air smelled of campfire smoke and brine. That was weird.

Opening an eye, he saw a calico cat looking back at him. She licked him on the nose.

That's not the cat.

Beyond the cat, he could see a pair of sunburned legs. One foot of which was in a green flip-flop, the other in some weird mangle of blue rope.

Suddenly he was back on the island, not back in Ellensburg. Thank God.

Sunny bent down, looking through the shelter entrance.

"Hey, you."

"Hey," he said in reply.

Why was he lying in here, feeling so awful? He remembered getting up in the night to puke, but after that was a mystery. This felt like one hell of a hangover.

Sunny came in and was leaning over him with a strange expression on her face.

"What..." His voice was husky, and he swallowed, "...what happened?"

Stepping inside, she smoothed her damp t-shirt over his forehead; it felt good. Then she put an arm around his shoulder and hefted him up.

"I think we got food poisoned. Drink this."

Instead of being the usual spring water in the soda bottle, today it tasted different. Warming? Not unpleasant, actually.

"I put wild ginger in the water for a day—to make a kind of sun tea. The ginger should help with the nausea."

"A day? How long have I been out?"

"A day." She took the bottle back from him.

"You need to drink a lot of this, then eat something."

To Kit's amazement, he found he was actually hungry. Sunny looked exceedingly pleased when he told her that. Reaching behind her, she smiled then produced a green lump.

"This will help."

He sniffed it warily. "Seaweed?"

"Yep, it's got all kinds of minerals and things in it. Come on."

She was virtually shoving it down his throat.

"OK, OK."

Chewing a little doubtfully, he was happy his stomach remained calm. After another couple of minutes, he concluded he actually quite liked the taste. Sunny squatted back on her heels and smiled at him.

"Good! Now move your butt. You smell, and I want to clean up in here!"

Kit smiled to himself—Sunny being bossy was good. She wasn't making a fuss, so he couldn't have been all that ill. But why then, in the back of his mind, did he have a vague recollection of her leaning over him and crying? He must have dreamed it. In his dream, she had been crying and telling him she needed him, that he mustn't leave her.

The following days were slow. As Kit recovered from the terrible poisoning, Sunny did the majority of the work. She'd make him coconut and ginger mash, with piles of dried out seaweed with lychees to follow, and Pinky delivered them another booby, which gave them meat for a day.

131

They discussed eating fish again. They had to presume the fish was what poisoned them. They needed protein and couldn't rely on Pinky's catches all the time. Kit said they should throw back any fish that looked similar to the one he'd caught on that fateful day. Sunny said they would cook all the fish more thoroughly in future. They both had a strange metallic taste in their mouth that lingered for a while, though that eventually faded, and Kit's hands and feet were tingling. But nothing too bad. They had survived, and the strange remaining symptoms were tolerable.

On the third day of Kit's recovery, he felt well enough to return to fishing.

As the days continued on, they were mostly filled with routine activity, but Kit was never bored. He continued to revel in the peace and satisfaction that were new to him.

In the downtime, he rested or swam, thought up jokes to entertain Sunny with, still aiming for that perfect ten, or took occasional walks into the jungle to see what was there. He'd noticed that Sunny didn't seem to like downtime.

"Relax, why don't you? All the chores are done!"

She'd sighed long and deeply, then explained that her fingers felt itchy with longing for a paintbrush or drawing tools. If she could get lost in some drawing, island life would be much more bearable.

Pinky was obviously also enjoying island life. Some days Kit did not see her at all, but almost every morning, she delivered a freshly caught breakfast. One morning she brought a rat. They had both declined to use it as a meal, but chopped up, it had made excellent fish bait.

"I hate rats," Sunny told Kit. "So did my dad, so mom had to be rodent control at our house!" Sunny then went on to tell Kit a story of a huge rat running loose in the diner where her mom worked.

"Andrea was on a table screaming, and mom was in a pair of waders with a baseball bat; she was worried it could be rabid." She had him in stitches as she described the local highway patrolman entering the diner to pick up a coffee and thinking he'd walked in on a hold-up.

In the evenings, they would lie under the stars and tell each other actual bedtime stories. Sunny continued reciting *The Incredible Journey* from memory. She just got to the section where Bodger was attacked by a bear. Kit was on tenterhooks to find out whether Tao would be able to save him. Sunny told her bedtime story every other night, and Kit, she'd declared, had to tell her a story of his own on the alternating nights.

Kit racked his brains for any story he knew thoroughly enough to stretch out into many nights under the stars. He'd eventually settled on retelling the plot of *Fury of Flames*. It was something he'd poured his life into for years.

"Oh, I've heard of that show! I never watched it, but some kids in my freshman class were crazy about it!"

"Freshman class at college, not high school I take it?" Kit hoped so; otherwise, he was going to feel extremely old.

"Yeah, yeah, it was big back then." My friend Ronnie was always doing fan-art about it, pretty hilarious stuff. The lead guy on the show was some prima donna, so Ronnie did this parody blog. It was hilarious—he got quite the following."

Slightly stunned, Kit didn't respond, not sure how to feel about this bit of information.

"Anyway, yeah," Sunny continued, "tell me the *Fury of Flames* story. I have to warn you, though, I'll probably have Ronnie's spoof in my head the whole time—hard to take something like that seriously."

Chapter 14

Sunny

According to the heap-of-stones calendar, they'd been on the island for two weeks when Kit returned from fishing with an exciting development—he'd caught a crab! In the simple world of the island, a crab was big news, and Sunny decided to mark the occasion.

She had been working on a mysterious project, which was to be a treat for the both of them. When Kit left to go fishing, she would go about the daily chores, and as soon as they were done, she would go off into the jungle to where she had set up her "still."

Kit's numerous remarks about wanting a whiskey, cold beer, gin and tonic, or glass of wine hadn't gone unnoticed, and she thought trying to brew something would be good for his mental health (*fermental health*, she chuckled to herself—Kit's bad joke telling was infectious). Vaguely remembering an article about monkeys making their own alcohol, fermenting sap or fruit or something like that, she'd left mashed lychees and wild ginger in a container with a makeshift lid for several days, hoping the fruit would ferment into a wine of sorts. The first batch had been poached by some wildlife, so the second go-round she made the lid much more secure.

Pulling the stones off the lid, she drew the container up to her nose and checked on the brew.

"Oof! Hope it tastes better than it smells," she said to Pinky, who was accompanying her.

Putting the container back in its spot, she thought back to the last time she'd gone drinking. She wasn't much of a drinker, but every now and then, a rum and coke would hit the spot.

Sunny was assistant manager at the Bagel Bubbe, and nearly always worked the early morning shift. Her tasks were organizing the deliveries, checking on the night shift production, and then getting started on a new round of baking for the afternoon service. The

134

small crew was a tight-knit bunch, and either Clive or Dennie was often in the bakery during the morning as well.

Dear Clive and Dennie, who were always on her case about dating...

"I don't have the time or space!" she'd declare, a little exasperated.

"I wouldn't leave it too long, or you'll be growing cobwebs you-know-where!" Clive had teased her.

Sunny had thrown a dish towel at him.

Her bosses were not to be deterred, though, and they had noticed that she chatted easily with Toby, the "sandwich artist" on the breakfast shift. Toby—highly egged on by the two older men—really wanted to enjoy Sunny's company outside of work, so every couple of weeks would ask her out.

After the cobweb crack, Sunny had finally caved, and she and Toby spent a night at a local karaoke bar. Nervous about singing, Sunny had consumed way too many rum and cokes. The rum and cokes had then led to sloppy dueting on the karaoke stage (to Abba's "Dancing Queen"—Toby's idea) and an even sloppier end to the evening—back at Toby's house. Waking up the following morning, Sunny came to, and felt as though her head was being crushed in a vice. Tiptoeing through Toby's house while trying to avoid his roommates was also not an experience she would be in a hurry to recreate. As she'd stepped out into the busy Seattle street, the sunlight making her wince, she'd sworn off alcohol for the foreseeable future.

This life of being washed up on a deserted island was certainly not what she would call a future that was foreseeable. With the smell of the pungent potion still in her nostrils, Sunny decided drinking was back on the menu.

Back at camp, Sunny watched Kit sitting in the sand and poking at the fire. He presented a pretty disheveled figure. The expensive designer style he'd sported on the boat was a far cry from his current style. He'd finally stopped "popping" the collar on his button-up shirt, and it had been ages since he'd given his hair the coconut oil treatment. Being dirty and tousled made him look 100% more human, she thought.

An astonishingly handsome human, if she was being honest with herself.

Sunny had been determinedly ignoring how physically attractive Kit was, but every now and then, she couldn't help but admire the planes of his face and the form of his body—she was an artist, after all.

Watching him dexterously handle some skewered fruit, she nodded to herself. His cooking skills had really improved.

As Kit "plated up" the crab and coconut onto some plastic discs (one an old frisbee and the other a bucket lid), Sunny disappeared behind a tree to strain the lychee liquid into a soda bottle and add a little water. Hearing him yell, "dinner's ready," she stepped up to the fire with her hands behind her back.

"Ahem, I've made a little accompaniment to go with it..."

She hadn't tasted any of the potion yet—well, she'd stuck a finger in and licked it, but she had not taken a proper drink.

Hope it won't be as gross as it smells.

There had been some fizziness when she decanted the liquid, so that made her cautiously optimistic that the fruit had actually fermented, and producing the bottle from behind her back, she handed it to Kit.

He studied the muddled liquid in the bottle and looked up, perplexed.

"It's supposed to be some kind of hooch..."

Bringing the bottle up to his nose, he gave it a swirl and inhaled deeply.

"I'm getting floral notes, and maybe, an 'int of popcorn," he said in a French accent.

Taking a sip, he held it in his mouth for a second, then swallowed.

"Well?"

Kit started coughing. "Shit Sunny, this stuff is gross! Have you tried it?"

She shook her head, a little disappointed but not surprised, and took the proffered bottle from him. Her face wrinkled as the zesty liquid hit her tongue.

"Interesting," she said slowly. "Tastes terrible, but—I think it actually worked! Or maybe not. Maybe this is just nasty, tangy fruit juice that's going to give us the runs..."

Kit took the bottle back from her. "One way to find out!"

He took a large swig. "Bottoms up!" He coughed a little and grinned. "But not literally, I hope. Hooch and the runs go hand-in-hand."

Sunny put her hand out for another slug.

"I'm going to live dangerously."

Soon, the bottle was half-finished, they'd eaten their fill, and a billion stars glowed in the warm night sky. The crab had been buttery rich, and they both felt decidedly woozy—meaning that the booze was officially booze. As the fire crackled, Sunny leaned against Kit and watched the flames.

Kit gently bumped his head against hers. "When's your birthday, Sunny?"

"January 13th."

"Aha! A Capricorn—the goat!" He nodded. "Not surprising at all. Capricorns are loyal, practical, and realistic..." he looked at her slyly, "...but also workaholics, stubborn and uptight."

Sunny made a face. "Ugh, that sounds like the most unromantic, boring star sign possible."

Kit wheeled her shoulders around to face him and looked at her with fierce eyes.

"That is not true! The boring stuff is drama and attention-seeking. Being loyal and working hard is highly romantic!"

Sunny asked Kit when *his* birthday was.

"What day is it today?" he asked.

They calculated the date through the stone calendar—today was August 18th.

"Well, in that case, I am going to be 30 in nine days' time."

"Whoa! The big three-oh!"

He was five years older than her. If she'd had to guess, she would have thought him closer to her own age.

"What did you do for your birthday last year?"

Kit stood suddenly. "Nothing much; I'm going for a slash."

Sunny watched as he headed into the bushes, weaving slightly.

Sometimes she'd ask an innocuous question, and he'd just shut down. It was very annoying. There were not a vast amount of topics that the two of them could chat about if he always refused to talk about himself.

Get over yourself, buddy; I can't imagine your secret life is that special.

Kit

While Kit relieved himself, he thought back to his last birthday. He'd spent his 29th in Paris. The team had rented out the *Moulin Rouge*, and he had thrown an extravagant costume party. He didn't remember very much of it at all, but the press loved the carefully leaked photos of him and Madonna doing the *can-can*. He'd also bought himself a dark red Mercedes CLK as a birthday gift.

Bit different this year.

Turning to the glow of the fire, he retraced his steps. Sunny was always after him to share stories from his life, but he didn't want to. Firstly, because it would all come out that he was Nicky Kitson, and secondly because he was a Virgo, and they were not big sharers.

Kit had a soft spot for astrology and used to check his *Starry Susan* app first thing every morning.

Sunny, a Capricorn, he thought. *I should have guessed!*

138

He thought about Alexis—who was a Leo. If he'd been washed up with her instead of Sunny, it would have been a very different story. Kit was exceedingly pleased with his survival partner and wouldn't have swapped her for anyone.

Starry Susan could have given me a heads-up about being shipwrecked, he'd thought several times during the last couple of weeks. *Maybe Mercury was retrograde.*

Sitting down, Kit wondered if maybe he should just spill all.

Sunny handed him the booze bottle, and the moment passed.

This is better, just keeping it simple.

"I never got into zodiac stuff," Sunny was saying "If your birthday is coming up soon, what sign does that make you?"

Kit looked at her with surprise. "I thought everyone checked their horoscope!"

"Not me!" she laughed. "After mixing up astrology and astronomy in a class presentation, I got totally put off—so humiliating!"

"Aww, poor Sunny-bach..."

Sunny flicked him.

"I'm Virgo, the water bearer."

Kit counted off his zodiac assigned traits on his fingers.

"Organized, a perfectionist, guarded, intense, creative, and completely charming."

"Organized! Perfectionist! I knew astrology was a crock!" Sunny laughed. "Though, I can agree with guarded."

Kit mock frowned. "You may not believe in the stars, Sunny, but they believe in you."

"Oh, come on! Do you really think you are organized? I know I haven't seen you in action anywhere but here, but..." she grinned at him. "...organized? Really?"

"Hmm, agreed that you might not think I'm particularly a perfectionist or obviously organized, but if you saw my record collection, you'd think again. Alphabetized and by genre too, took me ages."

139

"I probably would really like that," agreed Sunny. "Nothing I like more than an alphabetized system. Do you know some people organize their books by color!"

Kit, who'd recently had his library shelves "Ombréd" by an interior decorator, said nothing. "Anyway, I want to hear more about your acting. Tell me about the best role you've ever had. Or tell me about things you've acted in—would there be anything I've seen?"

After a beat, Kit gave the first tangential answer that popped into his head. "Well, I was once in a play where all the cast had to tango. That was fun. We had lessons for weeks with this eccentric Argentinian dance coach. At the start of every class, she'd say 'no leetle practeese, no leetle passion, always beeeg, beeeg, beeeg!' in her thick accent."

"That sounds amazing. I wish I could dance; I'm hopeless."

Kit jumped up and put out his hand. "Come on; I'll teach you."

"No, seriously, you really don't want to. I have two left feet."

"Do you see anyone out here judging you? I insist, and anyway, it takes two to tango." He stomped his feet and clicked his fingers, flamenco style. "I want to dance!"

Sunny stood, obviously reluctant and muttering, "Well, don't say I didn't warn you."

"That's the winning attitude," he laughed.

Taking her hand, he started to hum the classic tango song *La Cumparsita*. "Now just remember, slow-slow, quick-quick, slow."

Kit was a pretty good teacher and whirled Sunny around enthusiastically. But the routine he and Sunny performed on the dark beach was definitely not going to win *Dancing with the Stars*.

"I wasn't kidding about my left feet," Sunny laughed as she picked herself up from the sand yet again.

Holding her close, Kit could smell crab, sweat, and fermented lychee. Her soft body was quite delightful to hold close, and he felt his body reacting as a result.

Guiding her into a spin, he tried to think non-sexy thoughts. She was a refreshing, lovely example of humanity and didn't need a cynical, world-weary man like him letching all over her.

"You must have at least danced at prom?" he asked. "What was your prom like?" Kit thought imagining Sunny in her high school setting might help him get a grip on his annoyingly lust-filled body.

"Oh, prom! I had a surprisingly good time at prom. The theme was 80s music. My friend Julian was my escort. He was my first love," she sighed. "Into drawing and bird watching too, but I never told him I liked him."

Stumbling around in another failed tango maneuver, Sunny continued, "Mom kept telling me to take a chance, but I didn't want to spoil our friendship."

At this point, the tango lesson had stopped, and Sunny and Kit were just swaying backward and forward together like palm trees in the wind.

"Me and Julian danced like this at prom. He was sweet and knew I was a crappy dancer, so we just planted our feet and swayed back and forth to Duran Duran and Blondie."

"Oh, the 'planted sway' is one of my favorite dance moves," said Kit, leaning in and then from side to side.

Warm waves ran over their feet, making them sink further down into the wet sand. Wobbling unsteadily, Sunny laughed, "even the ocean is trying to plant and sway us!"

As they struggled to maintain balance, Kit started to sing a spontaneous Blondie parody. "The tide is high, and my feet are stuck. I wanna get them out of this muck...I'm not the kind of boy who gives up just like that..."

Sunny joined in, and they roared together, "Oh nooooo, noooo!"

Collapsing in a giggling heap, Kit held Sunny's hand.

"You are definitely not the kind of girl who gives up, are you?" he said in amusement.

"Oh noooooo, no!" Sunny sang a little drunkenly in reply.

As the shallows lapped over their outstretched legs, Kit pointed out a satellite moving slowly across the sky above them. "Think of all the people in their homes watching TV because of that satellite."

"If we never leave the island, all we'll ever be able to do is watch the satellite and not its broadcasts," pointed out Sunny, then adding wistfully, wrapping her arms around her knees, "and I can't even watch the satellite, 'cos everything up there is just a blur."

Her shoulders slumped. "If we never get off of here, I will never, ever see the stars clearly again." A tear welled up in the corner of her myopic eye.

"Time for bed," said Kit, heaving her to her feet. "If you are taking a stroll down the drunk and maudlin road, it's definitely time for bed."

And I definitely have to get my hormones under control, he told himself firmly. He'd become really fond of Sunny. She was like a little sister, nothing more.

He had to shut off thoughts of stroking that soft skin on her thighs, which had appeared after the burned dermis had flaked off. *I've got to cool it. This line of thinking is not good.*

But what could he do to help keep her in the little sister role?

"How about we do another episode of story time before you go to sleep? It's my turn, and Morgain the Great is about to receive word of an assassination attempt on his queen..."

Chapter 15

Kit

ueled by the effect of unaccustomed alcohol on undernourished bodies, they both slept hard. When Kit stirred, the sun had been up for a couple of hours. He had been dreaming he was at a red-carpet event, paparazzi flashes dazzling his eyes, groping hands pulling at his shirt. He woke with a pounding heart, which slowed on realizing where he actually was. Kit nudged Sunny, who groaned a little.

"Wake up!"

"Sshh, dreaming."

He nudged her again, and she reluctantly opened her eyes.

"Morgain the Great had joined up with Luath, Tao the Cat, and Bodger and was now part of the incredible journey crew," she said, then added, "Wish we had some Tylenol," while rubbing her temple.

"I'd make Bloody Mary's if I could," said Kit, "but we are all out of Worcestershire. Why don't you go for a pre-breakfast swim; that'll knock the hangover right out of you."

Sunny slumped back onto the sand. Kit, who obviously had a much harder head, was feeling perky. Looking out of the shelter, the first thing he saw was two small dead birds. He picked one up and waved it at Sunny, who went decidedly green. "Pinky prezzie!"

"Ugh, that's great and all but—ugh!"

"She wasn't to know you'd be too hung-over to appreciate her gift, so rude!" Kit laughed, flipping the bird carcass up in the air then catching it one-handedly.

Then he told her he'd clean the birds. "You go swim."

Plucking off the tiny feathers, he watched as Sunny went for her restorative morning dip. As she always did when swimming, she walked a ways up the beach before taking off her shorts and t-shirt, entering the water in bra and panties. Normally, Kit played the perfect gentleman and never glanced in her direction, but this time his gaze stayed on her. Her arms and legs were now mostly a deep golden brown, with the odd angry red patch, while her torso remained pale. Watching her gave him a mix of sensations, a strong feeling of fondness mixed in with a burgeoning desire—also, a huge wave of protective worry. She came off all tanned, strong legs—but she was also pale, soft belly.

And he could tell by the droop of her shoulders that she wasn't feeling happy.

Kit felt happy, though. Being with Sunny made him happy. Living on the island made him happy. Kit was happy. *If I had a nickel for every time I've been truly happy, I'd have washed up on this island a pauper.*

Making breakfast, Kit pondered on his mental state. Was it weird that he wasn't worried about their current situation and was actually enjoying it instead? Francis, the therapist, had told him he lived in a state of extremes and didn't know how to function in the everyday.

Kit decided that he was functioning very well in this everyday island life. Being the extreme opposite of a life he'd come to hate, it made sense that he was happy here. No need to analyze it further than that.

Sunny

*S*unny floated on her back, looking up at the great expanse of sky. The water was soothing and cool— the perfect temperature to complement the warm island air, but it still didn't wash away all her aches. She'd realized that her pounding headache was not just a hangover, and she could feel a familiar nagging ache in the small of her back. Her period was coming.

The thought of having no sanitary ware was awful. Returning to camp, freshened a bit by the swim but still dragging, she found Kit plating up breakfast for her. He was also portioning out some for Pinky, who had come to hang out.

"Pinky's getting fat," he gestured to the cat. "She must be taking out half the wildlife on the island! No wonder she's bringing us so much of her catch, she can't shove anymore in her fat tummy."

Sunny stroked the cat under her chin. She looked splendid, thought Sunny, happy, relaxed, and yes, definitely a bit chubby. Kit also looked happy and relaxed. *Why can't I be more like them*, she thought miserably. She was trying to live in the moment here on the island, but thoughts of growing old and dying here haunted her.

She imagined Pinky would die first, then Kit, and then she'd be all alone.

Ugh, get a grip! One day at a time, Sunny.

Giving herself a mental slap, she turned to Kit. "What's your plan for the day?" She was not at all surprised when Kit announced his big plans for the day were fishing-related.

"I'm going to upgrade the fishing pole—I think I need something a bit longer—then I'll fish, and after that probably go on another crab hunt."

"Cool."

He dragged the red cooler toward her and opened the lid.

"Look, see how nicely I got it organized—thought you'd appreciate it!"

The cooler was filled with equipment and supplies for the day, and Sunny did appreciate that he was getting more organized. But giving him praise for doing something he should have been capable of all along was more emotional labor than she was currently willing to give.

"Have a good day," she told him, then did a series of stretches, trying to relieve her aching lumbar curve.

Just keep busy, work through the pain.

Today she was going to weave her and Kit a sun hat each. She'd already collected the long dry leaves that she needed and had made plastic hoops of the blue rope to attach her weaving to.

Through the afternoon, she halfheartedly worked on her project. She'd just finished the prototype sunhat when something caught her attention. A sound, a sound that didn't belong to the usual rhythm of the island. Some kind of buzzing.

Was it an airplane?

Squinting all around the sky, she couldn't see a thing.

No time to waste.

Sunny piled the stack of emergency green branches onto the fire, which instantly billowed, causing her eyes to water intensely. Running down the beach, wiping at her streaming face, she kept looking around wildly and trying to listen for the faint engine buzz.

Damn, it's gone.

Walking dejectedly back to the fire, she suddenly heard the buzz again. Where was it coming from? As Sunny took a deep breath, about to scream at the top of her lungs for Kit, a dark swarm of flying insects suddenly buzzed from out of the woods and surrounded her. Batting at the moving cloud, she ran toward the fire, hoping the smoke would get rid of them.

It did, but not without the bees stinging her several times first.

"Damn it all!" she shouted. It didn't make her feel any better. She dragged herself down the beach and sat in the ocean shallows. The saltwater felt good on her stings, but her mood remained defeated.

What an idiot she was to think a buzzing swarm was actually a rescue plane. It was so stupid.

I'm stupid. This island is stupid.

Her period was stupid, and those painful bumps coming up on her body were definitely stupid. Laying back on the damp sand, she wished for the millionth time that she hadn't lost her glasses to the sea—and also that she had a tampon.

Sunny lay there for most of the afternoon, in a state of numb misery. At first, she didn't hear Kit return from fishing, but eventually, his shouts penetrated her gloom.

"Hey honey, I'm home!"

Sunny rolled onto an elbow, looked at him, then rolled back again.

"I haven't got crabs!" he shouted at her.

She was usually a very appreciative audience to any of Kit's banter, but today she wasn't in the mood.

Kit walked over and stood next to her, his shadow shading her body,

"Hey, what's up? Are you OK?"

"No," Sunny said, she was definitely not OK. As Sunny explained her run-in with the bees, Kit put his arm around and pulled her into a hug.

"Oh, Sunny, I'm sorry."

She yelped and pulled away, his hug pressing on a sting. "I just can't stand that I'm about to get my period on top of everything else," she said, bursting into tears. After a few minutes of Kit ineffectually patting her shoulder, she looked up again.

"I'm alright now, sorry to lose it."

"No, no, I understand." Kit then gave her a small grin and asked, "I could get you some moss—make you an *Always Ultra Mossy*, or is it just regular mossy you need?"

"Oh shut up!" she reluctantly gave him a smile. "Just go do your thing, and I'll do mine."

"I'll shut up." Kissing the top of her head, he added, "I'm sorry I can't help you—but I did catch nine fish today, if that's any comfort!"

"That's great—because I get ravenous when I'm premenstrual."

Kit leapt to his feet. "Well, now that I know that, I'm going to start cooking immediately! Don't want you going even further downhill!"

She smiled but didn't say anything, turning her head back to the sea.

In the late afternoon, Kit cooked away and Sunny lay in the shade, feeling crappy. But the meal he eventually served her helped. He'd scraped some coconut out of a shell and stuffed it under the

147

fish skin and then rubbed it with some wild thyme. She appreciated the effort.

"I'm going for a walk," Kit said after clearing up, "you'll be O.K.?"

In her current mood, being on her own suited her just fine.

Well, not quite alone; Pinky was back again, so she snuggled up to the cuddly cat in the shelter and was soon asleep, not aware of how late it was when Kit finally joined her in their sandy bed.

Chapter 16
Sunny

*I*t was mid-morning when Sunny pulled herself out of the shelter, still feeling testy and snappy. She tried to shake it off—after all, it wasn't Kit's fault she felt like this—but Kit, who had just returned to camp, didn't seem affected by her mood at all. In fact, he seemed in remarkably high spirits.

Bully for you, thought Sunny grumpily.

The morning ritual of bathing and fruit-eating was comforting, and Sunny began to feel a bit more like herself as they returned from the water pool. Getting on with her chores would help her feel better, she decided.

But as she and Kit stepped onto the beach, Kit insisted they not head straight back to the shelter. Sunny rolled her eyes at him—*he's probably got some new stupid idea about fishing rods or something*, and followed him unenthusiastically along the tree line—not really in the mood for mysterious adventures.

Kit didn't lead her to inspect homemade crab pots or fishing tackle, though; instead, he led her to a shady, sandy nook between two palm trees. There in front of her was a pretty dangerous looking hammock, hooked between the two trees, a random stack of plastic sheeting, and an old soap bottle that was stuffed with a selection of extremely burned sticks.

Kit looked at her and seemed surprisingly nervous.

"I err, made you a studio. The sticks are charcoal for drawing, and I didn't know what to do about paper, but I thought flat plastic bits might work..." he trailed off then picked up again. "Oh, and I tested the hammock with my weight, so it's perfectly safe, and don't worry, I didn't use any of the good fishing nets."

For a moment, Sunny just stood there, but the next second she was flinging her arms around his neck. Kit extricated an arm to point out the water and pile of snacks he'd left in plastic pots under the tree.

"I just thought maybe you could take a break from working so hard on practical things and try to make yourself feel a little better in..." he looked a little awkward, "...in your soul?" Running his hand through his hair, he added, "Maybe do something just for you for once?"

Sunny was overwhelmed; outside of her parents, no one had ever done anything so lovely for her.

"Well, I'll push off and leave you to it. Enjoy your namast-day spa!"

She gulped and gave him a final squeeze. "This is perfect, thank you, and also six points for the namast-day spa."

"Six points? Yes!" he said, then gave her a pretend punch on the arm and told her to have fun. As he walked off whistling, he looked ridiculously pleased with himself.

Sunny knelt by the pile of charcoal sticks, rubbing them experimentally against her fingers. This really was the loveliest thing Kit could have done. She missed drawing and painting so much. She examined the plastic sheets. Hmm, she could probably find something better to draw on. Maybe she could make her own paper!

Picking up a large dry leaf, she doodled a tiny flock of charcoal sea birds on it, and as she drew, her mind calmed. Sunny decided she needed to get a bit honest with herself. She had known that, over the last couple of weeks, her regard for Kit had grown and grown, but now she knew she was falling for him, falling really hard.

He was often unreachable, not sharing his feelings or anything about his past, but he was also so sweet and caring, willing to learn...

Gazing around in wonder at her new 'studio,' she added, *and thoughtful.*

He's also a goofball—Sunny found the silly side of Kit so endearing—*and completely gorgeous.*

She kept listing Kit's positive traits; there seemed to be an awful lot of them now. When they had danced last night, she couldn't stop herself from feeling incredibly turned on.

Then she thought about how only minutes before he'd been pretending to punch her in a decidedly sibling-like manner.

He sees me like a little sister. I mustn't ruin anything, though, she told herself sternly. *It would just make him uncomfortable to know I was crushing on him.*

She wished she knew more about his pre-island life. Suddenly, a cold shiver went through her. Maybe he was married and had a bunch of children who were at home mourning him! Maybe he didn't talk about it because it hurt too much?

Oh shit, she thought, *I mustn't fall for him if he's already involved with someone.*

But reining in her feelings at this point was going to be a challenge.

Kit

Three days, and two more exciting crab finds later, Kit was relaxing at the camp, trying to juggle some coconut shells, when his peace was shattered by panicked shrieking. Heart pounding, he raced down the beach to where Sunny was kneeling in the water. She was next to a washed-up creature, which, on closer inspection, seemed to be some sort of dolphin. About four feet in length and with a very long nose, the poor creature had a jagged plastic ring jammed over its snout, clamping the mouth firmly shut.

"Dead?"

Sunny shook her head frantically.

"No, no, he's still alive—quick, Kit, help me get this off him!"

They tried to slide their fingers under the plastic, but the jagged tubing was too deeply embedded in the skin to get loose. The dolphin opened a dull eye and looked at Kit incuriously. Desperately

151

brainstorming a solution, Kit ran back to the campsite and grabbed several things, hoping they could figure out something to help.

"I've got your bracelet, the fishhook, the razor, some plastic string, and the sharp rock," he yelled, racing back to the waterline.

Laying the meager items on the wet sand, none of them seemed capable of freeing the poor creature. Sunny grabbed the completely blunt and rusted disposable razor blade and started to saw awkwardly at the constricting plastic band.

"That's not gonna work." Kit shook his head, watching as the only thing getting cut was Sunny's fingers.

"Well, at least I'm trying."

As Sunny continued to rub fruitlessly at the plastic, fat tears fell down her face onto the beast's head.

Gotta do something...

Kit was running through his catalog of knowledge. He'd learned so many weird things from the movies that he'd been in. Frowning in concentration, he recalled being in *Mission Impossible 10*. Specifically, he concentrated on a scene where Russian agents captured him and tied him up with zip ties, with a bomb countdown clock ticking beside him. In that movie, he had to use a shoelace to free himself. He'd threaded it through the zip ties and made a sawing motion. It had totally worked. They hadn't even needed to use prop zip ties.

Pushing Sunny to one side, he grabbed the plastic string and threaded it through the tiniest gap between dolphin and plastic. Taking both ends of the string, he told Sunny to keep the dolphin's head steady. Pulling back, he made the string taut, then began to saw back and forth. The pressure exerted was making the plastic cut even deeper into the sad creature, but it looked like the dolphin didn't have enough energy to protest.

I think we are too late, Kit thought to himself, but keeping that gloomy view quiet, he instead shouted out loud, "Come on, Flipper! Don't give up!"

Sunny stroked the dolphin and whispered encouragement, "I'm sorry this hurts, we are trying to help you...my name is Sunny, and that's Kit...we are your friends. Please hold on."

Finally, the plastic snapped, sending Kit tumbling back on the sand. Sunny began heaving the creature into the sea, and Kit hurried to join her. Together, they maneuvered the mammal off the shore and into the shallows, where it just floated, not moving at all.

"Do you think he'll survive?"

Kit detected a wobble in Sunny's voice and, though he thought the dolphin's chances for survival were slim, chose not to say that to Sunny. Instead, he took her hand and gave it a squeeze.

"It's up to him now. We've done all we can."

Sunny said she was going to stay on the beach and keep vigil, so Kit went back to camp to return the tools and collect her some supplies. He returned minutes later with water, fruit, and the lopsided sunhat she had woven from the dried fronds.

Putting the hat on her head, he asked gently, "Do you want me to wait with you?"

Kit was worried. He needed the dolphin to start doing cheery, healthy dolphin stuff again. If the dolphin died, he was afraid a part of Sunny would die with it.

Sunny shook her head. "No, I think I want to be alone for a bit."

Seeing the creature so terribly afflicted by the ocean trash had obviously shaken Sunny enormously, and she turned to Kit with pleading eyes. "Will you go and find Pinky, make sure she's safe?"

"Of course."

Kit understood that Sunny needed reassurance that the rest of her family was OK, even if the dolphin wasn't.

He stopped still, reflecting on that thought. *Yes, we are a family—me, Sunny, and Pinky. I don't know when it happened, but somewhere along the line, we became a family.*

I like it! He said to himself. *I like it a lot.*

He would do anything to avoid thinking about his biological family, but he, Sunny, and Pinky were not a biological family.

153

We're a logical family!
He smiled to himself—he liked it a lot.

*****

Kit followed the path to the waterhole that was Pinky's regular hangout, his brain occupied with thoughts of dolphin rescues and Sunny's happiness. A loud cat call suddenly pierced his daydreams.

"Pinky?" he called out. "Pinky?"

All of a sudden, he was filled with dread. He hadn't seen Pinky much recently. In fact, now that he came to think about it, he hadn't seen her at all over the last two days. She was always pretty elusive, but they normally caught a glimpse of her at least once a day.

Fear ran through him. "PINKY!"

Don't you be in trouble too, Pinky, he thought nervously, hurrying along the now well-beaten path. *Your mistress can't take any more distress today!*

In the glade, Kit stopped for a moment, then focused on an odd mewling sound. Dreading what he might find, he knelt down and pushed aside some foliage. There lay Pinky. She blinked up at him, looking rather like the cat that had got the cream, and nursing at her bosom were three tiny kittens.

"Pinky! Good grief!"

Kit sat back on his heels, grinning. Well, that's one for the books! The next second, he was flooded with concern for the cat and her babies. Rats and other predatory creatures were living in the forest. The day-old babies were incredibly vulnerable—and literally as weak as kittens.

"You are going to have to move home, Pinky," he decided.

Reaching down to pick up a kitten, Pinky gave him an annoyed swipe.

"Hey! This is for your own good."

Manfully bearing with the swatting and biting, Kit deftly put all three kittens into the pouch of his shirt. He stood up, and Pinky scratched at his leg some more.

"Follow me if you want them back," he commanded bossily and headed back to the beach, a furiously hissing Pinky at his heels.

His family had just doubled in size. He couldn't wait to tell Sunny! This was the perfect thing to comfort her if things went badly with the dolphin.

Sunny

unny had moved to sit in the shallows, and pushed by the tide, the dolphin had drifted closer until its head rested on her knee underwater. Stroking the dolphin continuously, she whispered to it.

"I know you are supposed to tell your secrets to the bees, but it would be great if I could tell my secrets to you instead. The only bees I've seen on the island didn't seem very friendly." Scratching at one of the red marks that were left over from the bee attack, she continued on, lowering her voice even further. "So here is my secret. I'm totally in love with Kit. I've tried my best not to be, but I can't help it. And it's not familial love, before you ask. I can't kid myself he's like my brother because the feelings I am having are definitely not appropriate for a sibling situation."

She sighed deeply and petted the dolphin some more. Suddenly she felt it stir beneath her hand. Springing onto her knees, she peered through the water.

"Hey—did you say something?"

Holding her breath, she saw the creature shimmy a little, then the creature seemed to spring back to life, nudging at her hand, and in the next instant turning one hundred and eighty degrees and swimming back out into the bay. Sunny sat back in the shallows, waves lapping over her, and whooped with joy.

At the same time, Sunny heard Kit bellow from their base camp, urgently beckoning her to come toward him. As she raced across the sand, she yelled the good news.

"He's O.K! Just swam off and seemed fine!"

She jogged up to Kit, wondering what he had in his shirt. Kit pulled out the material so she could see the bundle inside.

"Oh my goodness! What! That is the most lovely thing I've ever seen!" her voice choked up. "Pinky, you clever girl, congratulations!"

Kit explained his worries about predators at the waterhole, and Sunny instantly agreed. Stretching down to comfort Pinky, she suggested one of them must stay at camp with the cat family at all times.

Grabbing a new pile of soft, dry grass, Sunny made a nest for the family in the corner of their shelter. As soon as it was done, Kit plonked the kittens into the bedding. Pinky, relieved to have her kids back, started washing them with her tongue.

"Have we any fish scraps? She probably needs extra calories if she's producing milk."

Kit immediately said he'd go and catch a whole fish, just for her, while Sunny kept an eye on the gang. Just lying on her stomach, gazing at the postcard picture that Pinky and her kittens made, filled Sunny's heart with joy. The whole scene was just so perfect. When Kit returned with a fish, he asked her what she was going to call the kittens.

"You get naming input too you know," she said, her gaze not leaving the cats, "but I did think the one with the funny eye should be called Winky."

One of the kittens had been born with a droopy eyelid, which made it look clownish and extremely adorable. Another kitten was smaller than the other two, and after a careful inspection of the under-regions, the only girl in the litter. The third kitten was the biggest and most boisterous.

"Then how about Dinky for the girl?" proposed Kit.

Picking up the biggest kitten, he studied it. The kitten immediately peed all over his hands. "Well I guess the big boy is Stinky!" Kit laughed.

"I love it! Pinky, Winky, Dinky and Stinky! They could have their own TV show!"

Chapter 17

Sunny

The next week passed in a haze of sunshine, kittens, fishing, and fruit picking. They took turns guarding the kittens and also looking out for the dolphin, who had not been seen since the rescue effort. At one point, they noticed their SOS signal was almost completely unreadable, having been knocked around by wind and high waves.

"I guess I should fix it," said Sunny, but without any enthusiasm.

"If you like, I'm too busy tickling this soft tummy," said Kit, playing with Dinky. He then proceeding to make ridiculous baby noises.

Sunny did eventually fix the sign, but with no sense of urgency. Life on the island was so tranquil. Kit was becoming an adept fisherman, and he'd also found a place where breadfruit was growing, so their menu was ever-expanding. She had her studio where she spent the late afternoons sculpting and sketching, and even their injuries were virtually all better. Kit's hand had completely healed, just a patch of shiny red on his palm marked where the terrible burn had been, and her face burns were much better too. Kit said he still had the odd tingling feeling in his feet that had been there since the poisoning, but they were basically fine.

To her surprise, Sunny found herself in Kit's mindset of que sera sera.

"Whatever will be will be..." she'd often hum to herself.

Kit

*K*it was pleased Sunny liked her new studio; she was certainly spending a lot of time there. He'd really had to stretch his mind to find something nice to do for her and was enjoying the feeling it gave him.

When you had endless resources, doing something generous was easy, but that was often different from doing something thoughtful. Sending his assistant, Troy, off to buy some jewelry and flowers happened on a regular basis, but he couldn't remember the last time he'd actually put effort and time into a gift.

It was the world he lived in. People didn't hand-make anything. Why would you when you could buy something that would be better anyway? As Kit had taken the time to collect sturdy, straight sticks and char their tips in the fire to make them into pencils, he had found himself understanding the satisfaction of making something for yourself.

He wondered who he could have become if, as a blank slate at seventeen, he hadn't gone to LA but instead had learned a trade. There would have been a lot less sex, drugs, and rock 'n' roll, but would that be such a bad thing? As he chewed on a piece of seaweed, he thought that, sure, having a lot of money meant he could have whatever he wanted, eat whatever he wanted. But after a while, it all tasted the same. Now, on the island, Kit had taken over most of the cooking. Making their meals out of fish and foraging was way more satisfying than any Michelin-starred dining he'd ever had.

But if I hadn't gone down the acting route, I wouldn't be where I am right now—on a magical island, with all the petty bullshit left thousands of miles away!

Feeling relieved to be far from the small-minded ways of Hollywood, Kit noticed that Sunny had gathered some lychees that were slightly on the pink side of red.

Honestly! I told her to get the red ones! She knows I like very ripe lychee with the silver fish.

159

******

Several days later, Kit awoke completely unaware that it was his birthday. The first thing he saw as he got up was Sunny, ruining their breakfast. A few days ago, he'd found a banana grove and was set on perfecting a banana-coconut mash as their morning porridge. Now she was getting it all wrong.

"You were supposed to heat the coconut in the shell before mashing it in with the banana." Grumpily, he watched over her shoulder. He kept pointing out where she was going wrong.

"Do you want to take over?"

She moved aside and gestured to the cooking area, but by then, the breakfast, if not ruined, was at least less than optimal. Continuing to grump around, Kit gathered his fishing supplies to head up to the rocks. He didn't know why he was in such a bad mood.

Just got out of bed the wrong side—if you could call hard sand covered with itchy dry grass a bed.

They ate their breakfast in silence. Then Sunny retreated to her studio.

I'm being a dick, thought Kit, *better say sorry.*

As he approached her spot, he could see her hunched over a propped-up stone, charcoal smudges down her thighs where she'd wiped her hands. He opened his mouth to apologize, but Sunny spun round and told him to get lost.

I didn't deserve that! he thought, tromping up the beach, lugging the cooler.

His day didn't improve any from there.

Nothing was biting, except large mosquitoes, which got even fatter on the blood from his ankles as he stood disconsolately dangling a limp line into the water. He'd also stubbed a toe on a rock while trying to cast. Going back 'home 'empty-handed always made him irritable, and today definitely was not his lucky day.

"Christ, what a wash today was," he said, flinging the empty cooler and fishing equipment into their stores. He flopped moodily in the sand and picked at the dirt beneath his fingernails. "Sorry, Sunny looks like we'll be vegetarian again for dinner. Sucks."

"We can have more of your breakfast porridge and some seaweed," said Sunny, "and I'm sure you'll catch something tomorrow."

"Catch some more shitty mosquito bites, probably." He slapped his leg. "I'm definitely catching more flies than honey."

Sunny looked at him a little uncertainly. "I know you are in a bit of a mood, but will you come for a walk with me?"

Kit eyed her. "What's up?"

Sunny apparently had had enough of his moodiness and stood with her hands on her hips, telling him firmly, "Just come with me— no questions!"

Geez, she'll be tapping her foot and brandishing a rolling pin next.

"Sure, whatever."

Sunny picked up the kittens, then led Kit by the hand toward her studio. When they were almost there, she made him close his eyes. Stretching up, she pinned something in his buttonhole, then led him a few more steps to the clearing, telling him to keep his eyes closed.

Curiously, he could smell mingling sweet scents.

She gave him the command to open his eyes.

"Happy birthday!" she cheered, stretching her arms wide to encompass the scene.

Frangipani and hibiscus garlands were draped from tree to tree, and two small fires burned on either side of the glade with wild thyme tossed on them, making the air sweetly aromatic. On a tiny bench, made from fishing buoys and a flat rock, sat soda bottles filled with the familiar lychee booze and a couple of newly found plastic beakers. Another battered salad spinner was filled with an assortment of bananas, lychee, and coconut, and on a Frisbee were

161

balanced some small chunks of burned meat, wrapped in seaweed and skewered on tiny sharp sticks.

Sunny settled the kittens in a nearby nest of sweet grass, and Pinky immediately hopped in with them. As Kit gazed around the scene, all his earlier sourness instantly melted away.

"It's my birthday! I'd forgotten! And a surprise birthday party... I've always told people never to do this to me..." Sunny looked at him nervously "...but this is the best thing ever!"

He picked her up and gave her a tight squeeze, then readjusted the beautiful white flower she had pinned to his shirt. Meanwhile, Sunny raced over to get him a cocktail, then proffering the Frisbee like a white-coated waiter said, "Hors d'oeuvres, sir?"

Kit squeezed his face *Home Alone* style. "I haven't any money, so I canapés!"

Sunny looked blank, so Kit repeated, "canapés—cannot pay!"

Sunny tried to keep her face expressionless but then snorted. "Alright, you can have a six for that."

Munching on a meat chunk and grimacing as he hit a piece of gristle, Kit cooed, "OMG, I can't believe Pinky is here! This party is soooo exclusive! She only goes to the very best parties, you know."

Laughing, he walked over to the little cat family and pretended to make cocktail party small talk.

It was a beautiful evening, like most of the evenings on the island, but tonight was extra lovely as the moon was full. They watched its delicate milky glow appear in the darkening sky.

Kit took a deep sniff of his boutonniere. "This flower smells incredible."

"I think it's called a 'Tiare flower,'" said Sunny. "We had a lecture about Gauguin in art history class. When he lived in Tahiti, he would paint these flowers all the time."

"Is that where he had all the thirteen-year-old wives? Old perv—ouch!" Kit ducked as Sunny threw a lychee at him.

"Honestly, though, the stuff you know amazes me. Have you always been a deep well of obscure facts?" Kit hummed the theme from *Jeopardy.*

Sunny laughed. "I'll take obscure facts that are not particularly useful for $800, please!" She took a large gulp from her beaker. "It's true that I'm good with weird trivia, but just don't ask me to remember a math formula!"

Straightening the flower in his shirt pocket buttonhole, she added, "Another tidbit about the Tiare is that girls in Tahiti would wear them as a mark of their availability. Behind the left ear meant they were single, and behind the right meant they were spoken for."

"And in a buttonhole?"

"Oh, that just means your best friend wishes you the happiest of birthdays!"

The night was filled with a chorus of frogs and insects, accompanied by a low 'ooom ooom ooom' of a tawny frogmouth owl. The flowers scented the air with a lush, creamy bouquet. Kit filled up Sunny's plastic beaker from the soda bottle.

"Let's drink to health and happiness, Sunny."

"Let's drink to your birthday Kit."

They agreed to drink to all of it—health, happiness, and birthdays. Then they raised a toast to Pinky and one to the full moon. Several toasts later, they were both more than a little drunk and trying to throw food into each other's mouths from progressively larger distances. Sunny was obviously terrible at this game and found it an achievement if she could even get something to hit Kit's head, let alone his mouth.

"Another step back, Sunny. Open up!" bossed Kit, squinting in the dark and trying to line the coconut chunk up with Sunny's mouth.

As Sunny stepped back, her leg brushed against something. "Oh your gift, I nearly forgot!"

163

Kit threw the coconut, and it bounced off her nose. "I have another gift? You've already given me so much," then continued with, "...ooh, that was a close one."

Sunny pulled a flat piece of white bark from behind her and said, "I'm sorry I couldn't wrap it," as she shyly handed it to Kit.

Moving closer to the fire, Kit looked at the bold network of lines and shading that made up an exquisite portrait of Pinky dipping a paw into the water pool. Kit didn't say anything.

"It's no big deal, just something silly."

Kit looked at her in amazement. "I absolutely love it. You are so talented! It's the nicest present I've ever had. In fact, I think this has been the best birthday ever." He paused. "Well apart from the mosquitoes and the lack of fishing success."

Several drinks later, they lay on their backs and talked about birthdays from their past, or rather Sunny did. As normal, Kit wasn't inclined to share very much of his past life. Sunny asked him about favorite cakes or birthday traditions.

"Well, I'd like to start a tradition of birthdays with you, Pinky, and the kittens,"

I really would, he thought. *I love my family.*

"And as for birthday food, well, this was definitely the weirdest, and I've eaten some weird things in my time."

"Like what?" Sunny propped herself up on her elbow and looked at him.

Kit screwed up his face, "Well, um, black pudding, in Scotland. You know what that is?"

"A pudding that is black?"

"Ha-ha, good one. Nope, it's like a patty, but made out of blood."

"Mmm, fried food—even a blood patty sounds good. Just think about a patty melt right now, with curly fries and a strawberry milkshake."

"Strawberry milkshake?" Kit shook his head in amazement. "You are one of those weirdos who choose strawberry over chocolate?"

Kit did think a strawberry milkshake would be delicious right then, though. His mind slid over to what he would most like to eat if a miraculous kitchen appeared on the island. "Fried chicken, mashed potato, a side of coleslaw, and a cold beer."

"Tuna melt with extra mayonnaise," countered Sunny.

"Ugh, no. I'm ready to give up fish for good. What about a rack of lamb?"

"Ooh, la-di-da, Mr. fancy pants!" Sunny teased. "No, I think what I'd actually have, as my number one choice, would be any casserole that my mom would make."

"Yum, casseroles. Give me an example..."

"My favorite is Chicken Divan, or Chicken Divine as we called it in my family. Shredded chicken, instant rice, frozen broccoli, condensed soup, mayo, and cheese."

"Oh, that sounds so good—make it for me when we get off here?"

Sunny looked around at him with amazement. "You never talk about getting off here!"

Kit smiled, "I know. I don't know why. Maybe it's because life is just so much easier here." He rolled over and looked at her, "but really, will you make me Chicken Divine?"

"Only if we can also get strawberry milkshakes."

They were quiet for a while longer, then Sunny asked him another question, in a slightly strange voice.

"Do you have a girlfriend, Kit? I mean, you never talk about stuff outside of the island. Are you married? Kids? Dog?" She looked at Pinky and the kittens. "Cat?"

After several beats, Kit replied.

"No cat, no dog, no kids, no wife. A part-time girlfriend in a messy, not good for either of us relationship. I kept trying to break it off with her, but somehow I'd get dragged back into it all again."

Sunny frowned. "That sounds lame! You do have your own agency, you know. You probably subconsciously still wanted to be with her if you kept going back."

165

Kit could see Sunny was intrigued to get some details about his life, and the lychee booze seemed to have emboldened her to ask more questions than usual.

"Tell me about her. What's her name? Would I like her? Is she very beautiful?"

Kit sighed. "Really? You really want to know?"

"Yes! Spill some beans! I tell you all about Mom and Dad, college, Clive and Dennie, Andrea—you never share anything important!"

This was truer than she knew. "OK. Her name is Alexis, and yes, she is beautiful. She's a model and comes from a very wealthy family, and I guess you might like her, but I don't think you'd have much in common."

"Because she's rich, beautiful, and glamorous, yeah, nothing like me."

"No, not that. She just doesn't have the same...substance that you have. Like, you care about things that matter, and she cares about things that don't matter."

Just like I used to.

"She doesn't seem that objectionable. Why split up with her?"

Kit watched the stars twinkling in the sky, then replied, "We got together when I was...in a place that wasn't very healthy. I was spending lots of money on frivolous things, doing lots of drugs, partying all the time. Alexis and I were a great fit then, but over the last year, I've changed. I really wanted to get clean, change my life, and Alexis didn't want that. I'd make a huge effort to clean up my act, and she'd invite a bunch of friends over, and they'd party, and I'd cave and be back to square one again."

"That does sound terribly unsupportive. She's probably not the best fit for you." Sunny nodded. "I'm just being practical, not mean."

"I don't think you've a mean bone in your body! And you're right. That's why I came out here for the research trip. A chance to get away from everything and sort myself out."

"Well, this is away from everything alright, but, but do you think you're sorting yourself out?"

He looked across at her and pulled her into a side hug, "I really do, Sunny, and most of it is thanks to you."

Sunny

*S*unny basked in his embrace but then reminded herself that side hugs were for Mormons and little sisters. Kit held onto her for a moment longer as she saw a strange expression cross his face.

"What?"

"Nothing."

Sunny had mixed feelings about Kit not being married or having a girlfriend. She was mostly pleased because now she could keep indulging in her fantasies about him, but on the other hand, if he was already spoken for, it would have helped her get over her crush.

Kit also seemed to have marriage on the mind. He told her that when he'd hiked to the center of the island, he'd imagined up a whole future for her. He told her about Roger the Ranger, who would be her husband, and her career in animal rescue and painting.

"You'd be working at the shelter part-time, and painting lots. Roger would be very supportive. He'd do most of the chores around the house and also do volunteer work in the community."

Sunny sighed. "Hmm, Roger seems a bit noble and boring. Can't he have a wild side?"

"I thought you'd like a sensible, dependable out-doorsy guy…"

"Dependable yes, but Roger sounds a bit stodgy. I want my family to be full of laughter and silly jokes."

Sunny thought about all the silly jokes Kit told and was glad the darkness was hiding her blushes.

Kit seemed determined to sell his imagined future to her, though. "You like the kids, right? Girl twins and a boy is what I had planned for you."

"Oh, I can get behind the kid part, though I hope they are not too much of a handful. Roger had better be a very involved parent, drive them to 4H after school, that kind of thing, because I'll need plenty of time in my studio."

"4H? Really?" Kit laughed.

Sunny punched him in the arm. "Definitely! Don't laugh! One of them would do dog training like I did, another would raise chickens, and the third? Maybe the third is a rebel and doesn't go to 4H but does sports instead—tee-ball, soccer, ugh!"

Kit chuckled again. "No to sports?"

Sunny sighed, "I guess they can do sports if they really want to. It's just that I was so bad at them and always last to be picked. But I'll stand at the sidelines on a drizzly winter morning if I must. Roger and I can drink giant steaming mugs of coffee as we cheer for a winning goal..."

Kit gave her a look that she couldn't interpret.

After a moment, he said, "That doesn't sound too bad, actually."

"Eh—Pacific Northwest winters are definitely not something I miss."

Thinking about the monotonous, gray, rain-filled winters, Sunny got to her feet, impulsively declaring,

"Midnight swim time!"

Kit laughed as she stumbled over, one foot trapped in her shorts.

"Good idea! But because it's my birthday we are going skinny-dipping. No more swimming in your underwear then walking about miserable with damp, chafing thighs for the next couple of hours."

Sunny was again glad the dark hid her flushing cheeks. Skinny-dipping sounded heavenly—but also sexually charged. *Must think unsexy thoughts*, thought Sunny, then, *ugh, he's noticed that my thighs are chafing.*

Out loud, she said, "All right, but no looking before I get in the water."

At the water's edge, they both silently took off their clothes and went gliding out into the calm nighttime ocean. Trying to keep her mind on a wholesome path, she insisted that Kit tell her more of the 'bedtime story.'

"Where we left off, the army of bears had just retreated into the woods, and Morgain was looking for his injured cousin, the princess..." Sunny reminded him.

As they floated, Kit continued the *Fury of Flames* plotline. Handily the series had gone on for years, so he had many more hours of story still to tell. "...Morgain gets a message that his cousin has been captured and is being kept behind the lines in enemy territory..."

"She must be so terrified, poor thing," Sunny interrupted, floating closer to Kit.

"She's frightened at the moment, but this is going to be the making of her. She's a warrior in her heart. She just doesn't know it yet." Kit splashed water at Sunny. "A bit like you."

Sunny splashed him back. "I'm not at all a warrior princess! I'm one of the peasants hauling firewood and emptying chamber pots. You, on the other hand, are very much the handsome prince type, totally accustomed to being waited upon hand and foot."

"Princes aren't always all good looks and no substance, you know. Sometimes they are just trapped in tradition and lifestyle, the whole gilded cage thing. I bet a lot of princes would love to get rid of the courtiers and live a simple life."

"Humph—I'm not convinced Anyway, get on with the story. What happened to Morgain's Snow Leopard?"

"Ah, she is still living with the wolf on the mountain, and the moon is full, just like tonight, so the wolf tries to teach the leopard to howl..."

Startling Sunny, he did just that—put back his head and howled to the moon.

"Come on! It's a full moon; we've got to howl!"

Floating on their backs, Sunny and Kit howled until their throats were raw and fingers pruned. Giggling with laughter, they swam back to the shore, rubbing themselves dry on worn-thin shirts and carefully not making eye contact.

Chapter 18
Kit

The sun rose as usual, but today the sky, normally a radiant cerulean blue, was stained a strange shade of mineral green, and a bank of storm clouds hovered on the horizon.

Kit woke to wind whipping at the shelter and the palm fronds on the roof flapping incessantly. Going outside, he looked at the troubling dark clouds looming out at sea and bent down to grab Sunny's foot. Being tugged awake by her toe, Sunny crawled out, and a gust immediately blew sand in her face. Kit took hold of her head, as she spat out sand and rubbed her eyes. He moved her face to look in the direction of the horizon.

"What? What is it?"

"Can you see the darkness on the horizon?"

"Not really, maybe a bit."

"It looks like a storm bank."

"Is it coming this way?"

"I don't know, but this wind isn't normal, and those clouds are strange. And look at all the white horses on the waves."

"I would if I could," she replied.

Kit kept his eyes on the ocean as a kitten scrambled up his leg. Bending down, he scooped up Stinky, worrying about the approaching front. The island weather had been great so far, just the odd refreshing downpour and one minor stormy night early on. This looked to be way more significant, something new.

"I think we should prepare for the worst, Sunny. I don't like this."

Sunny asked Kit what he thought the worst-case scenario would actually be. His brow furrowed. Stroking the kitten, he looked up and down the beach.

"Sea surges, maybe? A cyclone? Hurricane? Shit, I don't know the difference, but we should move inland. We don't want to be on the beach if the sea does surge."

"What about the water hole? We could go there."

"Ah, but then we'd be surrounded by trees. They could fall on us, or at least some of the branches might."

Sunny spread her arms wide. "But everywhere is surrounded by trees, unless we stay here, and you think we can't stay here!"

Kit looked at her with apprehension. Raindrops were now starting to be blown in with the gusting wind, and the waves were crashing heavily on the shore.

"Maybe we should go into the thick of the jungle. It's so dense the trees could actually be prevented from falling?" Kit proposed, wishing he wasn't feeling at such a loss.

"Yeah, the trees might just lean against each other instead of on us. I'll start getting our stuff secured."

She started collecting together their belongings, throwing the fishnets over the collected heap and weighing it down with rocks. Pinky and the kittens mewed as wind buffeted the shelter.

Kit was still thinking furiously. "What if we hiked to the cliff face? Then we'd have at least one solid wall to shelter against."

Sunny shook her head adamantly. "No way, rock slides. If you'd ever lived in Northern California, you'd know that's a bad idea."

"Really?"

Sunny nodded her head vehemently, "Really-really."

"Ahh! I just don't know what we should do." He flung his hands up in frustration, sending Stinky flying. "Oh shit, sorry, Stinks," he scooped up the kitten and gave him a quick cuddle.

Dammit, thought Kit, *I have to protect my family—but how?*

The wind continued to build.

"It must be getting nearer," Sunny was looking in the direction of the dark horizon. "I can actually see the clouds now. We need to figure something out."

The storm was getting closer by the second. Now they had to shout to be heard. Looking at each other, Kit accepted that neither of them knew the right thing to do. Looking at the scavenged belongings that Sunny had weighted down with rocks, he thought how the random pieces of junk had become so important to them.

A huge wave crashed on the beach, the water pushing up to within feet of their camp.

"That's it! We have to go!" Kit yelled. "Get the bottles and fanny pack stuff. I'll take the kittens in my shirt."

Before he gathered the cats, Kit knelt and scrabbled in the sand for a minute, then he hurriedly headed into the shelter and scooped up the kittens, along with some of their bedding, and stuffed the whole wriggling bundle down his shirt. Meanwhile, Sunny clipped on the important money belt containing the bracelet and the fishhook and gathered some bottles for water. The sea had grown so fierce that the crashing waves were now reaching all the way up the beach.

Kit turned to Sunny. "Now! We've got to go! Come on!"

Sunny's face was white with fright as she and Kit, with Pinky at their heels, ran into the forest. Within minutes sheets of rain had begun to pour down and they were completely drenched. The trees heaved and groaned, and the path had turned into thick, sticky mud. Kit could see Sunny struggling, the quagmire sucking at her inadequate footwear. The deafening noise made communication almost impossible.

Kit pushed on in the lead position. They hurried past the waterhole and deeper into the forest, not knowing where they were going, but with instinct driving them forward, away from the beach. Thunder rumbled overhead and lightning flashed. Kit concentrated on forcing his way through the undergrowth like a human snowplow, then using his body to hold back the branches so Sunny and Pinky could pass more easily. Now they were going up a small incline, which Kit thought a good thing. Who knew how far inland the sea might travel?

173

Kit had a feeling that this weather was a hurricane rather than just a regular storm. The trees groaned, branches crashed, and dazzling flashes of white lit up all around them.

Suddenly the trees opened into a glade, and the deluge of rain fell on them even harder. The sky stretched over them was dark and angry, the daylight completely swallowed by black clouds. Lightning blazed again and again. All of a sudden, a flash reflected on something a few yards ahead. Kit slowed down, squinting through the rain. What on earth could it be? Again the sky flashed, and he made out the shape. He couldn't believe his eyes.

It was the fuselage of a small plane.

As they approached, even in the poor visibility, they could tell that the plane had been in the jungle for a long, long time. And it must have crash-landed. The torn-off wings and crushed, crumpled hull were almost completely covered in vines.

But it could give them shelter.

Shouting through the rain, Sunny said she would go through the small doorway first. Being lighter and smaller, she'd be less likely to fall through a rusted floor, she said; and anyway, Kit was tending to the kittens.

The door had long since disappeared, so putting her load of plastic bottles on the ground, Sunny pulled herself up and through the portal.

He hadn't considered Sunny falling through a rusted-out floor until she mentioned it, and now he was filled with anxiety. After a long minute, Sunny poked her head out again.

"Get in. It's solid."

She beckoned Kit and Pinky to get in.

Pinky instantly hopped up and into the plane. Kit climbed in next, setting his squirming bundle and their grass bedding on the metal floor. The kittens, being kittens, immediately started tumbling over each other, completely uncaring of the chaos going on around them, and Pinky went over to nurse her unruly offspring. The inside of the plane was mostly dry; just one corner was damp, where the rain was coming in through a patch of rotted hull.

Peering through the dim light, Kit watched Sunny clear piles of debris into the wet rear section of the plane. It made him extremely nervous.

"Please be careful. Glass or nails or anything could be in there."

"I know. I'm just clearing a space for us." She gave the pile another kick, which resulted in a hollow metallic clang.

Brushing off a pile of leaves, Sunny pulled out a heavy enamel tea kettle. She picked it up and wiggled it at Kit. "Fancy a cuppa?"

Kit gave a sigh. "Yes, with a shot of brandy in it." He felt completely spent.

Sunny gave up on clearing the floor and plonked down on the dirty metal. She patted the space beside her, the light from outside nearly completely gone.

"Come and rest, Kit. It looks like we are going to live to see another day."

Sunny

The wind shook the rusty airplane all afternoon and into the night, but eventually they all fell into an exhausted sleep. It was still storming and dark when Sunny woke suddenly. Pinky was letting out a series of anguished meows. She groped around and shook Kit.

"Something's wrong."

Then, "Pinky, Pinky, what is it?"

Pinky wove between her kittens and the doorway of the plane, meowing frantically.

Kit sat up and immediately joined Sunny shuffling across the floor, arms stretched in front of them in the darkness as they made "pusssss pussss" noises.

Again Pinky cried out, accompanied by tiny mewling sounds from the kittens.

175

"What's wrong Pinky? You scared?" Sunny heard Kit ask the cat.

Pinky skipped out of his reach as he went to pet her. "It's OK kitty," Kit continued.

Pinky swiped at him as he once again tried to stroke her.

"That's not what she wants," said Sunny. She reached around the cat nest, and groped around blindly.

Sunny's heart almost stopped.

No!

Pinky yowled again.

"One of the kittens is missing!" she yelled at Kit.

No! No! No!

Pinky meowed and went to the doorway again. Lightning flashed, giving a moment of illumination—Pinky at the doorway, Dinky and Winky further back in the plane snuggled together. Missing from the scene was Stinky.

"He must have got outside," she shouted at Kit.

Pinky obviously thought her son was out there somewhere too.

Stinky was so adventurous, always climbing trees (then getting stuck) or clambering inside Kit's fishing cooler, even playing in the shallows of the ocean. He had no concept of danger at all.

"I'll look outside," said Kit.

Sunny couldn't see him but heard a thump as he jumped out of the doorway into the night.

"It's OK, Pinky; we'll find him..."

This time the cat did allow herself to be stroked. Finally, the message had gotten through.

After a minute, Sunny couldn't stand it, and she also scrambled to join Kit outside, telling Pinky to stay put. Her mind was racing with thoughts of the dangers—the predators, falling branches, the soaking rain, and who knew what else—that the little kitten must be facing. Outside was pitch black, she couldn't see anything, and the noise was terrible.

"Stinky, Stinks, come here, Stinky-boy."

Sunny, instantly drenched, yelled and yelled at the top of her voice, but she could hardly hear herself over the din. *If I can't hear myself, how can Stinky hear me?*

Couldn't hear, couldn't see—finding him seemed impossible.

Might as well be blind.

"I can't find him! He's gone!" Kit stumbled out of the dark and knelt beside her. They clutched each other's hands, rain falling down their faces, plastering their hair to their heads.

Thunder rumbled, the trees swayed, and the wind blew the tears from Sunny's face as soon as they appeared.

"He can't be gone. He can't be. Keep still, Kit—try and... I don't know, try and *feel* where he is..."

Wind, rain, thunder, crashing branches—nothing but noise and chaos. She knelt in the thick mud, her hands raking through heaps of leaves, musty smells released by her stirring fingers. *Oh, this was useless.* Through the gale, she listened as hard as she could but still could only hear the storm.

Wet earth, decay, musty smells.

And there, another scent—a putrid, rotten smell.

"Do you smell that?" she yelled at Kit.

"It's from that direction," Kit gestured to the edge of the glade, "stinks."

"Can you see anything at all?"

Kit moved slowly toward the smell, peering through the darkness. As he got closer, he called out, "Nothing."

"Get closer."

Kit edged slowly to where the smell was coming from. "It's coming from here," he said, then very gently he parted the dense greenery.

"AHH!"

Kit's scream was shocking.

"Kit? Kit?"

Sunny rushed over, stumbling toward Kit, who was lit up by another lightning flash, ghostly white with a long dark line drawn down his cheek, and a tiny kitten in his hand.

"I got him! I got him!"

Then, "Something clawed me, ahhh shit, my cheek!"

Sunny threw her arms around them both. "Stinky, is he OK? Are you OK?"

"I don't know—come on."

He got to his feet, and the three of them dove back into the plane. As soon as they were out of the gale, Sunny took Stinky and tried to examine him; he was soaked through but didn't seem to be injured. Pinky didn't give her a chance to examine the little kitten more thoroughly; she barged between them and grabbed him by his scruff, carrying him off to the other two kittens.

"What happened? Had something got him?"

"Yeah, it looked like some weird ferret. It had him by his neck, dropped him when I startled it, and then it swiped at me."

Sunny put out a hand to feel the scratch, but Kit pulled her hand away.

"Leave it, Sunny. It's not too bad. We should just get some rest."

Kit moved his body to sleep across the entrance of the plane.

"You get some sleep. I'll stay here, make sure he doesn't get out again—and make sure nothing gets in."

Sunny shuddered at the thought but was too exhausted to do anything else but lie down. As the adrenaline seeped from her body, Sunny looked up to the dark ceiling of the rusty plane. They had been lucky—again. She wondered how long their luck could last.

Chapter 19
Sunny

ometime toward the morning, the storm eased, then faded completely. When Sunny opened her eyes, it was to see a bright shaft of light coming through a hole in the metal roof. *That's where the rain was getting in last night.* Dust motes danced hypnotically in the sunlight. She studied the hole some more. The dark interior made the shape glow like a neon sign.

Next to her, Pinky and all three kittens slept.

Quietly getting up to pee, Sunny examined the sleeping Stinky. He seemed perfectly, miraculously, all right. Next, she stepped over a gently snoring Kit. In the daylight, she could see the jagged scratch that ran down his face.

Oof! Nasty!

Outside the plane, the forest was steaming.

Rich smells oozed from the soil, and hundreds of flowers had popped out overnight. Condensation dripped from overhead, and the smells and colors meeting Sunny as she emerged from the fuselage were almost overwhelming. Looking up, she saw the sky had returned to its customary blue. Stepping down on the forest floor, she could feel the wet heat through her flip-flaps (as she called her strange footwear).

After a trip to the bushes, she went to set their plastic bottles to fill under the dripping fronds and pulled bananas off a nearby tree. Sunny felt Kit deserved to sleep in. Kit, though, had awoken, and poking his head out of the doorway, called out to her.

"It's like a flower festival out here!"

In the daylight, his injury seemed much worse. He had a large jagged scratch that went from just under his left eye all the way to his chin. Crusts of blood made a dark vertical line, and his cheekbone was slightly swollen.

179

"Your face!"

He hopped down. "It's not too bad."

Sunny tentatively touched it. "It looks sore."

"Honestly, compared to how my hand was, this feels like nothing."

Squatting on the steaming jungle floor, they ate their breakfast, mostly in silence, just listening to the bird chatter and the kitten mews. From time to time, she glanced at Kit's profile and the angry scrape running down his cheek.

"What do you think the animal was?" he asked at one point.

"I've been thinking about that—I reckon it must have been a mongoose. They are all over the south pacific and are known for having a terrible smell."

"Ironic that it was a stink that saved Stinky."

Sunny gave his hand a squeeze. "You were so brave—don't make jokes—you did great." Passing him the bottle of water, she added, "We're so lucky it didn't kill him. It must have just picked him up."

"Yeah—luckier than whoever was flying this thing, poor guy."

Kit and Sunny looked at the plane somberly.

That there might well be a corpse in the cockpit was obvious to both of them. No one could have survived the crash. They'd concluded, though, the pilot would wish no harm to a couple of weary travelers.

They both wandered over to the plane, and Kit swept away some of the vines. What paint remained was a dull yellow, but she couldn't see any other obvious markings. The crushed nose was buried in thick bushes.

"What's the plan of action now? Get back home?"

Looking at the fallen branches that were scattered all around the glade, Sunny said glumly, "Yeah, we should. I'm kinda afraid to see what's happened back at the beach. But also, we need to see what useful stuff is in the plane."

"Whatever has happened to our camp, we can rebuild it. You know we can." Kit threw a banana skin off into the bushes and began peeling another.

"Yeah, I guess." Sunny let out a long and unhappy sigh.

"What's going on in that head of yours?"

Sunny moved to sit on the lip of the plane doorway, petting little Winky. Sitting on something other than rocks, logs, or sand was strange. It made her think of the world outside the island.

She was silent for a minute, then looked up.

"I think I'm scared. We were organized. We had control of our situation..."

She plopped Winky back onto the floor of the plane.

"...but then along comes a storm—and it's a wake-up call. We nearly lost Stinky. We are not in control—of anything."

She looked around the storm-battered glade.

"And the home we made, it's probably gone too."

Kit went over and curled his arms around her and kissed the top of her head.

"Home is where the heart is and all that, right? We can make a home anywhere, as long as we are all together."

Sunny's heart swelled with a huge rush of love and affection.

Damn it. Kit wasn't making it any easy to not just be fully in love with him.

Reluctantly she untangled herself from his embrace. "OK, I'll stop whining."

Squaring her shoulders, she made the mental decision to banish her fears and just get on with the process of surviving. "So let's check what useful stuff is here before we go back."

Kit nodded enthusiastically. "I keep thinking of all the potential new fish hooks I can make! Having a source of metal is going to be huge."

Sunny brightened. "And don't forget the tea kettle. We can boil water and make fish and breadfruit stews!"

181

Sunny wanted to go through the plane and organize it right then and there, but Kit said he wanted them to return to the beach first, to check out the damage at home and rebuild the shelter if necessary. Sunny suggested she stay behind by herself, but Kit frowned.

"Look, we should come back another day, maybe even tomorrow. Today we get the camp organized." Giving Sunny a wink, he then added, "after all, what would your dad say?"

"PPPPP," she grumbled, then smiled to herself as she noticed their attitudes seemed to have switched. Now Kit was being the organized one and she was being impulsive!

Even though her fingers were itching to strip the plane down to its bones, she knew she'd have more success if she planned out everything first. Maybe build some bags, or a sled to load everything on to transport back to the beach?

Her practical mind hummed.

"I wonder what new stuff has washed up on the shore." Kit added as he picked up the teakettle.

Sunny brightened at the prospect of beachcombing and began loading the kittens down her t-shirt, but Kit offered to carry them in the teakettle, which was both practical and very cute. Pinky leapt onto Sunny's shoulder for a ride home, too, obviously not liking the sticky mud on her paws.

The trek back to the beach seemed a lot quicker, and much less dramatic, than it had on the way in. Stopping briefly for water and lychees at the pool, they were soon back at their beach camp.

The storm, as predicted, had completely wiped out their shelter, the SOS sign, the storage shelves, and the studio.

"It's all gone," said Sunny sadly.

"Not everything, hopefully," said Kit, digging around in the sand. A moment later, he triumphantly held up the slightly smudged and damp portrait of Pinky.

"You saved it!"

"Of course I did! After you and the cats, your drawing is the most important thing on the island."

Sunny's eyes welled with tears. If only she could tell Kit how much she loved him. Instead, she set about trying to restore order to the camp while the kittens frolicked on the sand, quite unconcerned by the surrounding disarray.

Kit

*K*it watched fondly as Sunny, once more full of gritty determination, pulled logs up the beach and then started collecting firewood. Her hair was back in its customary lopsided bun, made by thrusting sticks through the knotted mass, and loose wisps of hair were glued to her cheeks with sweat. The t-shirt she wore was worn so thin it was now coming apart at the seams, a large gap ripped from armpit to hem on the left side.

Completely focused on her tasks, she was humming away to herself, and as he got closer, he heard the familiar tune that was becoming their island theme song.

"Que sera sera..."

He passed her a bottle of water, "Make sure you are drinking enough water, please."

"I will, thank you."

As she looked at him, Kit thought he could see something different in her eyes, but he wasn't sure what. She reached out and stroked the jagged scratch on his cheek. Her touch stirred a desire inside him. Out of nowhere, he suddenly wanted to take her hand and press it to his lips. *Whoa there, easy boy.*

Together they set to work to repair the camp. The re-made shelter came together easily, and Kit found himself knowing what to do without Sunny's instruction. When she examined his section of roofing and just gave it a nod of approval, Kit felt ten feet tall.

It took all afternoon to get things straightened out, but sweating and exhausted, they'd finally got it somewhere close to done. With no fish, they dined on the bananas and some freshly fallen coconuts. The teakettle had a hole in its bottom, but angling it on its side made it possible to heat water. Sunny made a warm ginger brew, which they both agreed was the most comforting thing they'd ever had.

But the tea couldn't stop their bodies trembling with exhaustion as they lay down for the night.

*****

The next morning Kit was sore and aching. His muscles protested as he collected more wood for the fire, and his knees had a decided tremble. Pinky, also exhausted, had slept through the night instead of hunting for a bird-catch breakfast. Everybody was finding it hard to get moving. Seeing Sunny moving sluggishly around the campsite, Kit sat poking at the fire and came to the conclusion they had been over-extending themselves.

"We are simply not eating enough calories."

He poked Sunny in her newly concave stomach. "I know we talked about going back to the plane today, but I should probably fish, and then we can rest and go back to the plane tomorrow. We've got to get some protein."

It was disappointing because they were both anxious to see what the cargo hold actually held. But both knew getting more food was the right decision. It took Kit much longer than usual to prepare for his fishing expedition, but finally, he was packed up and ready to go. Sunny walked beside him along the sand, listlessly picking up seaweed, as Winky, Dinky, and Stinky—the only ones among them who still had energy—nipped and chased each other, tumbling over rocks and scrabbling in sand heaps.

Perched on the rocks, Kit cast out his line and thought about how he was taking their well-being for granted. With just a small disruption in their routine, they had become horribly depleted within a matter of hours. Also, his cheek was throbbing. He really hoped the heat coming off it didn't mean an infection was forming. Watching the shimmery flashes of small fish in the water, he tried to will them onto the precious hook.

"Maybe we should go about preserving some fish, smoking it or something? Fish jerky?" he suggested to Sunny

From her spot near the tide pools, she nodded in agreement. "Hmmm, smoking. The humidity might be a problem—but we should definitely try it."

Slowly as the day went on, Kit finally hooked a small catch. Back at the camp, Kit cleaned the four fish as Sunny attempted to weave a "grill basket" out of bendy green sticks. The idea was to put a fish in it and hover the contraption over the smoke.

" How's the cheek?"

"A bit sore actually, hot to the touch." Kit patted his face very gently.

"There must be something that we can do to help it." An expression of extreme concentration crossed her face.

"What?"

"Shhh, I'm thinking..."

Kit smiled, "Very well! I'm going to pee. I'll leave you to your deep thoughts..."

"PEE!"

Kit laughed.

"Yes, I'm going to pee—you are very weird sometimes, you know."

"No! Wait! Pee! That's it! We have to put fresh pee on your scratch—that should stop any infection!"

"Are you trying to prank me?"

"No, no...I'm sure I read about it once."

She tossed him a plastic beaker. "Pee in this, then pour it on your cheek."

Kit was still not one hundred percent sure Sunny wasn't joking.

"Am I allowed to wash my pee-face afterwards? I'm going to smell gross."

"You really are. I think maybe leave it on there for an hour or two, then wash..."

Looking doubtfully at the cup and then at Sunny's earnest face, Kit nodded. He would give it a try; anything would be better than getting an infection.

Returning from the bushes, Sunny told him to sit downwind from her.

"Are you taking the piss?"

She giggled, "Sit downwind or urine trouble!"

Kit reflected on how Sunny was so aptly named. Being with her was like standing in a ray of sunshine, while all around you were gray skies. He gave her a generous seven points for her joke.

Serving up three now cooked fish, leaving one in the smoking basket, Sunny told Kit that she wanted to be the one to go to the plane and that he should stay on the beach to mind the kittens (and keep pouring pee on his face). This was not what Kit had in mind.

"I should go. I've got better footwear..."

"I'm better at finding things... and more organized."

"I'm not half-blind."

"Low blow! You got to do the exploration to the peak, so now it's my turn!"

Neither conceded, so it seemed they had reached a stalemate.

"Let's sleep on it," they agreed.

Relieved to have fish in their stomachs but still worn out, they snuggled down together, and after some more pee jokes at Kit's expense, they were asleep within seconds.

Chapter 20

Kit

inky must have also got some reasonable rest, as the next morning she resumed breakfast bird delivery, this time some kind of young duck.

"What on earth! How are there ducks here? And why haven't we seen any yet?"

"This probably serves us right for being lazy and not exploring around the island properly. There's probably a herd of goats and wheat fields somewhere too. Not to mention duck eggs."

After the comparatively sumptuous breakfast, Kit went off to give his face some more 'treatment.' When he returned, Sunny declared she had worked out how to decide democratically who was going on the plane salvage expedition.

"We will have to decide through the time-honored tradition of roshambo!"

"Really?" said Kit, "this is how we make big decisions in our family; rock, paper, scissors?"

"Well, it worked when I was growing up!" said Sunny, as she pulled at Kit's hand.

"Come on, stand up and let's do it!"

Kit reluctantly agreed, and Sunny reluctantly agreed to accept the outcome when Kit beat her three times in a row. She would stay on the beach and keep going through the flotsam the storm had deposited and make another grill basket.

"But if I stay here, you *have* to bring back as much stuff as you can. Don't miss any small thing that could be useful."

"Yes, mistress! What about your idea for bags or a sled?"

"I changed my mind about the sled. The jungle floor would make it impossible to drag. I did have a thought about a bag, though."

187

Kit watched her face rosy up as she took off her t-shirt, tying the bottom together with rope, and explaining he could put items in it through the neck hole.

Taking the shirt bag from her, he nodded toward her arms. "That's quite the farmer's tan you've got there."

Sunny's torso and upper arms were still surprisingly pale, especially when compared to her dark brown forearms.

"Oh shut up. Just make sure you come back with some good stuff! Getting my shoulders burned needs to be worth it!"

"I'll happily rub aloe on them in appreciation of your sacrifice…quite happy to rub you wherever you need to be rubbed, actually!" Her full white boobs straining out of her tatty bra were suddenly hypnotizing him.

Sunny's eyes opened wide.

Oh shit, shouldn't have said that.

Quickly offering her the use of his shirt, he made a joke about rubbing Pinky with aloe too, trying to defuse the tension that had suddenly sprung up. Sunny went back to being all business." Keep your shirt on. Then you can stuff more objects in it as a second bag if need be."

Kit nodded and took the tee. "All right then, I'm off." He gave her a salute. "See you later. See you later, cats," he yelled and took off into the forest.

As Kit trod the path inland, he thought about his reaction to a tee-shirtless Sunny. He really had wanted to rub aloe all over her body. And then really had wanted to lay her down in the sand and do all kinds of things to that same body.

This was not a road he should go down. She was alone on a deserted island with a man she barely knew, which was not something to take advantage of. He was not going to jeopardize everything just because he was horny.

Little sister, little sister, little sister.

He smiled as he thought about her playing rock, paper, scissors and making him wash his face in pee. All that was definitely little sister territory.

But Sunny wasn't a child; she was a woman. And she was like no other woman he had ever known. She had no subtext. What you saw was 100% genuine Sunny.

And he liked all 100% of her.

In the three? four? weeks they'd been together on the island, Sunny had become his best friend. Being around her made him a better person. He was becoming someone that he quite liked.

He had found a family and home for the first time in his life.

Kit felt a lump in his throat when he considered the shipwreck not happening.

He would never have bothered getting to know her at the research station. He'd have considered her someone to avoid, a person who was of no interest and without anything to offer him.

What a shit person Nicky Kitson is.

It made Kit sick to think of all the times he had dismissed people, just because they didn't walk the same walk as him. Talk the same talk.

I don't want to be Nicky Kitson ever again.

Sunny definitely didn't talk or walk the same as him, but she was exactly who he wanted to walk and talk with, now and always. But always should not just be here on the island. Always should be back in the world too. What if she got hurt, got really sick? We have been so lucky, but what if our luck doesn't last?

For the first time, Kit really considered how to get them off the island. He weirdly loved this retreat from reality, but Sunny—well, he wanted her to be safe. Safe and have the future she deserved, out in the world.

He hoped she would have room for him in that future. He wanted to be in her life forever. A life without Sunny seemed pointless.

Trekking on, he did not come to any conclusions on how they could be rescued, so he turned back to the job in hand. The path he'd beaten down two days earlier was straightforward to follow, and as he walked on now, he trampled it even further. The route to the plane would probably become a regular journey, and he didn't want Sunny getting lost if she was doing it on her own. Finally entering the plane glade, he looked at the sun and estimated how long the journey had taken him—*less than an hour, not bad.*

Looking back to the rusted-out aircraft, he paused for a moment to take it all in. Shuddering, he imagined the pilot's terror as he dove from the sky toward the thick jungle. Maybe he was already unconscious, thought Kit hopefully. Maybe he passed out and never knew what hit him.

Taking a circuit of the glade before entering the plane, Kit muttered, "PPPPP," to himself, remembering Sunny's dad's motto. In the body of the plane, the light was dim. Withdrawing his head, Kit considered his strategy. *I'll start at the front*, he thought. *Pay my respects first. I don't want to just loot the bounty and ignore whoever delivered it to us.* Pushing through dense bushes, he looked at the nose of the plane. The door to the cockpit was crushed and buckled, and when Kit kicked at it, nothing happened.

"OK, plan B."

Everything at the front of the plane was in a terrible state. The nose had half grown into the surrounding trees and was crumpled almost beyond recognition. Kit was almost inclined to give up getting into the cockpit, but he could hear Sunny's voice in his head, chiding him for not being thorough.

Climbing up on the wreckage, Kit shoved aside greenery, at last finding a way into the mangled space through a front window frame. Taking a deep breath and preparing himself to come face to face with a skeleton, he put his head through the gap and peered around the gloom. He could make out some metal springs draped in some kind of rubber, the pilot's seat possibly? No skeleton, though. He withdrew his head and squeezed his arm through the small space, feeling around with his fingertips. As his fingertips touched something metal, he extracted the object to reveal a belt buckle, covered with a film of tarry matter.

Setting it aside, again he reached in, groping blindly until he found another loose object. The shape was odd and he couldn't make it out at all by touch. But bringing it out, he gave a yell of excitement—a pair of glasses! Of course, they wouldn't be the right prescription for Sunny, but maybe they would help. He looked at them. They were also coated in a greasy tar. The next second the cogs in his head tumbled into place, turning to a sobering conclusion. A belt buckle and a pair of glasses were on the pilot seat. Ergo, the pilot was still there, only his body and bones had rotted away in the humid atmosphere of the jungle.

He wiped his fingers on his shorts, trying not to wonder what the goo was. *Sorry about that, Sir.* Not wanting to fumble around in the pilot seat any further, he swung his arm around in a different direction. He extracted wads of rotting rubber and the odd mystery metal piece, but nothing else of note. Opening the fanny pack, he very gently placed the glasses inside.

Out loud, he said, "Thanks, buddy. I hope you are resting in peace."

Moving from his uncomfortable position atop the nose, Kit went back around to the fuselage. The body of the plane held no trace of seating. *Must be a cargo plane...the question is, did it crash before or after delivery?*

Starting at the front, he carefully combed through the floor debris, delighting over various finds. The small things were easy to collect; a screwdriver and several dozen screws, a hand mirror, wire from who knows what, and some large square batteries. More large objects turned out to be several vehicle tires. The rubber was soft and falling apart, but the metal rims and hubcaps could be extremely useful. He kept going methodically down the body of the plane, finding a metal fountain pen and a clip that was obviously once attached to a clipboard. At the rear of the hold was a tangle of dark

191

objects, nearly invisible in the gloom. Putting his hand out tentatively, he touched something smooth and rounded. He poked it and it rolled toward him. The cylinder was a tin can. The can was sealed with no markings to say what was in it, but it looked like the kind of can that food would be in. Dozens of these cans were scattered around the tail of the plane.

Kit collected as many as he could carry in Sunny's t-shirt and decided to call it a day and head back.

He was so excited to show Sunny his haul!

Chapter 21
Pinky

The human lay unconscious, half in and half out of the shade.

She was lying just where the sand met the trees, a place that had left her arm and torso burning horribly in the fierce sunlight. Ants were feasting on a trail of blood that led from the female's head to a nearby coconut.

Flies bit at her mercilessly.

Pinky snapped at the flies, then tried again to nudge the human awake. Nothing happened. Pinky didn't like it; her human was normally extremely responsive, so this behavior was out of character. Pinky let out a loud meow, then bit the girl on the thigh.

Nothing.

Where was the other human?

Keeping a sharp feline eye on both her kittens and Sunny's still form, Pinky ran to the tree line and called out again.

She didn't know what else to do.

Chapter 22
Kit

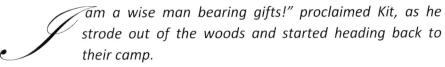

I am a wise man bearing gifts!" proclaimed Kit, as he strode out of the woods and started heading back to their camp.

"Sunny?" he yelled.

Hmm, she can't have gone far, he thought, stopping at her newly-reconstructed studio space and unloading the collection of goods from her t-shirt and hiding them behind a tree so he could do a dramatic reveal later on. Then, as if handling a newborn baby, he gingerly placed the fragile spectacles on the branch of a nearby tree to keep them away from clumsy feet.

Feeling very pleased with himself, he ambled into the camp and was immediately met by a volley of loud meows.

"Hey Pinks, what's up?"

He grabbed a banana and flopped back on the sand next to the kittens. Pinky immediately leapt on him. He pushed her off gently as he peeled the fruit and gazed around the beach.

Pinky mewed and circled, her tail flicking back and forth.

"Chill out kitty," he said through a mouthful of banana.

Pinky hissed in reply.

What was wrong with her?

He raised the banana to his mouth then stopped.

Where was Sunny? Not like her to be out of earshot of the cat gang.

He looked at the three kittens—not like her at all.

A chill shot through his body, and he got up slowly.

"Don't be alarmist," he told himself, "she's probably just peeing in the bushes."

"Sunny?"

Pinky mewled.

He couldn't stop himself from giving a yell.

"SUNNY!"

Now he really did begin to panic. Running a few yards along the beach, something bright green, something that looked like a flip-flop, caught his eye. He ran and dropped to his knees beside Sunny's unconscious body. Carefully, Kit lifted her head and shoulders into his arms. She moaned slightly and almost opened her eyes, muttering something that he didn't quite catch, then fell silent again.

Kit tried to keep calm.

"It's OK; you're OK now. Just lie still. Don't try to talk."

Checking her body, he couldn't see anything obviously wrong, but as he stroked her hair, his hand came away wet with blood. Paling, he parted the knotted strands and saw blood oozing sluggishly from the ugly gash and a large raised lump.

Pushing down his fear, he took stock of the situation. Sunny had been hurt, a head injury. She'd probably been unconscious a while.

What if she'd been like this all afternoon? What if she's dying?—Oh please don't die, my sweet Sunny, please.

Kit's thoughts started racing again, but he heaved them back into order. OK, she is unconscious; she is probably concussed and probably in shock. But also, her brain could be bleeding or swelling, and what about blood clots?

As gently as possible, he picked her up into his arms and carried her to the shelter. Laying her down, he rested her head on the stiff life jacket. Then he pulled off his shirt and tucked it under her to make a softer cushion. Frantically, he tried to remember anything he knew about treating a concussion. Dammit, if only he'd had a movie role as an E.R. doctor. Kit was pretty sure that lying in a darkened room and resting was recommended for head injuries.

He thought hard—limiting stimulation—that was it!

Taking Sunny's own t-shirt, which had been serving as his bag, he dampened it in Wilson and very gently sponged her face and neck.

"I'll not clean the wound yet; it might hurt, and the blood is clotting into a scab...don't want to disturb that," he muttered to himself.

Sunny moaned again as he passed the cool cloth over her burned chest, arm, and thigh. Speaking softly, Kit whispered to her, trying to think of as many comforting things as he could to tell her.

"...I got some really great things from the plane. I can't wait for you to see them...I saw that parrot bird again; she was looking splendid and followed me down the path for a while...The bush by the water pool has come into bloom. You were right; the flowers are purple, which means I owe you a fried banana..."

Kit's heart was racing so fast that he thought he was going to have a panic attack. He tried to slow his rapid, shallow breathing. *Pull it together, pull it together*, he repeated to himself like a mantra.

Sunny's eye's fluttered open slightly.

"Hurts," she croaked.

"Oh my darling, lie still. I'm here. Just rest. Have some water." Kit put the bottle to her lips, overwhelmed with relief that she was speaking.

"Steve, must put Steve out..." she whispered, passing out again.

Kit was terrified; she had seemed delirious. What if she shouldn't go to sleep? But also, maybe sleep was actually what she needed? He felt completely useless. Sunny had to be alright. She just had to be. He prayed with every ounce of him, "Please, please let her be OK... I'm sorry for everything, please, please..."

His eyes filled with tears as he looked down at Sunny. "I don't know what to do... I just can't lose you..."

Kit kept vigil all night, and Sunny would moan and stir but never fully awaken. He'd just closed his eyes for a minute sometime around mid-morning, and of course, that's when she woke up

Sunny

The sun was high in the sky, its rays piercing the shelters' gloom through gaps in the roofing. Must do some roof patching, was her first thought as she opened her eyes.

Oooh, I feel terrible.

Raising a hand to her head, she felt a damp cloth, and she could hear Kit next to her, snoring lightly.

I think I should sit up.

As she did, the world tilted, and she retched violently as soon as she raised her shoulders from the ground. Immediately, Kit was by her side, grabbing a bowl, holding back her hair, and then laying her back down.

"Ohhh, my head hurts so much. What happened?"

"I'm not 100% sure, but I think a coconut fell on you. I came back to the beach and found you unconscious. Let me see your eyes for a minute... your pupils are uneven. I don't think that's a good sign."

Sunny couldn't really take in what Kit was saying.

Eyes? Coconut? Coconut eyes?

A plastic beaker was brought up to her lips, and some water was dribbled into her mouth. Immediately she retched again.

It's so cold.

Sunny began to shiver.

Steve, he can't be out in the cold.

"Can you bring Steve in?" she asked Kit through chattering teeth.

She could almost see her little terrier now.

Hey Stevie, come here, boy. Come keep me warm.

Why couldn't she stroke him? She put out her hand but couldn't find the wiry coat.

Steve! What's happening!

197

*****

The next time Sunny woke, she had a raging thirst, but trying to sit up triggered the most terrible headache. She closed her eyes and waited for the shelter to stop swaying. Movement activated the terrible head pain, so trying to keep her head motionless, and with eyes closed, Sunny groped around to feel for water. Her hand knocked over a bottle, but she managed to right it before all the water escaped. Sipping the water made her stomach lurch, but at least she didn't vomit. Sunny tried to get her bearings. She was in the shelter, she heard the kittens in the corner, her head hurt, and her whole body ached...oh, and she had to pee, really, really badly.

"Kit," she whispered.

"Kit."

Sunny cautiously sank back down on the pillow and gingerly put her hand round to the back of her head. She could feel a huge lump and clots of sticky stuff. It made her dizzy to touch it. Feeling nauseous, shivery, and still desperately in need of a pee, Sunny didn't know what to do or if, in fact, she could do anything at all. She'd never felt so bad in her life.

Chapter 23

Kit

With the fruit, water, and aloe supplies running low, Kit had made the hard decision to leave Sunny alone while he raced to the water hole. As he ran through the forest, his heart pounded from the exertion and also the worry.

What if she did have a brain injury? And how can she be shivery in this sweltering heat?

Go faster...

Kit was away from the shelter for about 20 minutes, and he'd prayed Sunny would stay asleep. But on his return, he heard moans coming from the shelter and rushed inside. Sunny was trying to swing her legs around to get up, and she was groaning terribly.

"What are you doing? Lie back. You've got to lie still." Kit crouched beside her, gently stroking her forehead.

With her eyes closed, she was muttering something—Kit strained to understand. "What is it, honey? I can't make out what you're saying."

"Pee, got to pee."

Kit gently cradled her into a sitting position. "We can do this together. Come on, baby."

He couldn't pick her up in the low confines of the shelter, so he half dragged her outside as she moaned and groaned. They'd just made it outside, when he said. "Enough."

Kit slid down her shorts and underwear, then looping her arms around his neck, they squatted together face to face. They squatted and swayed, and Kit waited patiently for Sunny's body to relax enough to let go. She was crying, and he buried his face in her hair, murmuring sweet platitudes while keeping her balanced.

"It's OK, honey. Everything is OK. You're so strong. You're incredible."

199

After she was finished, Kit led her back to the 'bed' in the shelter. He'd taken off her shorts and underwear completely, as now they needed to be washed. Taking off his own shorts, he drew them up her trembling legs, then urged her to drink some more water. Sunny just turned away, mumbling, and within seconds she was asleep again. Kit ran a hand through his hair, trying to think what to do next.

First, more aloe.

Gently, so gently, he rubbed the gel from a fresh leaf. Her left arm, the left side of her torso, and left leg had been scorched by the merciless sun. Being careful not to scrape her, he eased up the straps of her bra, wincing at the blistered, angry flesh.

Oh, babe, I'm so sorry.

He was worried about dehydration. Sunny's skin radiated an unbelievable heat, and she was hardly keeping down any water. He rinsed out her t-shirt, wrung it out, and moistened her lips.

Heal Sunny, heal.

She slept on and off for most of the next two days, aware enough to sip water and occasionally pee, but nothing more than that.

At least she was drinking a little, thought Kit; that's positive.

Kit had been trying to sleep in small snatches by her side, but his subconscious was on alert and ready to react at any time. While she was awake, he would coax her to drink or try a little fruit, and every few hours, he reapplied aloe to her incredibly burned arm, chest, and thigh.

In between, he would talk to her, retelling the *Fury of Flames* plot or reciting more of Shakespeare's *Tempest*.

"Be not afeard. The isle is full of noises, sounds, and sweet airs that give delight and hurt not."

Oh Sunny, you are the thing that gives me delight and sweet airs.

While nursing Sunny, Kit had only been eating the odd snatched piece of fruit and had hardly slept at all. He knew he couldn't last much longer without something more substantial. He needed calories to be strong enough to look after Sunny. Maybe Pinky would bring something in the morning?

Pinky hadn't been hunting that much either; being a single mom was exhausting. Kit didn't want to despair, but he knew their situation was not good. He needed another human to help him take care of Sunny. Or he needed a freshwater spigot just outside the shelter. Or he needed a truckload of food delivered to their beach. So many problems and no easy solutions.

Wearily he thought about grilling delicious burgers, mouth-watering burgers and a can of cold beer. His foggy brain twitched, groping at something—can of cold beer... can...beer...can...can!

In a flash, he suddenly remembered the battered cans he'd brought back from the plane. How could he have forgotten them!

Making sure Sunny was sleeping peacefully, he went outside and along to her studio space. The cans he'd left hidden behind a tree were now half covered in sand. He picked one up. *Please, please let there be something edible inside.*

The small cans had a ring-pull type of lid, so he took the least dented one. *Just one break, just let us have one break.*

He eased the can open. A strange savory smell wafted out, not particularly pleasant, but not actively awful either. Peering inside, his eyes grew round.

Oh. My. God!

Unless his eyes were deceiving him, in his hand, he was holding—*Vienna freaking sausage!*

Now the big question—would they poison him?

He decided to take a small bite, and if he didn't get the runs or throw up, it would be canned sausage go time. *I'll wait until sunset...*

As the evening drew close, Kit felt optimistic that the food wasn't tainted. Trying to be zen and not give in to impatience, he watched as the sun finally sizzled down into the ocean, and as soon it disappeared in a flash of green gold, he popped open the can in his hand and devoured the lot. All the cans scavenged from the plane were the same size, with the same distinctive ring-pull, so he wagered them to be all sausages. And dozens more of the cans were waiting to be collected back at the airplane!

Sunny

n the third day, Sunny woke, and this time she opened her eyes without throwing up. The first thing she saw was Kit's face hovering over her.

Through cracked lips and in a husky, unused voice, she said, "You look awful."

Kit's face was lined with worry, and his eyes ringed by deep, bruised shadows—the mongoose scar, now a dark purple ragged line.

"You're back!"

Sunny sat up gingerly. "Ugh, I feel gross. Can I have a drink?"

He passed her a bottle, and she gulped down the whole thing.

"What happened," she croaked, laying back down again.

Kit explained he'd found her on the beach and that she'd been out of it for the past three days.

"Oh."

It was a lot to take in. She still felt horribly ill. She had completely lost three days. She would have died if Kit hadn't been there. She looked at Kit.

Kit looked like he'd been through hell.

"Are you OK?"

"Me? I'm fine—it's you who's the concern here!"

She peered at him. He was so gaunt. She could count his ribs.

"Where are your clothes?"

"Well, princess, you are wearing my shorts, and I sacrificed my shirt to make a cushion for your poor head."

Looking down, Sunny realized this was true. She was wearing Kit's shorts and her bra, and her cheek was resting on his cotton button-up. Her whole left side was on fire, the tight, burned skin swollen with purple blisters.

She closed her eyes. She just needed to rest for a minute more.

It was the next day before Sunny woke again. And this time, she felt well enough to get out of the shelter and sit in the shade for a while. The cats came over to sit with her. Sensing her fragile state, the kittens were uncharacteristically mellow.

Kit said he was going to freshen up the shelter while she was outside and went to take out the old grassy bedding and replace it with fresh.

Sunny watched his homemakerly efforts and smiled a little.

She loved him so much.

*****

The days passed, and on a prescription of lots of rest, Vienna Sausage, and sunshine, Sunny slowly improved. She was still weak, had bad headaches and dizzy spells from time to time, but she was definitely improving. Kit had taken over running the majority of the camp; breakfast in the morning, followed by gleaning and cleaning the camp, collecting firewood and straightening the SOS sign, and then making dinner. He had told Sunny that they were going to live on sausage, not fish, until she was well enough to accompany him to the fishing spot.

He was not going to leave her on her own again.

As the full moon approached once more, Sunny was delighted to have a whole day without a headache, so the next day, Kit resumed fishing while Sunny watched from the shade and trailed her fingers in rock pools. They only stayed out for an hour but returned to camp with three of their favorite silver fish. Their hands had brushed together as they'd strolled in the sand, making Sunny's heart squeeze.

203

While Kit cleaned the fish, then cooked, she wandered down to the tide line. She hadn't been beachcombing for ages, but today felt like a good day for a gentle glean.

Wandering along the shore, kicking up soda bottles and yogurt pots, she thought about Kit. These days she was always thinking about Kit. *Would I have fallen in love with him if we hadn't been shipwrecked—no, of course not.* Sunny tried to imagine doing her art residency at the research station. Kit would have been there researching for his acting role.

But it wouldn't have been this Kit.

No, it would have been the cold, hard Kit she'd met on the boat, someone who was interested in sneering and manicures, not a person who she would ever be attracted to. But this Kit was her best friend, the person who made her laugh and who occupied her every thought. This Kit she trusted to the ends of the earth.

That Kit wouldn't have even given me the time of day, and I would have thought him awful.

Sunny marveled at it all. *I wonder if this means that inside every person is a sweet, warm person waiting to emerge?* Maybe it's just a case of finding the right circumstances for the prickly layers of a person to slough off.

As she mused, her eye caught the shape of something unusual. Digging at it with her bare toes, she uncovered a purple plastic dinosaur. Picking it up, she looked at it with a feeling of deep poignancy, transported back to her happy childhood.

"Mom loves you, and you love me," her mom would sing, then Sunny would join in. "What a happy family."

I love Kit. Does he love me? Argh, it's all so damn tricky!

If we are going to live the rest of our lives on this island, can I really not tell him I love him?

Sunny considered the matter in her best PPPPP manner.

I don't tell him, and we continue as we are forever until we are dead.

I do tell him, and he's kind and a bit embarrassed for me.

I do tell him, and he laughs at me.

I do tell him, and he's mad that I've spoiled our dynamic.

I do tell him, and he says he loves me too.

"Urgh!" she groaned out loud.

Picking up the plastic toy, she shook it.

"Barney! Tell me what to do!"

Heading back up the beach to the camp, she called out to Kit.

"See what I found today!" she said, holding Barney the Dinosaur up for him to see.

"Whoa! Super dee duper!"

When he grinned, the jagged scratch on his face pulled taught on the newly healing skin. Kit had said he didn't care a bit if it left a scar. That mark was his war-wound in the fight for Stinky, and he'd take a thousand more to save any of them.

"How are you feeling?"

"Way better. No headache at all!"

She really didn't have a headache, but she didn't mention that she still felt dizzy and nauseous if she turned around too quickly. If she told him, then he'd never agree to her next suggestion.

"Hey Kit, I haven't swum in ages. It would be so lovely. What do you think?"

Kit agreed, as long as she just floated around and didn't try anything fancy.

They waded into the water naked. After Sunny's accident, shyness about seeing each other without clothes seemed to have completely evaporated. Sunny floated on her back and watched a blur of white cloud scud along in the blue sky. Kit must have been doing the same thing.

"Those clouds look like a thought bubble." He pointed upward. "One big thought and the smaller ones are like the little bubbles that go down to your head, like in cartoons."

Sunny, who obviously couldn't see this, didn't reply. Instead, she imagined a thought bubble appearing above her head. In it were the words "I love you, Kit."

She let out a groan.

"You OK?" asked Kit.

"Yeah, just got water up my nose."

Sunny thought about all the things she actually wanted to say to Kit. Maybe she could find a way to tell him that she cared so deeply about him without actually saying 'love.' She swallowed nervously and practiced some phrases in her head.

They floated on in silence.

Suddenly a large splash made them jump.

"What was that?" Sunny squeaked.

"Swim!" yelled Kit, "Shark!"

Panicking, Sunny started to swim with Kit just behind her. In a few seconds—seconds that felt like hours—they flung themselves onto the safety of the sand. The late afternoon sun glinted on the ocean, but now all they saw were gentle, unthreatening waves.

"Ahh, what was that? Really a shark?" Sunny's heart was beating out of her chest.

Kit was on his knees, staring hard at the water, looking to see what had made the splash. As if on his command, the water broke again, a crest of white foam pushed up only a few yards from him.

He sat back hurriedly.

"I definitely saw something big and black," he paused, "and I think I saw a fin."

Gulping, Sunny went to join him at the water's edge but could only make out the blurry shapes of waves. Then, all of a sudden, the water broke, and a long, rounded, scarred nose poked out and made a trilling sound.

"The dolphin!"

The friendly beast swam backward and forward playfully in front of them.

"Do you think he wants us to join him?"

"It looks like an invitation to me...let's do it." Kit put out his hand, and together they waded cautiously back into the water.

Almost immediately, the dolphin nudged on Sunny's thigh, toppling her over. Kit roared with laughter, but the next minute the dolphin had done the same thing to him. Sticking its head out of the water, it made a chattering, laughing noise. Much to Sunny's delight, a second dolphin then appeared and began frolicking and playing with scar-nose.

The four of them giggled and splashed in the water, but then Sunny stumbled over, and Kit immediately took her hand and pulled her out of the water.

"Rest a while? You don't have to say goodnight to the Flippers; just take it easy, please!"

They waded out of the sea and walked a little way onto a dry part of the beach. Kit didn't let go of Sunny's hand until they lowered themselves down to the sand. They lay back in tandem; then Kit took hold of her hand again. She watched the sun lower down the sky and the stars begin to emerge.

Sunny told herself to be in the moment.

This perfect moment.

Don't think, just be, she told herself. *Enjoy the handholding, enjoy the stars, don't ruin it by running your mouth.*

But she couldn't. She just couldn't. She just had to say something.

Chapter 24

Kit

K't reveled in the simple feeling of their interlocked fingers. He was feeling grateful to his bones that Sunny was recovering. As he'd tended to her sick body, he'd realized she wasn't only his friend and companion; she was his love. Nothing would make sense without her. The simple fact was he loved her. Loved her like crazy, actually.

Sunny was making some weird gulping noises, and she kept clearing her throat.

"Are you sure you are OK?"

"Err, Kit?" She sat up abruptly, not looking at him, instead turning her head to look up at the night sky.

"What is it?" He looked at her profile, lit up by moonlight, but couldn't read it.

"I just, err—thank you for looking after me—I feel..." she paused, blinked a couple of times, then continued, "I feel so lucky to have you here..." she gulped "...I feel, I mean I think, I think..." she flopped back in the sand.

"Ahh! You mean a lot to me, OK?" she almost yelled.

Kit tried to look into her eyes, but the dark night was shrouding them. *What's the worst that could happen?* he thought. *I'm not going to hold back any longer.*

"You mean a lot to me too, Sunny. You mean everything, actually."

His heart thudded so loudly he was surprised Sunny didn't comment on it.

"What do you mean, everything?"

Allowing his emotions to guide his actions, Kit reached over and took her chin in his hand. Slowly he leaned toward her and gently pressed his lips against hers, filling the kiss with every unsaid feeling inside him. His heart was being drawn through his body and into his lips, leading him to the most perfect moment of his life. His lips and her lips were everything, an endless ocean of feeling.

Eventually drawing back, Kit took her face in his hands. "Sunny, I am totally in love with you."

Looking back at him, keeping her eyes locked on his, she replied, "Kit, I'm completely in love with you too—completely."

They stared into each other's eyes, reveling in the exquisite energy flowing between them. Love was pouring out and connecting them, making the hairs on Kit's arms stand on end. Taking Sunny gently into his arms, he showered her hair, neck and face with kisses.

"I want you to get 100% better really soon, Sunny, because as soon as you are, I am giving you fair warning that I am going to have you six ways to Sunday."

"I don't really know what that means, but I'm absolutely sure I'd be game!"

Running a hand down his chest she added, "and I do feel much better, right now come to think of it..."

"Nope—not a chance! We've all the time in the world, my sweet love. And however desperately I want you, you are still recovering and..." he stopped suddenly, a question making him concerned.

"Hey, it's not the whack on the brain that is making you say you love me, is it?"

"Idiot," she said, then broke into a yawn.

Looking at her tired face, he swept her up into his arms, saying, "you've done too much," and carried her back to the shelter.

Laying her gently in their sandy bed, he made an observation. "You do realize I just crossed the threshold of our home, with you in my arms? I think that traditionally means that you are my bride now."

"Are you saying we just got married?" Sunny exclaimed, wriggling in his arms. "I mean, is that what you just said?"

"Damn right we did," replied Kit with a grin as he lay down beside her. "Now, wife—go to sleep!"

*****

The next morning Kit was awake before Sunny, and he watched her sleep, his heart skipping when he thought of the night before. Eventually, he forced himself to get out of bed and stoke the fire. As he began to organize breakfast, he heard the moment Sunny woke. She had obviously been attacked by kittens.

"Hey, you menaces! Leave my toes alone!"

The exclamation was followed by some rustling and several small meows. Then Kit listened as she continued talking to the cats.

"Guess what, Pinky—Kit said he loved me!"

Kit grinned to himself, then poking his head into the shelter, said, "Certainly do!"

Sunny grinned back, then turned to the cat. "See, I told you!"

He put out his hand and pulled her out of the shelter. "Also, I've got a wedding present for you."

In all the drama of Sunny's accident, he'd totally forgotten about the glasses rescued from the pilot. He'd retrieved them from the tree branch and now produced them from behind his back.

"Ta-da!"

"What on earth? Glasses!"

"They must have been Pilot Pete's. I found them on my first day back at the airplane. But then everything got crazy, and I just now remembered them."

He slid the fragile metal frames up her nose, and then she peered around.

"Not bad! Not perfect, but wayyyyy better than nothing—Oh Kit, I love them, thank you, and thank you, Pilot Pete." She paused, then looked at Kit a little sternly, "or Pilot Patricia, we are not going to assume..."

"Very true."

She stretched up and kissed him on his ruined cheek. "I can see your beautiful face clearly—it's gross how beautiful you are!"

He laughed, then replied sincerely, "You are the most beautiful person in the whole world Sunny-bach."

"Maybe you're the one who needs glasses…"

"Don't say that! Don't insult my wife! Babe, you shine through with beauty from every bit of you. It's dazzling."

"I know I'm not traditionally pretty, but I like the idea of beauty shining through my pores."

"Oh, it does, babe. It really does."

"Oh Kit, I can make out the leaves on the trees!"

Adjusting the earpieces to get a snugger fit, she stood on tiptoes, and he closed his eyes as she kissed him on the cheek. As her lips stayed there, he swung her gently around to continue kissing her in a much more thorough manner. Eventually breaking away, Kit laughed when she turned to him with a comedic wail, saying, "Oh no! I didn't get you anything!"

"Just get 100% mended, babe, and that's all the gift I need." Running his hands up and down her body and winking suggestively, he added, "Know what I mean?"

Sunny certainly did.

Kit and Sunny spent the rest of the day in a haze of love—or, as he declared, 'honey-marooning.' They lay in the shade, and as Kit fed Sunny pieces of fruit, she wrapped her fingers in his dark curls pulling him closer. He had never in his life felt such an intense need to protect someone, and this was what made him draw back and tell her to rest.

So, lazing in the shade, her battered head resting on his chest, Sunny quizzed him about his past. He told her about being a very mediocre student in high school. He told her about Brian and how the two of them lived in the VW bus for one whole, cold winter.

But he still hadn't told her of his fame. He planned to do it sometime, but it didn't seem important, here in this place, at this moment, the whole truth. The truth that was important was that he loved her.

Here on this island, he was just Kit, not Nicky Kitson.

211

He was Kit the Fisherman. Kit the Cat Dad. Kit the Husband.

*****

Two days later, Kit watched Sunny walk across the beach—Winky, Dinky, and Stinky nipping at her heels, and thought, *this life is paradise. We may have water and fruit instead of milk and honey, but it's paradise all the same.*

Then he watched her stumble, a little unsteady on her feet.

Damn, she's still not right.

He'd just returned from the water hole with fresh supplies as well as a large bunch of flowers. The sun was warm, and the sky was blue. He tried to suppress his worry as he waved to her. Sunny waved back, wonky glasses sliding down her nose for the nth time. As she approached him, he offered her a lychee and asked her how she was feeling.

"Ooh lychee, that would make a lovely change—and I feel fine."

He placed a lychee in her mouth and asked her if she still had a headache. Sunny shrugged. Kit gave her a look, and she admitted her head was actually bothering her a little.

"I know you don't want a fuss, but you have to keep me in the loop, babe."

"You just want reports so you can get into my shorts," she laughed back.

They'd reluctantly decided to hold off on lovemaking until Sunny's concussion was better. Three days with no headaches, dizzy spells or double-vision, then it would be game on!

"Oh you know I've got my eyes on the prize," Kit replied. He reached out a finger and traced it down her cheek and over her lips. He watched her forehead wrinkle into a frown.

"Babe?"

"Just these stupid zaps in my head," she replied." They come out of nowhere, but only last for a couple of seconds."

"Oh sweetheart, hang in there," he replied, "in a few days, this will all seem like a dream."

Then Kit brought his arm out from behind him and presented the bunch of flowers.

"Tah dah!"

"For me?" She playfully clapped her hands to her chest and opened her eyes wide.

"Well, I didn't bring them for the cats."

She buried her nose in the bouquet, and Kit plucked out a flower and placed it behind her ear.

"Oh, putting it behind my left ear, hey? Trying to tell me something?"

Kit was lost for a moment, but then he remembered the Gauguin story and how the maidens wore their flowers.

He growled, "Give that back to me. I don't want you thinking you're footloose and fancy-free."

Sunny's heart thudded as she thought how much she loved him.

Kit's heart thudded as he thought how much he loved her.

They looked at each other. What was that thudding sound?

Time slowed, and Kit tilted his head back and looked into the sky.

Thud, thud, thud.

"Oh shit!"

Helicopter.

A dark spidery shape was descending downward, aiming to land right next to their SOS sign. They looked back at each other in shock. Sunny started to sway. The next moment she dropped into Kit's arms in a dead faint. He looked down at her, then back at the approaching helicopter, not knowing how to feel.

They were rescued.

Chapter 25
Kit

louds of sand raced across the beach, and Kit bent his body over Sunny, his back to the beating black blades. Sunny lay unconscious in the cocoon of Kit's embrace, and he felt frozen with shock. The deafening engine noise, the smell of jet fuel exhaust, and the scouring sand pierced the tranquil bubble of the island. Kit's mind scattered along with the sand, having trouble comprehending it all.

"Babe? Sunny?" He leaned over and checked her breathing.

Had she fainted, or was it something more? He brushed the hair off her face, and she gave a small moan.

A hand reached out and touched his shoulder.

Kit jerked his head around, still shielding Sunny with his body.

Three men in matching turquoise t-shirts were there on the beach, standing right beside him. They all wore mirrored aviator sunglasses and had clean-shaven faces and crisp clothing.

Kit saw his reflection in their lenses.

Gaunt, scarred face, rough beard, and a network of scratches and stings all over his body.

"Nicky Kitson?" said the first.

"Oh God, we actually found you!" said the second.

The men were bubbling with excitement, but Kit turned his back on them and concentrated on Sunny. As she began to regain consciousness, he snapped to the newcomers.

"Water, now."

Instantly a bottle was unsnapped from a belt and handed to Kit. The rescuer then turned to the other men yelling, "get the stretcher."

"Hey honey, it's OK, take a drink," Kit said to Sunny, helping her take some sips from the bottle.

A stranger knelt down next to Kit. He said, "It's OK; we can take it from here."

Kit growled at him.

Sunny became fully conscious, and Kit was horrified that the first thing she saw was an unknown man looking down at her.

"It's OK, baby. It's OK." Kit stroked her hair, his head spinning and heart cracking. Everything was going to change, and he could do nothing about it.

Kit leaned close and told her to keep her eyes shut.

"Babe, I know it's loud and strange; just keep your eyes closed and hold my hand."

The rescue team was rushing around and yelling. The flower from Sunny's hair had fallen and become trampled underfoot as she was strapped to the stretcher. With a man at either end, the stretcher was lifted up, ready to move.

Despite his urgings to keep her eyes closed, she opened them, looking at Kit in a state of complete panic and confusion.

"Kit, Kit, don't let them take me."

She struggled to sit up, but the efficient strangers pressed her back down again. Kit was nudged out of the way, and he lost grip of her hand.

"Kit! Help me! Kit!" she screamed and then, "the cats!"

Kit ran in front of the stretcher carriers and put out his arms. "Wait, wait, this is too much. Slow down; who are you? What's going on?"

The largest of three men stepped forward. "I'm Mike Gazabine, team leader. I know you must be in shock, sir; we are with SafetyFirst Security. We have been searching these islands for nearly seven weeks now, trying to track you down."

He nodded toward Sunny, "Now we should get the lady into the bird. We have medical supplies and an EMT aboard."

"We're leaving?" said Sunny weakly.

"Yes, ma'am, we are taking you home."

Looking at their campsite, Kit felt himself torn.

They were going "home," but home was right here.

The island was where Kit had learned what an actual home was. What family was.

I don't want to leave, he thought. *Being here and having nothing allowed me to find everything.*

But looking at Sunny, he knew it was time to go, and go immediately. She needed medical attention, and she was what mattered most. And the cats, of course.

Now that Kit had shifted into this mindset, he wanted to get them going as soon as possible. He explained the feline situation to the man called Mike, who told him not to worry. Collecting a lidded box from the helicopter, he helped Kit with a hectic twenty-minute cat hunt, finally capturing Pinky and the kittens and getting them safely inside the box and then into the helicopter.

Mike punched air holes into the box, then secured the lid with duct tape. "Safety First! It's in our name!"

Kit didn't respond. He stood in the wind of the rotating blades for a moment, and looked along the beach.

Their beach.

"Is there anything else you want, sir?" Mike asked doubtfully, looking at the piles of junk around him.

Kit wanted to take it all with him, everything on their wobbly supply shelves, the woven roof of their shelter, Sunny's ridiculous sun hat and flip-flops (or flap-flops as she had named them). Instead, he turned and just picked up the charcoal drawing of Pinky, then followed the man back to the waiting helicopter.

The blue and yellow helicopter soared up and over the island, giving Kit a bird's eye view of his temporary home before it disappeared into the sea haze. Sunny had been hooked up to an IV of fluids and given a tranquilizer, so she was drifting off to sleep. The medic kept trying to jam him with a needle too, but Kit waved him off irritably. Over the thrum of the whirling blades, the security team filled Kit in on what had happened over the last two months.

A faulty diving tank, the team leader explained, had caused the supply vessel accident. It had exploded and caused a chain reaction with other flammables onboard. The entire crew, including Farhan (who was now completely recovered) and Dr. Stokes, had made it safely onto the lifeboat. From there, the story got muddled.

"Most of the lifeboat occupants said they saw you go up in flames when the third explosion hit—but Dr. Stokes and the first mate were convinced they'd seen you go overboard," the security man continued, nervous of the stony expression on Kit's face.

"The lifeboat was picked up after a few hours, well after dark. Searching for you was pretty fruitless at that point, but at first light, the local rescue agencies coordinated with the Australian Navy. That took a while to get organized, but by the next day, we had planes and ships from all over, looking for you."

The security man told Kit that, back in Los Angeles, Kit's personal assistant and security team had recruited SafetyFirst to set up an independent seek and rescue mission, with orders to scour the South Pacific Ocean and every one of the 1000 atolls on which Kit could have washed ashore.

"And Sunny." Kit growled.

"Oh yes—the girl. She didn't have any family that we could find, but we have been in touch with her ex-employers in Seattle, and with her college."

Dismissing Sunny as not really relevant, the man continued to tell Kit of the thorough and amazing job they had done searching for him.

"Our CEO has been on the news several times; Oprah even had him on to talk about the search efforts. You've been pretty much headline news every day since you disappeared."

Kit wearily leaned his head against the vibrating window and closed his eyes. The next moment he heard the click of a photo being taken.

"Just one to show the wife! Can we do a selfie too?"

Chapter 26

Kit

The helicopter made its way determinedly back to Fiji where SafetyFirst had set up their base. Kit had been pleased to learn the crew was flying straight to the local hospital; Sunny needed to get to a doctor immediately. Nothing else was important. She was awake now but a little loopy on the tranquilizers. And the security team looked on curiously as she held tightly to Kit's hand.

Landing in the parking lot—the hospital didn't have a helipad— Kit was happy to see that no satellite-dish-topped news vans were waiting for them, just a small group of people standing around a hospital gurney. Within a minute, the scrub-wearing staff whisked Sunny away, her stretcher disappearing through double doors, while Mike steered Kit, who was holding the box of cats, toward two officials waiting to greet him.

Kit suppressed his urge to follow Sunny and gave a tired smile to the waiting party.

"Thank you, everyone, for your support. I appreciate it greatly."

An elderly man with kind eyes stepped forward. "Jo Bula, Hospital Chief. We are very happy to be of service, should you be standing? Do you need a wheelchair? That scratch on your face looks like it needs attention."

"I'm fine, honestly. Thanks for your help."

Turning to a crisply dressed woman next to Dr. Bula, he was introduced to Olivia Wainiqolo, the governor of the island. In a deep, comforting voice Olivia told him that she'd been talking to the US Ambassador in Papua New Guinea to coordinate travel and documentation needs.

Again Kit thanked everybody.

Mike had added, "I've just had a word from your personal assistant..." He looked at his notes. "Troy Weathers, is already on his way here, should arrive tomorrow. When you've had a chance to rest, we can talk about added security."

Kit was relieved he would have a team assisting his and Sunny's return to the USA. But mostly, he was concerned with the well-being of Sunny—and the cats.

Dr. Bula beckoned an orderly to take the cats and look after them in the staff lounge, then suggested they should get Kit out of the sun to be checked in to the hospital. Inside the building, another doctor approached them and explained that Sunny was having tests.

"She's in for a CAT scan, but we don't have an MRI here, so I would recommend she has one when you get to the mainland. We are also running her blood work and setting her up on a course of antibiotics. I would like to do the same for you too, if you would consent."

"Later." Kit swallowed his impatience and did his best to be polite. He knew everyone was trying to help, but he really just wanted to be with Sunny.

"Can you just take me to her room first," he added, "please."

Sunny

*A*fter several scans, blood draws, and IV insertions, Sunny was wheeled back to a room where Kit was waiting. He was slumped in a chair with his eyes closed, an empty plate on the table next to him. He had a band-aid in the crook of his arm and patches of stained yellow skin where iodine had been daubed on bites and scratches.

Sunny was able to see these details because the friendly x-ray technician had lent her his spare glasses. The pilot's fragile glasses had been lost during the rescue, which wasn't surprising. The scene had been hugely chaotic.

The past few hours had also been chaotic and overwhelming. The noise, the people, the smells and textures, all left Sunny's poor head spinning. Her wounds had been cleaned and dressed, the cuts

219

and burns attended to, and she was so filled with painkillers and antibiotics she felt a gross mixture of spacey and nauseous. What she really wanted was food and a shower.

And of course her family.

As the orderly helped her into the bed, she poked Kit in the arm to wake him up.

"Kit! Ooh, you ate—what did you have?"

Rubbing his eyes, Kit then leaned over and kissed her.

"Mmmm, I can taste sugar on your lips," she ran a tongue over her own lips. "I'm desperate to eat, but they won't let me in case I need surgery. It's torture finally being surrounded by food and drinks—drinks filled with ice—and I can't have a thing—and the cats! Where are the cats!" she gabbled.

Kit laughed, gathering her into his arms.

"Slow down, babe."

The hovering orderly asked if they needed anything else.

"No, thank you. And thank you so much for your help," she replied.

When they were left alone, Kit immediately told her the cats were safe. They were all safe now.

"But isn't everything strange? Sitting on furniture, hearing machines and other voices."

"Yeah, I don't think I like it."

Sunny agreed with Kit. She didn't think she liked it either.

They lay in the narrow hospital bed, holding each other, talking about this and that, but nothing important, while the hospital buzzed with life around them.

Did you know aloe is antiseptic?" asked Kit at one point.

"No, no I didn't," replied Sunny.

"Hmmm, apparently so..." said Kit.

"So the face-pee spritzing?"

"Completely unnecessary."

Sunny giggled.

"Well, I always suspected you liked toilet humor," Kit said, grinning.

"Two out of ten. Anyway, I guess we'll know for next time…" replied Sunny.

"Next time we are marooned on an island and in the middle of a hurricane, while searching for a lost kitten, and a strange creature attacks my face?"

"Exactly!"

Kit gently cupped her head in his hand, to go in for a kiss, but immediately withdrew it again.

"Whoa babe! What happened?"

"You like my bald spot?"

The doctor had shaved a patch of Sunny's skull to get at the wound.

"Hmm, very Sinead O'Connor," said Kit, leaning over her and peering at the now clean wound. "Make sure they don't give you a tiny wig to put on back of your head—that would cause big trouble…"

"Huh?" said Sunny.

"In fact, there would be hell toupée!"

Kit cracked up, and then so did Sunny. The more they laughed, the more they couldn't stop. "Ten," gasped Sunny at one point, "you've finally made it to ten!" Tears were running down their faces, and Kit was hiccupping as the door opened.

A small doctor in a long green surgical gown entered, holding some transparencies. He stood patiently as Kit and Sunny tried to collect themselves. Eventually, they were calm and the small doctor gave them a tired smile.

"Well, Ms. Evans, it looks like you had a small brain bleed, but it has stopped on its own. You'll need to have it carefully monitored, and you must go and see a neurosurgeon when you return to the USA. But for now, we are not going to do anything about it here on the island."

"That's good news, isn't it?" asked Kit.

"It is, sir," nodded the doctor.

Sunny had other priorities, though." So I can eat now?"

The doctor's kind eyes crinkled." Yes, my dear, you can eat."

Sunny was given a plate of sweet potato and fish, which though delicious, was a little disappointing because it was fish. She'd be quite happy to exclude fish, coconut, and bananas from her diet for a while yet.

"I can't believe how tired I feel. I think I have to close my eyes for a minute."

Kit moved her food tray out of the way away, gently scooting her over until he could get back in the bed beside her. Two nurses and an orderly bustled in, ostensibly to take the tray and close the blinds, but in reality they just nudged each other and stared at Kit.

Sunny didn't notice, though. Her eyes were closed, and the last thought she had before passing out was simply to wonder what was for breakfast.

Chapter 27

Kit

The next morning, Sunny told Kit that the breakfast of eggs, bacon, and toast was truly the best thing she'd ever eaten. As she devoured the food, merrily chatting about her new friend, the orderly called Matthew, who had snuck the kittens into her room for a visit, Kit smiled, but the anxiety of "revealing" his true self was hovering like a heavy, humid cloud. A storm was coming. He just knew it.

"Seriously, Kit, that was so good! It's weird, though. My body feels more achy sleeping in a proper bed than it did in the sand."

"Yeah, I know what you mean. Amazing how you can adapt so quickly to something like that."

"And now we have to adapt back to the real world. I'm not sure I'm ready," said Sunny.

The Real World reality show flashed into Kit's brain. He shuddered. "Babe, you've got nothing to do today but rest. Get all the sleep you can," he paused, then took hold of her hand. "Worry about the real world when we leave here, not before."

"Sounds good to me. But if I'm lazing around all day, will you be OK? Are you sure you don't mind doing all the work?"

Kit had told her he was going to work out travel plans and logistics for their return to the states.

"It's fine, babe. I've got it."

Within minutes Sunny had fallen back asleep, so Kit went off to a small empty office where, on a borrowed laptop, he video-chatted with various members of his over-excited team. The squeals and gushing taxed his brain. He knew they meant well, but it was all a bit much. On a pause between meetings, Kit took a moment to check his horoscope. He could really do with some astrological advice; "Storm clouds are gathering on the horizon, do what you can to prepare."

That sounds about right, sadly.

Next, he clicked on Sunny's Capricorn sign. "Your world is changing, Capricorn. When you feel lost, look to your roots." Kit hoped desperately that Sunny was going to be OK with the new changed world she was entering.

In the late afternoon, when Sunny was awake again, over cups of hot tea and a sticky honey cake—which overtook breakfast as the best thing she had ever eaten, apparently—Kit filled her in on the plans he'd made. Flights were booked, temporary IDs were on their way, and he now had access to his bank account.

He also told her the hospital gastroenterologist had said he and Sunny had likely suffered Ciguatera fish poisoning.

"It happens when fish eat dino-something-or-others after a storm...I didn't really follow it all."

"Dinoflagellates! That's what Dr. Stokes studies. She told me she'd been poisoned by them—how weird, it all comes full circle."

"To think I was so pleased with myself, catching that fish—the only one I could get after that rainstorm—wish it had been 'the one that got away'."

"We survived it, though."

"We did, but we'll need more check-ups about it all. There's boring long-term stuff like low blood pressure, things like that."

"Well, if that's the worse thing we have to face back in the real world, that's really not too bad."

That reminded Kit of someone who hadn't made it back to the real world. He had been talking to the authorities about the crashed aircraft in the jungle. A plane—a 208A Cargomaster—had gone missing after leaving Fiji in 1987, and the Fijian government thought their plane must be it.

The pilot's family was going to be extremely grateful to finally know what had happened to their loved one, the minister for transportation had said.

Finishing the final morsels of the sweet pastry, Sunny pushed her plate to one side.

"I need to let Andrea know I'm OK, and Clive and Dennie."

Kit pulled a borrowed cell phone out of his pocket. "I thought you'd need to do that—use this."

Kit leaned back in the chair and closed his eyes while Sunny, not wanting to run up a large international phone bill, made a very quick call to Weaver Creek.

"I told Andrea to call Clive and Dennie, and she said she'd call the college too. But Kit, there's something else we need to talk about. It's really stressing me out. I got travel insurance before the trip, but I don't know if it will cover all this. We need to check on that before they do anything else. I'm so scared the CAT scan isn't covered. That must be thousands of dollars."

Kit picked up her hand; this was it.

"You don't need to worry about money..."

"Kit! We do have to worry! What's the point of being rescued if we end up destitute and living on the streets?" She bit her lip and continued, "if we are homeless, I'd rather go back to the island."

He squeezed her hand.

OK—gotta do it. Gotta talk about everything...lay it all out in the open.

But before he could say a word, they were interrupted by a knock on the door, followed by a suave-looking young man peering around it.

"Nicky! It really is you! Geez, you scared the crap out of us!"

225

Sunny

*S*unny watched the young man step swiftly toward Kit and mock-punch him on the shoulder.

"Gotta say, the Robinson Crusoe look isn't too bad on you. The press are going to go nuts—you've gotta keep the beard for the press conference."

The newcomer made Sunny feel a mixture of confusion and shyness. Firstly, she had no idea what he was talking about, and secondly, he was as crisp and clean as a laundry detergent ad, with the same polished air that Kit had had when she first saw him. His eyes were the same blue as his popped shirt collar. The stranger's pristine appearance made her hugely aware of her battered, grubby self, so she shrank back into the cool sheets of her hospital bed, pulling them over her beaten-up body.

The startling blue eyes then focused on her, and the man stuck out an enthusiastic hand. "Troy Weathers, Nicky's personal assistant."

Extracting her own hand from the sheets, Sunny took his and shook weakly, now completely confused. She looked round to Kit with questioning eyes. "Nicky?"

Kit was completely still, like he'd turned to stone.

What on earth? thought Sunny.

Troy was looking from Sunny to Kit and back again, still with a large smile on his face.

"The press are going to love you too, Sunny-D, don't worry. If we spin it the right way, you can sell your story for a fat fee!"

"College Kid says 'being a Castaway with Kitson was no Catastrophe, I'm coco-nutty about him!.'"

As he spoke, he stretched out his hands as though mimicking a tabloid headline.

"Kitson?" whispered Sunny.

"Troy," Kit hissed.

Troy turned back to Kit.

"Think you are going to turn the whole thing into a movie Nicky? Paramount and Universal are already putting out some juicy feelers to Mattie."

Sunny had a dreadful feeling welling up inside her. "Paramount? Universal? Mattie?" she whispered.

"That's enough," growled Kit, his face thunderous looking.

"Sure—I know it's a lot, man." Troy winked at Kit, and turning back to Sunny, continued on, "Mattie is Nicky's agent."

Sunny just lay there, watching him swivel back to Kit, twisting like a tornado, destroying everything in its path.

"Oh man! You should have seen the premiere of *Mission Impossible 11*! Everyone wore black armbands, and they had a minute's silence for you—though Gwyneth sobbed very theatrically through the whole thing, so the minute was far from silent."

Not getting any response from either Kit or Sunny, he continued, "Man, you need a plastic surgeon ASAP! Hope that face of yours can get back to perfect—though if anyone can make face scars fashionable, it's Nicky Kitson."

Sunny looked at Kit again. He wouldn't meet her eye.

"Nicky Kitson," she said slowly.

Even Sunny had heard of Nicky Kitson. The name Nicky Kitson was more familiar than Johnny Depp or Tom Cruise. Nicky Kitson—the Oscar nominee. Nicky Kitson—the wild man of Hollywood.

Nicky Kitson, Nicky Kitson, not Otis Kitson, and not her Kit at all. At first, she'd thought he'd seemed familiar, but he'd never said anything. He'd had that hat on, and then she'd lost her glasses...

"You didn't say," she whispered.

"Go away, Troy," snarled Kit.

Troy gave a salute. "Right away, boss, got stuff to organize."

Giving Kit yet another wink, he rushed out of the room, pulling his cell phone out to answer a call as he did, "... Conan dude, let's pencil in a date..."

The hydraulic door hinges hissed as Troy left the room. She heard Kit take a deep breath, and a wave of panic traveled through her body. Sunny buried her head into her pillows. She didn't want to look at Kit. Or should she say Nicky.

She was completely shocked—and hurt.

"Sunny, baby, please..."

"Why didn't you tell me? I don't understand," her voice muffled under the covers.

"Baby, please, it doesn't make any difference. I love you. I didn't tell you because, because you just knew me for me, and you loved me for me. You didn't love me for my career or my money, so it didn't matter."

Sunny could feel his hand stroking her back through the sheet.

"On the island, who I was in the world didn't matter."

Sunny rolled over and sat up again.

"But we're not on the island now, are we."

Into the silence of the room, Sunny then added, "I'm going to sleep now."

She closed her eyes, and after a while, she heard Kit sigh and leave the room. Lying in the bed, Sunny's heart and head were racing. One minute she was filled with outrage and fury, the next with panic and embarrassment. She tried putting herself in Kit's shoes, but that just made her crosser.

I wouldn't lie to Kit. If you love someone, you don't lie.

She grimaced, the pain in her heart making her shudder.

Maybe he doesn't trust me? Maybe he thought I'd just like him for his money and fame? Stupid, stupid, stupid man!

Sunny once again felt all at sea; she'd told him everything, and all he'd ever told her were half-truths or lies.

Chapter 28
Kit

As they prepared to board the plane back to the USA, Kit went over everything he still had to do; increase the security team, and also set up some extra help at his home in LA—Sunny might need a residential nurse while she regained her strength—and he had to figure out his contracts and get out of the stuff he was committed to filming.

He'd got Troy to buy some new clothes for them—they couldn't travel in hospital scrubs—and there should be new glasses waiting for Sunny in L.A. The temporary travel documents were sorted, but he still needed to talk to his PR company. The world, he knew, would be waiting for a statement.

As Kit worked through his list, he watched Sunny sitting in a departure lounge chair, looking out of the window with a glum expression on her face. She'd been very quiet during the last 24 hours, only the cats eliciting real smiles from her.

She'll probably be pissed for a while.

He knew he shouldn't have kept the truth from her—but she'd come around.

If I could go back in time and do things differently, I would. But it's too late now.

He just had to mitigate it all as best as he could and hope she would soon realize that nothing was going to change.

*****

LAX was a heaving mass of paparazzi and fans who were crushed up against security barriers like the most die-hard of black Friday shoppers. A grim-faced security team escorted Kit and Sunny around the crowds and through the terminal. Troy ran ahead like an eager puppy, high-fiving members of the press and tweeting about their re-entry into the USA. Hashtag—JustInTheNickyOfTime. Troy knew his boss appreciated a punny hashtag.

Kit was shielded behind a new pair of dark glasses, and Sunny had on the new pair of spectacles that had been waiting for her at the airport. With one hand clutching the cat carrier, he had Sunny's hand tightly gripped in the other. Kit felt that if he didn't keep a tight hold, she might bolt at any second.

The flashing lights and people screaming were probably overwhelming. Sunny looked dazed, and she was trembling. He could feel it through their linked hands. Kit was used to it all, but Sunny would be having a very different experience.

Hungry-eyed men and women called out to them, as their every movement was documented on cameras and phones.

"Nicky, Nicky over here..."

"... Sunny...what was it like....marooned with Nicky?"

"Nicky...new film?"

"... The President... Nicky, Nicky"

"Miss Evans...exclusive... hundred thousand..."

"Sunny...*Oh Wow!*... photo shoot..."

Escaping through sliding doors into the LA sunshine, Kit and Sunny were ushered forward by the security team to a black Range Rover with tinted windows. Another Range Rover in front, and one more behind, made a convoy of three. The driver held open the rear door, and Kit put the new cat carrier, with its full load, between him and Sunny.

The cats mewed plaintively, and Sunny tried to comfort them.

He wished he could comfort her in the same manner, but every time he tried, she pulled back, so he decided to give her space. She was under enough pressure as it was. He didn't want to add to it.

Sunny

*T*he cats cried and Sunny stroked them gently.

It's OK, kitties—I'm lost and bewildered too.

Pulling away from the concourse, she glanced at Kit. He sat white-faced and unreadable on the far side of the vehicle.

We are losing him, thought Sunny miserably. This Kit, remote and cold, was the one she had met on the very first day on the boat.

The convoy took them along the slow-moving I-405 until they eventually passed through tall automatic gates and down a long driveway. At the end of the drive, Sunny saw a beautiful house surrounded by rich grass as smooth as velvet. Trees dappled the light, and lush foliage spilled over curving, paved paths. She could see sparkling blue water through a brick archway and an expanse of tennis courts to her left.

The door to the house, set between two white columns, stood open.

The Range Rover came to a perfectly smooth halt on the raked gravel, and suited men sprang to open the doors on either side. Kit immediately stepped out, but Sunny hesitated, pulling the cat carrier toward her.

"I can take that for you, ma'am," an impassive-faced man said to her.

"No thank you," she mumbled, reluctantly getting out and hugging the carrier in front of her like a shield.

An older man with rolled-up shirtsleeves appeared in the doorway of the house.

"Welcome home, Mr. Nicky."

"Thanks, Tony."

Sunny remained frozen by the car, awkwardly holding the cat carrier, while behind her the security team was disappearing smoothly to who-knew-where.

This is Kit's real life? she thought numbly, and then she corrected herself, *Nicky's real life?*

Kit came over and put a hand on the small of her back, trying to usher her up the steps. Finally, she moved, stepping wearily into the cool entrance hall. Tony, who must have been the housekeeper or something, followed them, saying, "I've put some refreshments in the library, but if there is something you particularly wish for, please let me know."

"I'm sure it will be fine, Tony."

He paused for a moment, and Sunny saw a look of uncertainty cross his face.

Clearing his throat, Kit said, "Tony, this is Sunny. This is, err, her home now."

Sunny stood stock-still.

This is my home now?

Tony inclined his head and gave Sunny a pleasant smile. "A pleasure to meet you, ma'am, please let me know if I can help you in any way."

Tony's professional demeanor never dipped, even though he was probably riddled with curiosity. "May I take the cats for you?"

Sunny wanted to refuse, but Kit told Tony to take Pinky and the kittens up to his bedroom and release them from the carrier, adding, "they'll need all the normal cat stuff. Can you see to that please..."

"My pleasure," answered Tony.

Sunny didn't believe for a second that organizing kibble and cat litter would really be Tony's pleasure, but she obediently handed over the cats. With her arms now free, she hugged them around her body and gazed about her. The house was cold—cold, white, and unfriendly.

Kit must have seen her shiver, because he took her by the hand and led her up a gracefully curved staircase and along a landing to a bedroom where Tony was depositing the cats.

Kit's bedroom?

Silver and gray sofas surrounded a fireplace and huge white fur rug. The vast bed was covered in white pillows and silver throws. In fact everything in the room was white, silver, or pale gray, apart from a few attractively placed bouquets and a very battered skateboard propped in the corner.

The AC was on max, and she shivered again.

"AC setting 75 degrees," said Kit.

"With pleasure Nicky," replied a female voice, making Sunny jump. She knew it was just Siri or whatever, but the silky smooth computer voice doing Kit's (or really Nicky's) bidding was, well, off-putting.

Turning back to her, he said, "We'll send someone to buy you proper clothes tomorrow, but for now, come and grab one of my sweaters."

The walk-in closet must have been organized by Tony because the jackets and shirts hung in groups of the same color, not how Kit would organize things at all. She imagined heaps of expensive clothes thrown carelessly onto the floor. But here, sleek sliding shelves opened to reveal shoes and boots. She watched him pull open a drawer, which was filled with folded cashmere sweaters. Choosing a soft dark blue one, he passed it to Sunny.

She pulled the sweater over her head and it snagged on her glasses. Kit helped her untangle herself.

"Hey look, I'm trying to pull the wool over your eyes!" he said. His joke sounded forced to Sunny, and it was a little too on the nose for their current situation.

She stood back, the sweater hanging almost to her knees, and said "Thanks."

"You OK?" asked Kit.

Sunny nodded. "I'm OK, just tired is all. Is it alright if I rest for a bit?"

"Of course! You don't need to ask permission!"

"Oh, and maybe borrow a phone, so I can call Andrea?"

"Babe—this is your house. The phone is here," he said, gesturing to a white handset discreetly tucked into a built-in niche.

Sunny nodded, then looked around the room, "I'm sleeping in here?"

Kit ran a hand through his hair, and Sunny thought he looked frustrated. "I hope you'll sleep in here with me? If that is what you want..."

Sunny looked at the cats, who were asleep on the fur rug, and said again, "OK."

"Call Andrea, lie down for a bit." He moved to kiss her on the forehead, pressed his lips to her brow, then added, "come find me downstairs when you've slept."

The door shut behind him, and Sunny stood alone in the middle of the glamorous bedroom feeling more marooned than she ever had on the island.

Pulling the soft wool of the sweater up to her nose, she breathed in deeply. It didn't smell like Kit. Well, it didn't smell like the Kit she knew. It probably smelled like Nicky.

And this room was almost the size of the house Sunny had grown up in.

I wish we were still on the island.

Island Kit had loved her. She didn't know if Hollywood Nicky would.

Taking another deep breath, Sunny tried to think logically. Kit hadn't given her any reason to believe things had changed. Except things *had* changed. He was different now—he was like the sun, and everyone in this orbit rotated around him. He just had to raise an eyebrow, and everyone went running to do his bidding. She didn't like seeing him like this. And what would a relationship be like with a superstar anyway? There would probably be press and fans everywhere, like at the airport.

She shuddered.

And would she have to live in LA? In this huge, intimidating house? On a deserted island, in a rickety homemade shack, Sunny knew she and Kit were a perfect fit. But here, in this shining, opulent life, she was a square peg in a world of round holes.

How can I be happy here? Be myself?

It was just so complicated, and Sunny wasn't sure if she could handle it. Kit was comfortable in this world, but if he had to spend all his time trying to keep her happy or making concessions, that would be awful.

To make it work, one of them needed to change, adapt; could she?

She paced around the bedroom miserably, picking up Stinky and wishing she had his courage. While the rest of the cats huddled in the corner, Stinky was roaming and exploring all over. Looking at the bouquets, she was aware that she shouldn't be nosy, but she couldn't resist lifting the flaps on the white envelopes to look at the notes they contained. The first arrangement was a tasteful mix of lilies and green ivy, subtle but upscale.

"Dearest Nicky, So pleased to hear the news, let's catch up sometime soon. Archie says hello. H & M". At the bottom of the card was a royal crest.

The next arrangement was massive, an explosion of color, with confetti-filled balloons attached to it.

"We love you! Welcome home!" The card bore dozens of signatures and had a *Nicky Kitson Films* logo at the bottom.

The last bouquet was dozens of flawless white roses, tied with silver ribbon and arranged in a heavy pale gray vase. Looking around the arctic bedroom, Sunny thought, *this one seems to belong here.*

Extracting the card, she read the details. "Darling, I burned a candle for you every day! I'll love you forever. You are my yesterday, today, and tomorrow, Alexis."

Sunny's fingers froze on the card. Kit had been economical with the truth for the whole time they'd been on the island. He was a very famous actor but had pretended to be relatively unknown. He had said he and Alexis were broken up, but was that the truth? How could she trust him? He only told her parts of his story, not ever the whole. For all she knew, Kit and Alexis were madly in love and engaged to be married. She certainly didn't know if she could trust Kit to be fully honest with her.

Getting into bed, Sunny pulled the cold white covers over her head.

Chapter 29

Kit

Kit shut the bedroom door softly and returned to the study, completely ignoring all the flower arrangements, balloons, and bottles of champagne that were cluttered on a credenza in the hallway. White envelopes bearing the name Nicky Kitson were taped to each of the gifts.

The study was his favorite room in the house. The walls were dark green above the rich, polished oak wainscoting, and over the fireplace was an Andy Warhol print of Elizabeth Taylor. On the floor was the antique Aubusson rug he'd spent a lot of time tracking down, and his favorite leather recliner was next to a wall dominated by books. This room was his sanctuary and where he could slough off the worries of the outside world and just read, listen to music, and drink whiskey, completely undisturbed.

In the center of the room, a table was loaded with an overflowing charcuterie board, salads, and warm, yeasty breads, which Kit side-stepped, heading to the bar and filling a glass with whiskey and ice.

He was doing a very poor job of making Sunny's entry into his real life easy. It was hard. He just didn't know how to play it. Looking around at all the expensive things in the room, he tried to imagine how Sunny saw his life.

Overwhelming and gross, probably. Now that he was seeing it through Sunny's eyes, he could see that the study wasn't a retreat. It was a fortress designed to keep people out. The room was filled with precious objects that he'd carefully collected, but he didn't allow anyone into the room, so the pieces in his carefully curated collection were captives also.

All those thousands and thousands of dollars to buy a rug, a vase, a book—things that had at the time seemed ultimately important, and far more important than any people in his life. Remembering how he'd fought tooth and nail to get a signed first edition of *Fahrenheit 451*, his favorite book, Kit cringed. He'd treated the auction room staff like crap, so determined was he to have the winning bid. Now the book was on a polished shelf, and he never took it down to read, just kept it there as a trophy, a captive.

I made a prison and locked myself inside. Now I'm asking Sunny to step into the prison with me, which is crazy—I just got free! Why am I back here?

No wonder Sunny was shutting down, shutting him out.

He took the book down from the shelf and flipped it open at random.

"But Clarisse's favorite subject wasn't herself. It was everyone else, and me. She was the first person in a good many years I've really liked. She was the first person I can remember who looked straight at me as if I counted," he read out loud to the empty room.

Sunny was totally Clarisse. An odd, life-changing girl.

And she made me see how fake all this is. We've got to make a plan, figure out how we work now, off the island. I don't think we should be here...I've got to talk to her.

As Kit closed the $25,000 book, putting it back on the shelf, the phone in his pocket vibrated—it was Mattie.

"Nicky-Baby! We gotta meet—Paramount are back onboard for Plague World..."

"Hey Mattie, yes, I'm doing O.K. after being missing, presumed dead for months, thanks for asking..."

"Yeah, yeah, want me to get a ticker-tape parade organized? Seriously, that could be great—put you on a tropical float, girls in bikinis throwing out plastic beads and coconut candies like Mardi Gras, or a ticker-tape parade, but we could call it a Nicky-tape parade and have confetti printed with your face on it..."

"Mattie?"

"Yes, Nicky?"

"No."

On the other end of the line, Mattie chuckled, used to the fickle nature of the celebrities he managed." Sure, we'll think of something else—you want something a bit less ostentatious? What about a live streaming church service of thanks? Churchy stuff always goes down a treat."

"I'll see you at the press conference, Mattie. Tomorrow, 5 P.M. right?"

"You got it Nicky. Just keep your mind open. I've got all sorts of plans for you."

Hanging up, Kit refilled his whiskey and took another look around his study.

I don't want this life anymore.

Kit suddenly realized that he was master of his own destiny. What had Sunny said to him? "You do have your own agency, you know. You can make your own choices..." her voice echoed in his head.

I'm going to retire. I'm going to retire and sell this house and then buy something for me and Sunny in the countryside. That'll work; we can work. I know we can.

The relief in deciding to step away from it all was incredible.

"I'll announce my retirement at the press conference," he told Elizabeth Taylor, who was looking down at him from her spot above the fireplace. It seemed to Kit that she was giving him a look of approval. "Maybe I won't tell Sunny beforehand. I'll just do it live at the conference. That way she'll know I really mean it.

He lifted his glass back to Ms. Taylor, the epitome of Old Hollywood. "To retirement, Lizzy! Tomorrow is a whole new day!"

Sunny

*S*unny had a restless night, pretending to sleep but mostly staring at the ceiling. She had never felt awkward sharing the sandy bed with Kit, but in this mansion, she found it impossible to relax. In amongst all the craziness, so many huge things had never been discussed. And they'd never even had sex yet! She had imagined it many times. On the beach, under the stars, warm air on their skin. But here? In this air-conditioned ice palace?

That morning Kit had sat on the side of the bed and explained that he had to go out for most of the day. First to see his PR team for a press conference planning session, then he needed to see his lawyer, and finally, he was headed to the Hotel Luxe to do the damn press conference.

Left to her own devices for the day, Sunny wandered around the house. Dinky and Winky, still overawed by the last few days, played and slept under the watch of Pinky in the corner of the bedroom. Stinky, though, followed Sunny around the house, tiny paws scrabbling on polished hardwood floors and clawing up stuffed brocade sofas.

It's all very tasteful, but I don't recognize it as Kit at all.

When Sunny had learned of Kit's fame and fortune, she had half expected him to have a Hugh Hefner style mansion, with shag-pile carpets, a sunken living room, and a revolving dance floor. That would have almost made more sense than this grand, bleak palace.

She paused to study a framed photo of Kit shaking hands with President Obama. Next to that was a framed tabloid front page, the headline reading—*'Kitson Keeps his Kit On!'*—accompanied by a picture of Kit holding just a fig leaf in front of his genitals. A few steps on, Sunny sucked in her breath, a beautiful glowing painting depicting sharp concrete lines around a glittering blue swimming pool. The colors were almost luminous under subtle, hidden lighting. She'd never seen a David Hockney artwork in real life before, and she lost herself for a while in the strange beauty of the painting.

In a way, it's a painting of Kit's life, she thought—a *beautiful, unnatural, expensive environment. The only softness is the water, and even that is trapped by its surroundings. And if you fall, that incredibly hard boundary is unforgiving...*

"Can I bring you anything, Ma'am?" Tony's voice interrupted her thoughts.

"Oh, please call me Sunny." Sunny didn't think she'd ever been called Ma'am in her life. She added nervously, "If it's not too much trouble, would it be all right to have some toast or a bagel?"

Sunny would have loved to go and fix her own breakfast but wasn't sure of the protocol.

Later, she walked around the gardens, holding a mug of coffee in her hands. A groundskeeper nodded to her as she rounded a corner, finding herself at the sparkling blue swimming pool. Sitting on the concrete edge, she dipped in her feet while watching a pair of house finches dance around the courtyard.

It was too simple to draw an analogy from the birds, she thought—the glossy male with his shiny red chest, and the dumpy female in shades of dull grey and brown. She watched the female gather a tiny twig, probably to shore up the family nest. The male, meanwhile, was swooping onto the cherry tree, enjoying the fruit and the sunshine.

Was she capable of living in these walled gardens?

Sunny sighed. The warm water, comfortingly familiar among all the strangeness, was soothing on her feet. But within a few minutes, a pool boy arrived to sprinkle chemicals into the water, so Sunny listlessly wandered back inside.

I know; I'll watch some TV in Kit's screening room.

The room had a giant projector screen flanked by red velvet curtains. The seats were plush and wide and could tilt back so you could recline while watching a show. Tony showed her how to operate the controls, and Sunny flicked through all the choices on the screen—so many choices, too many choices. One button showed her things that Kit actually owned rather than had the option of streaming. It was mostly a catalogue of Nicky Kitson movies, but then she realized she could watch *Fury of Flames*, take up the story from where Kit had left off at the island. The Winter Princess was still being held captive, so she could finally see how that worked out.

Kicking off her shoes, she reclined her seat and wrapped herself in a blanket, tucking her feet underneath herself. Despite the Californian climate, she was still having trouble keeping warm. As the show played, Sunny was aware she was just killing time.

Killing time before that stupid conference.

Sunny had said that under no circumstances did she want to be involved in the press conference. In the end, Troy had persuaded her to write out a small statement, which he would read on her behalf.

"You will watch it live, though, won't you, babe?" Kit had asked her.

"Yes, I told you I would."

"Great, I really don't want you to miss it. I think you might find it interesting."

Kit was looking more excited than she'd seen him all the time they'd been back.

"What's making you so happy? Being back in the limelight?"

"Hardly! I'm happy to be getting this press conference done so we can then get on with our lives. You will watch it, won't you?" He asked her again.

"Yes! Geez!"

Chapter 30

Kit

Kit's PR office had arranged for the press conference to be held in the ballroom of the Luxe Hotel in Beverly Hills—Invited press only, with limited questions assigned to specific outlets. Troy had also had the PR team develop a PowerPoint presentation, with maps of where the boat exploded, the route they had drifted, and the location of the island.

Kit's eager assistant had also gotten them to include some candid snaps of Kit and Sunny's rescue. Unbeknownst to Kit, the security team had been snapping away during the evacuation. The shelter, the storage shelves, and the fire pit had all been immortalized in pixel form. One of the crew had also captured pics of Sunny on the stretcher and Kit caringly holding her hand.

"Hey Kit, you ready for this?" Troy asked.

"Yeah, I just want it done with."

"The PowerPoint is killer! Wanna check it out?"

"Nah, I trust you," replied Kit.

"OK! Well the press are gonna go nuts, be prepared!"

Outside Hotel Luxe, the streets were lined with paparazzi and onlookers hoping to catch some of the action before and after the conference. Inside the hotel, producers and staff swarmed around busily. Kit was having makeup powdered on his face and his hair tweaked by one team, while another hooked him up to various mics. He didn't even seem to notice all the bodies patting and pulling at him, so used was he to being the eye of a media storm.

A woman with a clipboard pushed into the room.

"Places in 5."

"Check," said Troy, "ready, Nicky?"

"Oh, I'm ready."

*****

Kit stepped out into the ballroom, and the press surged forward, cameras clicking, shouting for his attention. Large TV cameras lined the back of the room and hot lights shone down, making sweat appear on several TV reporters' foreheads and upper lips, which were blotted away by efficient assistants before going live. The venue atmosphere was electric. This was probably the biggest celeb story of the decade; the handsome movie star becomes a real-life hero, risking his life to save a bystander, and then surviving nearly two months on a deserted island.

They were all also hoping that they would learn about a scandal. Had Kit deflowered a virgin? She wasn't underage, but could they spin it that way? Hero stories were great, but anti-hero stories or stories with a bit of deviance were even better. The congregated members of the press rose to their feet, clapping and whooping as Kit entered the room. Troy stepped up to the podium and read a short opening statement and then invited Kit forward to speak.

Sunny

*S*unny reluctantly switched off *Fury of Flames* and turned on the press conference. She watched Kit appear on the TV screen. He seemed relaxed and poised, so different from the detached, awkward Kit of the last few days. *He's totally at home in front of the cameras*, she thought. He also looked mouthwateringly gorgeous, his beard trimmed back to a roguish stubble, hair tamed, skin glossy with lotions and treatments, and the scar on his cheek hidden by make-up. As he put his hand on the podium, she noticed his nails had been manicured. She scanned her own stubby, torn-up fingers. When had that happened?

Kit

*K*it looked at the sea of faces in front of him, paused a beat then, looking straight into the cameras, launched his famous movie-star grin.

"Well, I must say it's nice to see you all again," he said.

The press roared their appreciation.

Like riding a bike.

After that, Kit was off, making them laugh, making them cry. He hooked them with a poignant moment one second and then had them rolling with laughter the next. He'd been doing this a long time and knew exactly how to tell a story and captivate an audience. And, of course, leave them wanting more...

"I'm going to pass you back to Troy now. He's going to explain the geography of my little vacation; I think he knows more about it than I do!"

Troy stepped forward and pressed the remote control. The press oohed and aahed when they saw how far, and for how long, Kit (and Sunny) had drifted at sea. The following photos of the burnt-out supply vessel were also satisfyingly dramatic. Next up, Troy moved on to the rescue. Here is a map of their search grid, here is the base of operations, here is a photo of the crew who actually found Kit.

And here is a photo of Kit, at the moment of rescue.

Kit was stunning—gaunt and shirtless but mahogany brown and muscled. His long hair was blowing in the breeze and his green eyes piercing out of his dark tan. Beside him was Sunny, lying on the stretcher. Sweat had stuck frizzy hair to her ruddy face, and her gleaned glasses were skewed and smudged. The angle of the shot was foreshortened, so her head looked tiny, and the entire bottom half of the picture was taken up by her peeling, chafed thighs, and shins covered in swollen insect bites.

The space between them was only an inch or two in the photo, but, appearance-wise, the space was unfathomably vast.

245

Sunny

iving a howl of anguish, Sunny pulled the blanket over her head. Oh, what a dreadful photo! Taking a deep breath from beneath the covers, Sunny then peeked another look at the screen. Oh no, Kit looked so beautiful and heroic, like the cover of a romance novel, but she looked the complete opposite. Tears pricked at Sunny's eyes. The tabloid writers were probably already planning some hideous headlines:

Beauty and the Beast? *Tarzan and Plain Jane*?

She hadn't been so bothered by her ordinary appearance for a very long time.

Her mom, Michele, was pretty. Her dad Glynn was not; in fact, Glynn and Sunny looked very alike. When Sunny had mooned over glamorous images in magazines or on TV, her mom would hold her hand and remind her about her own mother—Sunny's grandma. She had died when Sunny was seven, but Sunny remembered her easily. The soft laugh, slightly trembling hands that combed her hair, and the long white cane.

Being blind, Grandma had fallen in love with her husband without ever seeing his face. She had never seen her daughter, Michele, or granddaughter, Sunny.

"Fall in love in the dark," she advised anyone who would listen, "you don't need to see anything to know how beautiful a person is."

Michele would remind Sunny of this and that no one should get extra merit just because their features fell in a certain way.

Sunny had fully embraced this philosophy up until now. So, why did this seem different?

It's this place, she thought. *People only care about the outside. What's inside holds no currency.*

Physical appearance was so unimportant on the island, but standing beside Kit in LA, it suddenly became a huge concern. Sunny tried to tell herself not to think like that. *Kit is still Kit. He knows what is important and what isn't. We just need to adjust, that's all.*

Though looking up again at the photo—which the TV station was keeping on the screen for an annoyingly long time—she shuddered. *The island had scrubbed away Kit's superficial surface—but what if the mainland grew it back? On looks alone, it sure seems like we don't belong together...*

Her heart cracked a little further.

Chapter 31
Kit

Thankfully, the cameras went back to the live scene of the press conference, where Kit was looking thunderous. Troy, completely oblivious to Kit's wrath, was telling the press pool that in a minute he would open the floor up to questions.

The questions never happened.

In a totally dramatic crash, the double doors at the back of the ballroom flew open. A stunning girl stood frozen in the doorway. The light silhouetted her figure and made her hair glow like a halo. She was long-legged and slender, but as the clinging emerald green silk dress rippled around her body, it highlighted an unmistakable baby bump, swelling graciously at her midriff.

Having paused long enough for the camera operators to get a good shot, she undulated in a runway model walk, down the aisle and straight toward Kit. Her long blonde hair rippled down her back in perfectly manipulated beachy waves. Opening her arms, she threw herself at him. The reporters were going wild, and cameras were flashing like a disco ball at high speed.

"It's Alexis Ballantine, daughter of the media mogul Rupert Ballantine," the press pool gossip flashed around instantly. She was Kit's girlfriend, and now they had gotten to witness their reunion.

And, by the looks of it, she was preggers! This was money!

Pressing herself up against a stunned Kit, Alexis waved at the press, then turned and kissed Kit full on the mouth. Troy was grinning happily. He knew this would be a hit, and Alexis, who had a new reality TV series starting soon, had been very enthusiastic about the ploy.

Alexis's clear, piercing voice broke through the hubbub, "Nicky darling,"

The clamor of the room instantly quietened.

"I love you so much," pausing she placed a Madonna-like hand on her stomach, "...we love you so much. Thank you for coming home; this little one needs his papa."

Sunny

*S*unny fled up to Kit's bedroom and spun around in panic. She couldn't think; she couldn't breathe. Wave after wave of pain rolled over her.

"Oh Pinky, what should I do?" she implored the little cat, who looked on intently.

Pinky pushed her nose into Sunny's palm, nudged at her and let out a series of mews.

"I should go, right?" Sunny asked the cat.

She couldn't stay here, surrounded by Kit's world. She should leave... and leave immediately. Pinky returned to the kittens and started cleaning Dinky's fur.

"You have to look after your family Pinky, and Kit needs to look after his. It's just the way it is."

The panic left Sunny, and she felt strangely calm. Pinky was right; family first. It was time for Sunny to go.

Now she started to get practical. One of Kit's team had gotten the bank to overnight-express new credit cards, and she had her temporary ID, so flight was possible. Using the iPad that was lying around in Kit's bedroom, she checked her finances. To her surprise, the full amount of the RAMBO residency money was still in her account.

Looking around the room, she saw nothing that was hers to take, except perhaps the cats. But if she ended up at Clive and Denny's, there was no way she could take Pinky and the kittens. Brisket absolutely hated cats.

It wouldn't be right to take them, she thought. *I can't guarantee them anything.* Better for them to stay where they could live the life of luxury—sleeping on fur rugs and having a housekeeper to fetch their kibble. They would have Kit, Alexis, and the baby to be their new family. Sunny hoped that Alexis was a cat person.

But even if she wasn't, they'd have Kit. She trusted Kit to love them.

Having gathered her meager belongings into a tote bag she'd found in Kit's closet, she went downstairs.

Tony had not wanted to call her a taxi without Mr. Nicky's say so, but Sunny had threatened to call the police, accusing him of holding her hostage if he made her stay. So within a few minutes, Sunny was on the road and headed back to the airport.

First, she bought an economy ticket from an agent, then, after going through security, she went to a gift store and bought a large Dodgers sweatshirt and ball cap. The checkout clerk gave a practiced smile and waved a desultory fist in the air, "Go Dodgers!" She gave him a weak smile in return.

As Sunny pulled on the fleecy sweatshirt, it caught on the back of her head, where her shaved patch showed angry red scar tissue. She raked her fingers through her hair to cover the bald spot again, then gave up and just rammed the ball cap onto her head. She could see her reflection in the glass window of a store. Sunny didn't recognize herself.

Her face was mostly the same, just a bit gaunt, with a dappled mixture of golden brown and shredded red instead of her usual pale skin. But it was her eyes that she didn't recognize. Cheesy though it was, Sunny could see they were really the window to her soul. No longer filled with determination, just desolation. Hopeless, not hopeful.

I never thought I'd be like this, she thought. *Driven to despair over a man.* She stared at herself for a while longer, then sighed.

Where was sensible Sunny when you needed her?

Encouraging herself to be less pathetic, she wandered over to the concourse bookstore. Maybe she could get lost in a book for a while? It would be blissful to get out of her head. Sunny walked into the store and straight past the LA-themed books. No, she didn't want to read the History of Hollywood or buy a map of where the stars lived. Sunny was half expecting to see a book with Kit on the cover.

The next aisle over was biographies, and, turning a corner, that's exactly what she did see. *Nicky: The Nicky Kitson Story (unofficial biography).* Kit's green eyes blazed out of the glossy book jacket.

I should probably buy it. I don't really know anything about Nicky Kitson.

A girl squeezed past Sunny to pick the book up. "Oh! I love him!" The girl turned to her friend, "I nearly died when he disappeared."

"Right?" said her friend. "Can you imagine being that girl who was with him, lucky b-word."

The first girl nodded vigorously. "I'd be a damsel in distress, with Nicky Kitson as my savior, any flipping day of the week!" Hugging the book to her chest, she headed toward the cash register.

Sunny imagined waiting for Kit to be her island savior. It was so ridiculous she nearly laughed aloud. Then her smile fell off her face. She watched the girls pouring over some photos in the biography.

It's like Kit belongs to everybody, she thought, *everybody apart from me.*

Rounding another corner, she halted in front of a display titled, *Classics For Young Readers.* The book that was front and center was *The Incredible Journey.* A summary from the bookseller was taped to the shelf.

Staff Pick! A classic story of bravery and ingenuity. Three animals find their way home by sticking together and never leaving anyone behind.

Sunny's face crumpled.

"Are you OK, miss?" A sales clerk asked as fat tears fell down her cheeks.

"I'm fine. I'm just homesick," she sniffed.

The clerk handed her a tissue. "Are you a long way from home?"

Sunny pictured Weaver Creek, then Seattle. Next, she thought of the island, and then finally Kit's house.

She didn't actually know where her home was.

"You're far from home?" the clerk repeated.

"Yes," replied Sunny quietly. "Very, very far."

Chapter 32
Kit

*K*it was livid and determined to fire Troy on the spot. The end of the press conference had been a farce. Kit had stalked off the stage, leaving Troy and Alexis smiling and chatting with the press.

Mattie had come running after him. "I didn't know anything about this, I promise."

"Yeah," snarled Kit. "Pretty good for business, though, right?"

"Well, yes," conceded Mattie, "you'll be front page for weeks."

Clenching his fists and making a real effort not to punch Mattie, Kit waited icily for Alexis and Troy to leave the podium. He hissed to a nearby security guard to bring them straight to him as he paced up and down in the green room. The pair were definitely looking a little sheepish when they entered, but Alexis put on a bright smile.

"Darling!"

Kit ignored her and turned to his assistant. "Troy, you are fired. Get out before I wring your neck."

Troy spluttered, but Kit didn't allow him to say another word. Instead, turning back to Alexis, he said more gently, "Are you really pregnant?"

Alexis was silent and flushed prettily.

Troy, who wasn't going to take all the blame, sneered. "It's a pillow stuffed up her dress, her idea, not mine."

Alexis whirled round and shrieked at him. "Liar! You said that it would be the perfect dramatic conclusion to the press conference!" Turning back to Kit, she opened her eyes wide.

"Darling, I'm so sorry if I upset you, but we could make a real baby if you like. *People Magazine* said they would give us a huge spread about decorating our nursery."

"Are you both completely mad?" shouted Kit. His whole body was buzzing with anger.

Count to ten, he told himself.

If he didn't get a grip, Troy was going to be thrown through the green room window.

This is insanity.

Troy was making chill out gestures with his hands. "Oh, come on, Nicky, you know how the game is played. Fake an engagement, whirlwind marriage, or pregnancy, and your headline stock will quadruple."

Kit closed his eyes as Troy continued.

"We are capitalizing on the shipwreck story, got to keep the momentum going. Come on, Nicky..."

Kit stood in the center of the room, fists bunched and heart racing. What must Sunny be thinking?

He strode over to the door and flung it open.

"Hey!" he yelled to a group of nervous-looking security and producers hovering in the hallway. "Bring the car. Get me home now!"

He turned back to look at Troy and Alexis. A small part of him knew it wasn't really their fault. He had changed and they had not. He didn't want to play these Hollywood bullshit games anymore.

But the game was afoot.

Footage of 'Nicky and Alexis, Back Together?' was spinning around the internet before he'd even got back into the Range Rover.

Sunny

*S*unny had bought a one-way ticket to Seattle. That seemed the logical place to go. *That's where this story started, so it's fitting that's where I go when it ends*, she thought. Huddled in her cramped middle seat, she flipped through the channels of the in-flight entertainment screen. *Fury of Flames* was playing.

Sunny didn't have any earphones, so she just sat and watched a tiny Kit on the tiny screen. Fur was draped around his shoulders, and a scrap of tartan hung off his hips. She didn't even realize she was crying until her seatmate nudged her and passed some tissues. People are so kind, she thought, welling up even more.

In the scene playing, Kit was wrestling with some scary white creature and then plunged a crystal dagger into its heart. *This is where the snow leopard comes running back to him, the curse broken*, she thought. Seconds later, she watched a tiny Kit look up with amazement as his leopard friend came bounding up.

I miss Pinky and the kittens so much. I hope they are OK. And oh, I miss Kit so much too—Island Kit. I miss Island Kit so much, she thought desperately. Sunny had cried so much her temples pounded with dehydration. She touched the slowly scarring mass on the back of her head.

Or there would be hell Toupée.

She thought about her and Kit rolling around with laughter in the island hospital.

I guess I'll need to grow scar tissue on my heart as well, she thought.

Kit

Kit was fuming. How dare Tony let Sunny go! Tony protested that he could hardly have kept her a prisoner. Kit knew he was being unreasonable but couldn't stop himself. "Call the cab firm and find out where they took her!" he yelled. Kit had already decided she'd be headed north, either to Weaver Creek or to Seattle. Tony told him the cab had taken Sunny to LAX.

Now I just have to find out what flight she took...

But after a fruitless hour on the phone, Kit found that, no matter how easily heroes could track down fugitives in the movies, in real life one couldn't bribe their way to get passenger information out of a booking agent.

"I'm sorry, Sir, we cannot give you a passenger manifesto. It's just impossible."

Kit was at an impasse. She didn't have a cell phone he could track, and he had no idea what her email address was, let alone her password.

He tossed it over in his head. Where would she go? Weaver Creek would be comforting and homey, but in Seattle she had Clive and Dennie. He found the details of the bagel shop online and called the number.

A bored-sounding teenager answered. No, Clive and Dennie were not there. No, he wouldn't give out their home phone number or address. Yeah, sure, he was Nicky Kitson, the kid said, then said he had to go 'cause Elvis had just walked in. The kid hung up.

Kit cursed but then remembered his team had been in touch with Clive and Dennie soon after they had been rescued. Finally getting a personal number for them, he managed to speak to Dennie.

Clive and Dennie had been very agitated by Kit's call and the news of Sunny's flight. They had seen the press conference but had no idea that Sunny was romantically involved with Nicky Kitson. It was troubling to them, especially with all this drama with Alexis and Sunny having a head injury.

After a muted conversation, Dennie told Kit, "If she gets in touch, we will pass a message on, but we won't tell you where she is if she asks us not to."

In the background, Brisket howled in agreement.

Kit was a little frustrated but also pleased that Sunny had such loyal and protective friends.

His next call was to Weaver Creek, where he managed to get Andrea on the phone. A very similar conversation followed to the one he'd just had with Clive and Dennie. Andrea hadn't spoken to Sunny that day, but if Sunny turned up on her doorstep, she would be welcomed with open arms. Kit asked her if she would let him know immediately if Sunny called her.

"I will, because I think it's only fair that you know she is safe," said Andrea. "But don't think I'll let you speak to her or see her if she doesn't want to..."

What to do? Not willing to second-guess himself, Kit made decisions. He would send his favorite security guy, Jason, on the next flight to Seattle to see if she went to the bagel shop. *And I'll charter a plane to Redding. I might even beat Sunny if she is headed there!*

"Tony!" Kit yelled.

His housekeeper came running." Sir?"

"I'm going to find her—you take care of the cats."

"Of course," said Tony, looking poker-faced.

Kit paused and looked at Tony properly. Kit knew he had been an asshole to the man. It wasn't his fault that everything had gone wrong. "I'm sorry, Tony," he said. "I shouldn't have snapped at you. I would be very grateful if you could take good care of the cats."

Tony unwound a little, his face softening as he looked at his distraught boss. Remembering the last time he'd been given very specific instructions to treat guests like royalty, Tony replied, "I'll treat them with more reverence than young Archie, when the Sussexs come to visit."

Kit put a hand on his shoulder. "Thank you."

He slid back into the Range Rover as the security guards gathered around, awaiting instruction." Jason, you get to Seattle and stake out Clive and Dennie's," he said, then added "...and someone make sure there's a rental car waiting for me at Redding."

Leaning forward to his driver, he then told him to step on it. "Burbank—now!"

Chapter 33

Sunny

*L*anding in Seattle, Sunny's thoughts were a complete muddle. Had she done the right thing by running away? She had acted on instinct, not with her usual methodical nature. Seeing a payphone on the wall, she made her way over to it and dialed Andrea's number from memory.

"Honey, come home, let me look after you," Andrea had cried.

Andrea's sympathy nearly undid Sunny completely.

"No, Andrea. I just wanted you to know I was safe. I'm in Seattle. I'm going to take some time to figure out what's next."

When Andrea told Sunny that Kit had been in contact with her, Sunny's knees went weak. Sunny didn't want to talk to him. She thought Kit might feel obliged to stick with her, and she had to free him from their bond. He had to focus on Alexis and the baby. The baby was the most important part of the equation.

If she spoke to him, she knew she wouldn't have the strength to resist going back, so she had to flee. She had to flee so he could be free.

If he called Andrea, he'd probably think to call Clive and Dennie too. So, she had to avoid going there, but if she couldn't go there, where should she go? For once in her life, she had a little money and she could make some choices. But where to go? Where?

She slumped down on a concourse bench, completely at a loss. Her head hurt, and she was tired and hungry. *Well, I'll get a motel for the night. Then I can figure things out tomorrow*, she finally decided.

Kit

The plane rose above the clouds, and sunshine poured through the small windows. Kit blinked in the light. How could he be without her? The very sun that was in the sky every single day reminded him of her. She was his warmth, his light. If he couldn't find her and convince her to be with him, he would never have a sunny day again.

Kit tried to close his eyes and rest, but it was useless. He looked at his watch. An hour till they landed in Redding.

That hour had almost passed when Kit's phone rang. He looked at the number, heart pounding when he saw it was Andrea.

"Yes?"

"Hello Mr. Kitson. I'm calling to let you know that Sunny is safe," said Andrea's husky voice.

"She's with you?" Kit asked anxiously, "is she in Weaver Creek?"

"No, no, she's not with me," Andrea replied.

"Do you know where she is then?" asked Kit.

There was a pause. Kit could hear chatting and music in the background.

Just tell me!

Kit tried to stifle his impatience.

The pause continued. A voice in the background yelled out for a refill. "One minute..." Andrea yelled back.

"Look, you wanted to know she was safe. She told me she was; that's all I've got for you. I've got to go." Andrea abruptly hung up.

If Sunny hadn't gone to Weaver Creek, then he needed to get to Seattle.

Seattle.

Seattle was a huge city, and Jason had only the bagel shop and the art school as starting points. Kit would get a proper private investigator out there to find her if this didn't work. His sweet, no-nonsense girl was being surprisingly full of nonsense.

259

No, that wasn't fair. He should have known that this was going to be way too much for her. The Hollywood world took no prisoners—then Alexis faking a pregnancy in front of the whole world and that unflattering photo. He hoped he would soon have the chance to tell her the baby thing was all made up and also tell her how precious she was. The only thing in the world Kit wanted was to hold Sunny in his arms again.

Sunny

*E*verything relied on you having a smartphone, thought Sunny. She wanted to find a cheap motel and then take a taxi there, and the easiest way to do that was online. Glancing around, she saw a stand selling pay-as-you-go phones—thank goodness! And thank goodness for her bank balance. This was the most money she had spent in one day, ever.

The phone salesman eyed her maroon face, baggy Dodgers outfit, and puffy eyes curiously, but she was soon in possession of a smart-ish phone. *That phone is just like me,* she thought, *not as smart as all the other phones around it.*

Kit

*K*it checked his phone again. No new messages. The plane had landed and the pilot had been very unobliging and not just taken off again to Seattle. He said he had a charter to go straight back to LA.

Kit had tried waving his platinum credit card around, but it turned out the next charter passenger was equally loaded. The small Redding airport couldn't drum up another charter plane for eight hours.

Damn, I can't just sit here and twiddle my thumbs.

260

Kit decided to take a rental car and drive himself. Peddle to the metal, he could get there by 2 A.M.

Sunny

*S*unny sat in her first-floor Motel 6 room, close to the Seattle airport. She had fond memories of these kinds of motels.

Once a year, her dad would go to Susanville to re-key areas of the prison. Sunny and her mom would go along as well to make it a family vacation. While her dad worked, they'd swim in the pool then flick through TV channels, her mom zeroing in shows like *Friends*, then giving Sunny control of the remote so she could watch *Rugrats* or *The Wild Thornberries*. When her dad came home, Sunny would draw while her mom heated burritos in the microwave. After supper, she would fall asleep listening to her parents murmuring as they shared their day.

Sunny had no plans to swim or watch *Rugrats*, but she did get a frozen burrito from the 7/11, along with a carton of cheap Franzia wine to drown her sorrows with. She'd thought about drinking the whole thing, but her head was hurting.

I should probably limit myself to just a couple of glasses, she thought.

But in the end, she'd hardly taken a couple of sips when she passed out, exhausted.

Chapter 34

Kit

*K*it got onto the highway and started to race north on Interstate 5. He'd only gotten a few miles when a line of flashing lights indicated an accident ahead.

Damn it!

The stream of cars ground to a halt. Groaning, Kit pulled out his phone and googled the stoppage. A semi had jack-knifed. Estimated time until the road was clear again—3 hours!

Ugh. There was no way to get around the blocked road at all. Maybe something was trying to tell him something, trying to tell him not to go to Seattle?

If he was going to have a sign from the universe, he would appreciate it if it was nice and obvious, please.

His phone buzzed with an incoming text.

It was from Jason.

"Boss, overheard bagel dudes talking. One said Sunny had arrived in Seattle."

Kit instantly pressed a button and called his security guy back.

"Yeah, boss, I'm like having coffee and eating like my twentieth bagel here. Kinda turned into wallpaper, you know? Anyway, the short one, maybe Dennie, came scurrying in and said Sunny had called and she was in Seattle."

"Did you hear where she was headed? Was she going to the bagel shop?"

"I couldn't tell, I think they had spotty service or something. The soon back call to her expecting is one short."

Yes! Finally something to go on!

Unlike this road.

Traffic moved forward another few yards and then stopped again, but now that Kit had a bead on Sunny, he was moderately less frustrated. Not quite que sera sera territory, but majorly less despairing.

Slow and steady wins the race!

He felt sure Sunny's dad would appreciate that sentiment.

Sunny's dad.

Kit wondered if Sunny's dad would appreciate him.

I wish I could have met him, met them both. Got their blessing.

The traffic crawled a few feet more. As Kit finally rounded a bend, he could see a road sign ahead of him. It indicated that the next exit was for Weaver Creek.

Weaver Creek!

Weaver Creek, 20 miles.

Seeing the turn to Sunny's old home town gave him a further lift in spirits.

The traffic stopped again. He checked his phone. Still three hours until the road was clear. Kit's car was now stationary at the exit to Weaver Creek. He went back and forth in his mind for a minute, then swung the wheel.

Why the hell not?

He wasn't going forward, so he might as well go back in time, and take a look at Sunny's origins.

After turning off the highway, Kit raced along the winding mountain roads, arriving at the Weaver Creek sign 30 minutes later. Entering the town, he slowed and drove down the main street. First he passed the elementary school, then the bar, then—what the! A Bigfoot Museum!

She didn't mention that, he chuckled to himself.

At the end of the street there was a homely looking diner, the lit windows showed a packed house.

Must be where Andrea works, where Sunny's mom worked.

He gave Andrea a mental wave.

It only took a few minutes to drive all the way through the small town. After the last house, he pulled the car over to the side of the road.

263

He got out and inhaled deeply. This is where Sunny had grown up. The mountain air was pine-scented, and he could hear a rushing river, the Trinity River, flowing somewhere off to his right. These were the smells and sounds of her childhood. It smelled and sounded great.

OK. Now I go to Seattle. This felt good. It was a good idea to come here.

His phone rang again.

Jason! Yes!

"What you got for me?" Kit asked.

"Sorry boss. She called back and, from what I can gather, said she wasn't going to stay with them. They don't know where she's gonna crash. She could be anywhere in Seattle."

Feeling disappointed and not a little exhausted, Kit got back into the car. As he reversed to turn around, he noticed another, smaller road. It had a sign posted at the entrance. A sign to the cemetery.

Well, I asked for a sign.

Kit drove the short way up a winding gravel road to the top of a hill. He got out, and standing next to the car wondered where her parents lay. In the silent graveyard, Kit spoke out into the dark.

"I'll take care of her, I promise. I won't give up until we are together and safe."

For a second, he thought he heard the sound of a violin drifting on the wind.

Kit shivered, then putting his foot to the floor, he once again raced along the dark roads

Sunny

*S*unny had fallen asleep with the television on. She woke when the late-night movie had transitioned into breakfast news, and outside, the sky was early morning grey.

"And today's top entertainment news is still the dramatic rescue of Nicky Kitson and Seattle art student Sunny Evans," a perky presenter announced.

Again, the newscaster showed the photo of Sunny being taken off the island. She winced.

Yeah, that's sooo entertaining.

The news cut back to yesterday's press conference footage, and Sunny couldn't look away. She reached out a finger wanting to stroke the contours of Kit's beautiful face.

Picking up the not-very-smart phone from the nightstand, she was filled with a massive urge to call him. Maybe she should? No, no, she had to make a clean break. And anyway, she didn't have his phone number or email address.

I have absolutely no plan. I can't keep spinning out.

Sunny thought maybe taking a little action would make her feel better. Doing something was better than doing nothing.

Picking up the phone again, she wearily logged into her own email account. The inbox—usually a mix of art supply offerings and beagle memes—was overflowing. Media outlets of every kind were trying to get in touch with her. Also, as she scrolled, she saw she had several emails from Clive and Dennie, her old friend Betsy, and another couple from Dr. Stokes and RAMBO.

379 unread emails.

My inbox is as out of control as the rest of my life.

Though it pained her not to open, respond to, or junk her messages, she just couldn't do it. Sunny lay the phone back on the nightstand and then lay back herself.

Maybe I should go back to the 7/11 for more supplies and then just stay here indefinitely. The Motel 6 could be my new home.

That was as good a plan as she could muster.

Kit

*K*t arrived in Seattle just as the sky was beginning to lighten. He drove straight to an up-market hotel. He'd called Mattie from the road and had him arrange for the Presidential Suite to be waiting for him. Mattie had told him that this kind of work wasn't really in his wheelhouse, and Kit should not have fired Troy.

"Yeah, no. Let's not go there. Thanks for organizing," replied Kit.

Mattie had reluctantly done Kit's bidding. Kit was hoping for a couple hours sleep in his palatial suite, but it was not to be. Eventually putting on the TV, he flicked through the channels to find something to watch.

Tom Hanks, my old Castaway *pal!*

Kit quickly realized the movie playing was not *Castaway* but the last few scenes of *Sleepless in Seattle*.

Shaking his head at the irony, Kit ordered some coffee and watched the happy ending, hoping some of the energy from the movie would seep into his and Sunny's own love story and give them a happy ending as well.

After the movie ended, Kit called his team.

No one had made any further progress in finding Sunny, so he checked his horoscope app, seeing if the stars could guide him.

"You are apt to feel a major shift this week. All will go well if you listen to your intuition and make a plan—the answers are obvious if you just look around".

Roger that, Starry Susan, thought Kit.

This time last week, he and Sunny had been on the island, in their bubble of blissful love. Talk about a major shift.

Sunny

*I*n the morning, Sunny dragged herself out of the hotel room to restock on supplies from the 7/11. These included an egg salad sandwich, a box of cheerios, some milk, and a family-sized packet of Chips Ahoy. It was the comfort food of her childhood. The only thing missing was one of her Mom's famous casseroles.

I was going to make Kit Chicken Divine.

She cried her way through the morning and spent the afternoon eating cookies and sketching. The hotel room had a scratchpad and complementary Motel 6 pens to draw with, just as it had when she was a child. She drew the beach, the shelter, her studio. She drew Wilson and the waterhole. She drew the kittens and the crashed jungle plane. She drew the dolphin and his friend splashing in the starlight.

Then she drew Kit, his beautiful face lit up with pleasure as he tickled Pinky's fat tummy. She drew him floating in the waterhole. *Like Ophelia amongst the lilies*, she thought dramatically, *except I'm the one who is dead.*

She couldn't remember which play Ophelia had been in. Kit would know—he knew all things Shakespearean. He'd probably start quoting lines in his "Shakespeare" voice and then make some pun about Ophelia and lilies.

Sunny tried to imagine what the joke would be—but failed.

"His sense of humor is terrible," she told the grubby motel room, her tears splashing down on the little ink drawings, "and I love him so much."

She flopped back on the swirled, shag-pile carpet.

"But he's not mine to love."

Chapter 35
Kit

s Kit made a hundred calls from his hotel suite, he began to feel hopeful. He had a plan. He was listening to his intuition. But would it work? It had to! He called his agent, furiously outlining what he needed, Mattie reluctantly agreed. Kit's Hollywood PR firm had been in touch with their Seattle counterparts, and a representative would be joining Kit shortly. Jason, the security guy, recalled from bagel shop duty, met him at the hotel with a greasy paper bag full of warm rugelach. The sweet dough energized him. Things were falling into place!

Kit paced the suite, impatient for the new PR people and the extra security to turn up. He had to make sure everything was being organized in the manner he'd requested. He looked at his watch, not long to go!

Sunny

unny had found a rerun of *Friends*.
Oh Mom, I wish you were here.
It was the one with Phoebe's wedding. She was in the middle of getting married to Paul Rudd. At the moment he told Phoebe she was wonderfully weird, Sunny started crying again.

Kit thought I was wonderfully weird.

There was even a dog at the TV wedding.

And we had the cats...

After a moment, she said out loud, "I'm an idiot."

I shouldn't have run away. I should have stayed and listened to what Kit had to say. Maybe we could have stayed friends. Having Kit as my friend would be better than having no Kit in my life.

She spoke to the perky people on the television, "I could have been the fun aunty, maybe babysit for him and Alexis."

Sunny gulped. That wouldn't be too terrible, would it?

Kit

The conference room in the Crown Plaza Hotel was almost completely packed. Seattle's journalists, busily licking pencils and checking recording devices, thought they were in scoop nirvana. One of the Seattle PR team told Kit the last time they had any juicy celebrity stuff happening was when Sir Mix-A-Lot, one of the few famous Seattle residents, admitted that he didn't actually like big butts.

Kit nodded distractedly and continued to try and calm his breathing.

Sunny

Sunny rolled around on the bed to switch off *Friends*, stupid Phoebe and Mike, and flicked through the channels to find something else. The news channel had another segment about Nicky Kitson's rescue. She knew she was torturing herself but couldn't stop herself from watching it. The daytime TV hosts were talking about the shambolic press conference in LA.

"Yesterday's press conference certainly left more questions than it answered; don't you agree, Samantha!"

A blonde, tanned host trilled back. "It sure does, Buck. Are Nicky and Alexis Ballantine engaged as well as expecting? And the way the press conference closed down, right after her dramatic entrance, has kept us all guessing...daddy-to-be-Nicky is keeping his gorgeous lips pretty tightly closed."

"Well, it sure is difficult to learn of impending fatherhood on live TV, in front of millions of viewers no less. To give us an overview of the psychology of unexpected fatherhood, we have our favorite doctor joining us. Welcome to the afternoon show, Dr. Buzz."

Sunny muted the TV.

Kit

Kit was waiting to enter the conference room. The PR firm had done an excellent job, and the room was completely packed. He ran his hand through his hair and checked his inside pocket to make sure he had everything he needed.

Sunny

Sunny glanced grumpily back at the TV and, sighing, un-muted it. She guessed she'd listen to what Dr. Buzz had to say. He was rambling on about how the genetics of beautiful people were very likely to make a beautiful offspring. Well, duh, thought Sunny, an Alexis and Kit baby would be the most beautiful baby in the world, outshining every Gerber baby there'd ever been. She was about to mute again when Dr. Buzz was abruptly cut off by Samantha in the studio.

"And we have breaking developments in the Nicky Kitson story. We are now going to cut live to another press conference. Nicky has called a surprise second press conference, and we are all on the edge of our seats!"

The scene cut to a glamorous reporter standing in a crowded hotel room.

"Thanks, Samantha. I'm Rabbia Kazi with KING 5," the reporter said, looking a little nervous. "As you can see, I'm standing here in the conference room at the Crowne Plaza Airport Hotel in South Seattle." She gestured behind her. "Any minute now, Nicky Kitson is expected to join us on stage to share, as his press release put it, 'some extremely important and personal news.'"

"Thanks, Rabbia." The show host turned to her partner, "So Buck, what do you think? This has got to be about the baby, right? Maybe it's a marriage announcement..."

Cutting Samantha off, the scene returned to Seattle. Camera shots zoomed past Rabbia to focus on the front of the room as Kit stepped onto the small raised platform. Still a dark golden brown from the island sun, but with gray shadows under his eyes and a mouth that had settled in a firm line. Sunny couldn't look away from the TV screen. *He doesn't look well,* she thought. *Oh poor Kit, I hope Alexis will take care of him properly.*

Chapter 36

Kit

*S*tanding at the podium, Kit surveyed the rows of journalistic eyes beadily staring at him. *Like a venue of vultures, clacking their beaks in preparation to feed off my carcass,* he thought. The press edged nearer, quivering in anticipation as their recording devices and cameras whirred.

Kit took a deep breath. "Thanks for joining me today, and thank you to the hotel for accommodating this conference at short notice. I have a few things that need to be said, so if you'll listen first, I'll take questions after."

A hush—as expectant as Alexis wasn't—fell over the room.

"Firstly, I'm announcing that as of today, I am completely retiring from acting. I've bowed out of *Plague World* and also the Bond franchise. The studios have been very gracious, and I'm sure that we are all excited to find out who is going to be filling those roles."

Murmurs flew around the room but were immediately shushed. If this was the first announcement, what was the next?

"And secondly, I want to share the news that I recently got married to the most wonderful girl in the world."

Sunny

*S*unny looked up in despair. Kit had married Alexis, and together they were going to be King and Queen of Hollywood, with a troop of beautiful babies.

Kit continued. "And I am retiring to a location, which I'm not going to share with you all for obvious reasons..."

Sunny could hear the journalists in the room chuckle.

Then Kit pulled a slightly battered flower from his pocket. He laid it on the podium.

"...and my wife and I are going to have three babies. I am going to retrain as a park ranger and change my name to Roger."

The TV screen split in two, and Buck and Samantha, the daytime show hosts immediately started talking about the scene unfolding in the Seattle hotel.

Was this another Joaquin Phoenix thing? Nervous breakdown? Method acting stunt? Then their mics were cut off as Kit began to speak again.

Sunny was blinking rapidly, and her mouth had dropped open.

"And now," Kit said into his microphone, "to the main reason I called this conference. There has been a little miscommunication. Alexis Ballantine is not pregnant. That was just a misguided prank on her behalf, no big deal." He said it lightly, as though he had found the whole thing slightly amusing. "And in all the craziness of the last few days, I have actually mislaid my wonderful, practical, ridiculous new wife."

He picked up the flower and looked directly into the camera.

"So Sunny-bach, I have your flower here. Can you please come home, so I can tuck it behind your right ear?"

"Uhhgh...uhh...wah..."

Sunny made a series of unintelligible noises and sank down on the floor in a nest of her scattered drawings. She looked back up to the TV screen that still showed an image of Kit holding out a Tiare flower.

"Me?" she whispered, "it's me?"

Half crying and half laughing, she picked up a drawing of Kit and kissed it furiously until her lips were blue with cheap ink

Kit

O ne thing Kit had not thought of was how exactly Sunny could get in touch with him. The hotel was fielding hundreds of calls from people claiming they knew where Sunny was, or indeed, claiming to be Sunny. The outside of the Crowne Plaza was now ringed several paparazzi deep, which made it near impossible for anyone to enter or exit. Security had been placed at the door, and only registered guests would be admitted.

Damn, thought Kit, *I did not use PPPPP. Sunny's dad would have some stern words for me screwing this up so royally.*

Sunny

O n the other end of the equation, Sunny was equally stumped. At first, she'd thought to check out of her motel room and run straight to Kit, but then she realized she didn't know where he was to run to. A quick Google search on her new semi-smart phone told her that Kit was at a hotel only half a mile from where she was now. Looking at the live footage of the hotel, completely under siege by journalists, she realized she'd have to phone the hotel and tell him where she was.

Sunny, the PPPPP mantra, flooding back into her brain, jotted down all the things she wanted to say to Kit on her phone call. She knew she would be tongue-tied if she didn't.

1. She loved him.
2. She was sorry for running away.
3. He didn't have to give up acting if he didn't want to.
4. Was he 100% positive that Alexis wasn't pregnant?
5. Who was looking after the cats?

Kit

*K*it paced up and down, growling in frustration. He'd already spoken to a dozen "Sunnys." Each time his heart expanding in anticipation, only to deflate like a sad, week-old party balloon when the person on the phone was a phony, a journalist, or in one case a deranged sounding woman who said she'd "take him out for good" if Kit stopped acting.

After that experience, he'd got Security Jason to start screening the incoming calls, but he had to find a way to make it easier for Sunny to get in touch with him. She didn't know his private cell number or email address. And if he publicly told her where to meet him, the press would overrun them, just like he was at the hotel.

Pulling the penthouse curtains aside, he could see the rows of news vans and heaving masses of onlookers below him. Someone noticed the curtain twitch, and within seconds every lens was pointed his way. Kit tried to yank the curtain back into place but only managed to rip it from the runner, exposing him even further.

Sighing, he sat on the sofa and put his head in his hands. If only Sunny were here, she'd figure out a way. He needed her so badly. He thought about the bedtime story Sunny had told him on the island. *I'm like Tao, trying to find my best friends. I get so near, but there are still stumbling blocks everywhere.* Kit wished he was back on the beach where everything was simple, Sunny laying in the crook of his arm, kittens tumbling around on the sand, and Pinky taking a well-earned nap. He did miss the cats, and that made him even sadder when he thought how anguished Sunny would be, separated from the furry family.

What should I do, Pinky? he thought to himself.

Hmm, that gave him an idea.

Chapter 37
Sunny

*S*unny had tried to get through to the hotel, but the line was consistently busy. Every time, heart pounding, she dialed the numbers, she was met by the busy signal. Switching off the phone again, Sunny looked in the spotty motel mirror. Her face was blotchy from crying, and her skin was peeling off in drifts. The new glasses that had been express-delivered to LAX were a little too large for her face and made her eyes bulge like a startled frog. Her shoulder-length hair was a nice color now, and with plenty of conditioner, the dreads had come out. But yanked back into a ponytail, you couldn't see the shimmers of gold, just the bald patch of scar tissue.

Sunny considered for a moment running out to get some makeup and hair products, but she squared her shoulders, dismissing the idea. No, he liked her as she was. She wasn't going to pretend she was something she wasn't. Picking up her cell again, she emptied the warm wine box into a plastic beaker—just like the cups that she and Kit had drunk from on the island, she noticed—and hit redial. The phone rang, and a receptionist put her through to a bored-sounding man, who definitely wasn't Kit.

"Right, so you're Sunny Evans, sure you are. Just got to check though; can you tell me the names of the three kittens..."

What on earth! She reeled off their names, quite confused.

A stunned silence on the other end of the line was broken with a thud as the phone was dropped onto the floor. "Booossssssss—we got her!" she heard the man yell. In an instant, he was back on the line with her. "Stay on the line; don't hang up. He's coming. Oh geez, don't hang up, please; he'll kill me."

Sunny laughed out loud, "I promise I won't hang up."

Kit

*I*n the presidential suite, as the maintenance guy was re-attaching the curtains, Kit's head was pressed to the phone receiver. He was laughing and crying at the same time.

"My little darling, where are you? Let me come and get you." He ached to put his arms around her and know that she was safe.

Sunny explained she was at a Motel 6 close by.

"So close! OK stay put."

"I will, I promise. But Kit, are you sure about all this? Giving up acting, your Hollywood life?"

"100% babe. All I need is you and the cats."

"Oh, sweet babies, I miss them. Are they with you?"

"No, I left them with Tony. He swore he would treat them like royalty..."

"Well that seems reasonable," she replied. "So now just come and get me so we can get back to them, OK?"

"I'll be there in a flash."

Setting the receiver back on the hotel phone, Kit felt a rush of warmth flood his body. She was so close. In a matter of minutes, they would be back together. But how could he get to the motel with the press following him? He could go and get her in a convoy with his security, but he didn't think turning up at the motel like that would be the best way to reunite with Sunny. All that kind of thing was the problem, not the solution.

Mustn't scare her away again!

"There must be a way to get out of here discreetly." Kit puzzled over the problem.

Sunny and Kit

*S*unny looked up as a soft knock sounded on the motel room door. Through the peephole, she could see someone in overalls and a hat that read "Maintenance." She glanced nervously around the room at the scattered, tear-stained sketches, junk food wrappers, and empty plastic cups. She hoped she wasn't going to get in trouble for trashing the room! Taking the chain off the door, she looked at the floor, embarrassed, and stammered, "I'm so sorry about the mess. I was just going to tidy it up—I promise."

"What would your father say about this disorganization?" grinned Kit, pulling off his hat and then pulling her into his arms.

She shrieked and dissolved herself into his arms. "Oh Kit, I'm so sorry I ran away. I love you so much."

"Silly goose, it's me that is sorry. Everything was crazy. No wonder you split. But don't ever do that again, you hear!" He looked down at her swollen red eyes, peeling nose, and lopsided glasses and felt whole again.

"I won't. I don't ever want to be apart from you," sniffed Sunny, then, "I have to ask again, just to be sure, you are truly 100% sure about giving up acting? You don't have to..."

"I truly, truly do." Kit said firmly. "I am truly, truly over Hollywood." He tucked the now extremely crumbled Tiare flower behind her right ear. "I don't want the spotlight anymore. All I want is to be in the sunlight with you." He pulled at the strings on her Dodgers sweatshirt, "you, my art-full dodger, are everything that I want. We are going to live happily ever after, surrounded by cats and children."

Sunny beamed, a huge grin creasing her still burned cheeks. "You're not serious about being a park ranger, though? I don't want to hurt your feelings, but I don't think it's really in your wheelhouse."

Kit raised an eyebrow, "That's a relief. I wasn't wild about the idea. How about I chuck Roger completely out of the window."

"Yes, please," Sunny said, burying herself against him. "I don't want Roger; I just want you."

"Just me," agreed Kit. "And by the way, I'm chucking Nicky Kitson out of the window too. From now on I am just Kit, through and through."

He suddenly had a thought, "Or...how does Kit Evans sound?"

"Amazing," she giggled.

Holding her tight, he kissed her hair. "OK, that's settled! So, now we can do anything we want, Sunny. Anything. Go anywhere, do anything. What shall we do?"

Sunny pulled his head down and pressed her lips onto his. Her heart sang, as the kiss went on and on and on. Finally, pulling away, she gave him a smoldering look.

"You said we could do anything?"

Kit nodded.

Sunny glanced behind her at the motel room, then turned back to him.

"Let's go see the cats."

Getting into a large rented SUV, Kit reached across and clicked in her seat belt. "Would you mind if we took a couple of detours on our way back to LA?"

Sunny raised an eyebrow, waiting to hear what was coming next.

Kit coughed, "A-hem, well, I thought we might drive all the way back, take the scenic route. Andrea would love to see you, and when I did a mad dash from Weaver Creek to Redding, I saw this property, set back on a mountain. The view must be amazing."

He held both her hands. "And you know what else it had? A *For Sale* sign..."

Kit put his hands on the steering wheel.

"Just one more stop before we head south," he said. "We need some road snacks."

Sunny raised an eyebrow.

279

"And I've heard that Clive and Dennie's have the best bagels in town..."

Want a bonus scene from Marooned?

Sign up for my newsletter and get a sneak peek of Kit's last weekend before he heads off to the island:

Get your bonus scene here!

Book Two Coming soon:

To stay up to date on all Lost and Found Series news, subscribe to my newsletter:

Subscribe Here
https://bit.ly/3QDno3D

Please make sure to stalk me:

Facebook: https://bit.ly/3Piocvd

Instagram: https://bit.ly/3wnpCfl

Twitter: https://bit.ly/3Nc1nHM

TikTok: https://bit.ly/3evQMLW

My Website: https://www.louisejanewatson.com/

About the Author

Louise Jane Watson

Born and raised in the UK, Louise Jane Watson moved to the Pacific Northwest almost two decades ago. Over the years, she has worked at a clown school, founded an all-girl, cow-punk band and raised three kids. With a BFA in Fine Art, her artwork has been shown in museums and galleries, both nationally and internationally. Her passions include conducting extensive research projects, reading survival stories, and living room dance parties.

C

Acknowledgements

A lot of people have helped make this book come to life and I am so grateful for their time and their feedback.

Thank you to my beautiful beta-readers; Melia Donovan, Denell Graham, Ellie Peck, Kate and Andrew Phoenix, Chris and Stella Watson. Thank you to Multnomah County Library for research help into Welsh idioms, and if you want to know the origin of *Don't put the violin on the roof*, it comes from when people lived in tiny low stone cottages. They had no storage, so things they no longer used were tucked into the thatch—and then forgotten about.

Thank you to lovely Monica Drake for her first read and suggestions, and of course a massive thank you to Nathan Fayard for editing the book. Your insightful questions and sense of humor were such a part of making this book come to life! In fact, so much thanks to all the Foundations Books Team, I am so happy to be part of the Foundations Family.

Lastly an eternal thanks, of course, to my wonderful family; Mum and Dad, my husband Curly, the kids — Jess, Ellie and Finn, and lastly thanks to Pinky the cat. You may not like being picked up, but I hope you like being immortalized in this book!

More From Foundations

www.FoundationsBooks.net

Love or money?

Kate Toscano's life is upended when her sister Cassy is killed in a car accident. This jet-setting writer for a trendy Las Vegas magazine, is now the guardian of her five-year-old, autistic nephew, Jimmy. She's forced to move back home. Kate's mother, Lydia, is skeptical about bringing a young, special needs child into her well-structured and organized home in Avalon Bay.Sparks reignite for Kate when she runs into John Neal, her old high school flame. Is it too late for her? It appears John may already be in another relationship.Not everyone is accepting of Kate's new charge. Relationships, old and new, become transparent in her current reality. So, Kate must make a decision:

Choose security, or taking a bold chance on an uncertain future.

A recently widowed lawyer, pursued by three formidable women with casseroles as their calling cards.

Each woman has something tantalizing to offer him; all of them can cook up a storm. His own wife never bothered herself in the kitchen, he is needy enough to savor their dishes, but wary about where their overtures might lead.

Set on the shores of California's Central Coast, this alternately wry and wistful take on second chances is full of engaging characters who, in midlife, find themselves longing for new purpose—and more specifically, a lasting relationship. Unintended miscues and mishaps ensue. For him, rejoining the circle of life becomes a dizzying, if much desired, prospect. For the women, the pursuit becomes an unexpected journey to empowerment.

Twists and turns accelerate until, they find who or what most matters. Crucial discoveries come to light. Including how little the widower knew about his deceased wife, and a mysterious musician who lives along the boardwalk of the Pacific oceanfront.

Then the pandemic takes hold.

f

Foundations Book Publishing
Copyright © 2016 Foundations Book Publications Licensing
4209 Lakeland Drive, #398, Flowood, MS 39232
All Rights Reserved

10-9-8-7-6-5-4-3-2-1

ISBN: 978-1-64583-096-2

Lost and Found Series: Marooned
Louise Jane Watson

Copyright © 2022 Louise Jane Watson

g

Printed in Great Britain
by Amazon